HARD EVIDENCE

HARD EVIDENCE

MARK PEARSON

LARGE PRINT

Oxford

First published in Great Britain 2008
by
Arrow Books
Part of The Random House Group

Published in Large Print 2009 by ISIS Publishing Ltd.,
7 Centremead, Osney Mead, Oxford OX2 0ES
by arrangement with
The Random House Group

British Library Cataloguing in Publication Data
Pearson, Mark.
    Hard evidence [text (large print)].
    1. Prostitutes - - Crimes against - - Fiction.
    2. Missing persons - - Investigation - - Fiction.
    3. Police - - England - - London - - Fiction.
    4. Detective and mystery stories.
    5. Large type books.
    I. Title
    823.9'2–dc22

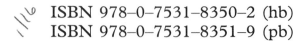 ISBN 978–0–7531–8350–2 (hb)
       ISBN 978–0–7531–8351–9 (pb)

Printed and bound in Great Britain by
T. J. International Ltd., Padstow, Cornwall

For Lynn with love

In 2004/2005 police figures indicated there had been 1,028 child abductions in England and Wales. That's three children a day. Or night. Abducted. Every eight hours a child is stolen in the UK.

BT press release

Each year in the UK more than 40,000 children under the age of 16 are reported missing — and after two weeks 1,300 children will still not have returned home.

BT Media Centre

ACKNOWLEDGEMENTS

The Ancient Mariner, it is told, could fix people with his beady eye in a room and, to a man and woman, they'd listen spellbound to his tale. If I fix people with my beady eye in a room they scatter like the thirteen tribes of Israel. So thanks are firstly due to you, reader, for letting me take you on this journey into Delaney's world. Not, it has to be said, a pleasant world, but made richer by your presence.

Louise Tam ordered me to write this book in the first place, Robert Caskie, the Lancelot of the publishing world, championed its completion and cause, James Nightingale made it far better than it was and Jane Selley polished it up like a shiny apple. Thanks to Caroline Gascoigne, Kate Elton and all the wonderful people at Random House for not booting me out of their door in the first place. And thanks, of course, to Mum and Dad without whom nothing much, least and most of all this, would have been possible.

Lastly, the careful reader may have noted that DI Jack Delaney is partial to an occasional drop of the fortifying spirit, and in this regard I must acknowledge the Wheatsheaf and Lobster public houses, of West Beckham and Sheringham respectively, for the invaluable assistance their excellent staff provided in this most vital area of research.

As for the city, Delaney's London is like a terminally

infected, sick man crying out for medical attention. Delaney is certainly no surgeon, but, as Bernard Cromwell might well put it, he will don his gown and march, scalpel in hand, once more.

MP

CHAPTER
ONE

Night-time on the river, twenty-five miles west of London. Kevin Norrell, a foul-breathed and acne-scarred man, hooded and sweating, pulled hard on the oars, really getting into it now. Years of steroid abuse had given him strength, if not wisdom, and his blades flashed across the dark ridges of the windblown river like scalpels slicing through mercury. He grunted as they dipped into the water and pulled the boat upwards and forward. In the cloudless sky above, the moon hung full and fat, the sickly colour of a dying man. The colour of Billy Martin's yellowing face, in fact, as he lay huddled in the corner of the small skiff. His hands were bound with twisted coat-hanger wire, his mouth was pulled into a painful rictus by a gag made from his own shirt. Trembling, he pulled his legs protectively in towards himself.

"For God's sake keep still!" A hooded man at the other end of the boat, holding a video camera.

Kevin Norrell pulled unconcerned on the oars, not missing a beat. He didn't know or care who the huddled man was; he was paid for his muscle, not his brains. Billy Martin cared about something, though.

You could see it in his rat-like eyes as they flicked from side to side like a warning finger.

"Never work with bloody amateurs." The hooded man with the camera again. "This isn't a steadicam, you know."

Billy Martin twisted his face and managed to move the gag a little. "You think you're scaring me? You're not. Who do you think you're dealing with here?"

"With you, dear boy. We're dealing with you. We're washing you away. Like a blot, like a stain."

"I've got insurance."

"You had insurance. I'm afraid the policy has recently been cancelled." He nodded to Kevin Norrell, who reluctantly laid down his oars and gripped Billy Martin's shoulders. Martin tried to shake loose, but Norrell's muscles bunched and his fingers dug into the struggling man's shoulders like mechanical claws and held him powerless.

"You can't do this."

"But we can," said the hooded man; he pointed the camera and nodded encouragingly. "Good. Let's see the fear."

Kevin pulled Billy Martin upright; he was screaming with pure terror now, desperately trying to escape the huge man's grip. But Kevin lifted him up, his feet twisting uselessly in the air, then threw him into the river as easily as passing a basketball and with the casual indifference of a refuse collector emptying a dustbin.

Billy Martin's scream rang in the night air like a steam alarm as he crashed into the cold water, his arms

2

burning as he strained against the wire holding him, desperately trying to stay afloat, and failing.

The second man nodded again, zooming in for a tight shot as the rocking boat steadied itself, and called out encouragement to Billy Martin.

"That's it. Wriggle like an eel, splash out with your legs."

Billy Martin's screams gurgled and faded as he sank beneath the water. The ripples gradually died away, the boat was still and the river was peaceful once more. The cameraman nodded to the rower, as if to praise a child, but the smile didn't reach his eyes. Eyes which were as cold as the water that had suddenly filled Billy Martin's lungs.

"Shame we couldn't get crocodiles," he said after a moment.

If Kevin Norrell had any idea what the man was talking about, it certainly didn't register on his face.

CHAPTER
TWO

The football. The cricket. The state of English sport in general. The bird off *Emmerdale* getting her tits out for some lads' magazine. They'd banned smoking, they'd be banning alcohol in pubs next, something else to thank the Californians for, no doubt, like the Atkins diet and low-carb beer, and the bloody Mormons who banged on your door with the sincerity and charm of house-to-house insurance salesmen, or cockroaches.

Jack Delaney let the conversation wash over him as he downed a shot of whiskey with a quick, practised flick of his wrist.

He was sitting on a cracked leather stool at the wooden counter of the Roebuck, a scruffy north London pub. A big mirror behind the bar, with thirty-odd bottles of spirit in front, bouncing different-coloured lights off it like a Christmas tree for alcoholics.

Delaney picked up his pint glass and let a sip of creamy Guinness soothe his throat if not his soul; even the door-to-door Mormons couldn't sell him that, even if he had been in the market. No new soul for Jack Delaney today; just the old, sin-spotted black thing at the heart of him. Forgive him, Father, for he had sinned. If women looked at him, which they did often, they'd try to guess his age and reckon it to be around the late thirties. He had dark hair, dark eyes, and if they got to know him they would get to see that dark soul. Mostly he didn't let them get to know him.

Delaney held his whiskey glass out and nodded with a wink at the barmaid. "Evaporation."

The barmaid took his glass, smiling but with no real hope behind it. She poured a generous shot of Bushmills and placed it in front of him.

"Cheers, Tricia."

"Any chance of getting a drink here!" A large man, a few inches over Delaney's six one, but carrying weight, and drunk. Delaney gave him a glance, dismissed him and returned to the solace of his Guinness.

"The fuck you looking at?"

"Minding my own business here."

"You seem to be minding my fucking business. And you" — to the barmaid — "get me a fucking lager."

Delaney sighed and flashed her a sympathetic smile. "Sorry about this."

The big man's eyes widened; he shook his head, disbelieving.

"You got a problem or something, you fucking Irish fucker?"

Delaney debated discussing the delicate beauty of the English language, but instead stood up from his stool, picked up an empty bottle and smashed it against the bar. Then kicked hard, very hard, with the side of his foot into the larger man's knee. The man grunted with surprise and blinked. He swayed back, and

Delaney flashed his left hand on to his throat, grabbing his windpipe and holding him rigid. Then he moved the jagged edge of the broken bottle towards the drunken man's now terrified eyes.

"If you wanted to dance, you should have asked nicer."

"Please."

"Too late for please."

Delaney's hand tightened on the bottle, his hard eyes telling the fat man the really horrible nature of his mistake.

A hand tapped Delaney's shoulder and he turned round to see a smiling man in his thirties. Dirty-blond hair, brown eyes, five ten. He clearly worked out, the muscles tensing in his arms as he balanced on the balls of his feet like a boxer, ready to move.

"Let him go."

The man dipped a hand into his smart leather jacket and fished out his warrant card, which he showed round the room like a warning. Nobody paid him much attention; a fight in the Roebuck was as unusual a sight as a G string in a pole-dancing club.

"Police. Detective Sergeant Bonner. Why don't we all calm it down?"

Those who had been watching turned back to their beers, losing interest.

Delaney stepped back and put the broken bottle on the bar. Bonner leaned in to the shell-shocked drunk, who had fallen to his knees and wet himself.

"I'd fuck off if I were you."

The man needed no second telling and limped as quickly as he could to the door. Bonner nodded at Delaney.

"Cowboy."

"Sergeant."

Bonner spun the broken bottle on the counter.

"Irish party games?"

"Something like that."

"You're going to have to come with me, I'm afraid."

"Ah, Jesus. Come off it, Eddie."

"Out of my hands."

"Don't tell me it's that prick Hadden again. What are you doing, Sergeant Bonner, kissing arse and running errands for that slag now?"

"It's not about the missing cocaine."

"What the fuck is it about then?"

"Jackie Malone."

Delaney was genuinely puzzled. "What are you on about?"

"She's been making a nuisance of herself asking for you."

"So? Since when do the wants of a brass like her send the Met's finest out on errands?"

Bonner gave him a flat look. "Since the brass got rubbed."

Delaney sighed, picked up his jacket and walked with Bonner to the door, Tricia giving him a grateful but nervous smile as he passed. Bonner opened the door.

"Would you have used the bottle?"

"Who knows? I try to live in the present."

Bonner shook his head. "You know your trouble, Delaney?"

"Yeah."

And he did.

CHAPTER
THREE

Bonner shifted gear and his fifteen-year-old Porsche Carrera growled slowly through the traffic. Camden Town on a hot and busy Monday night was not where he wanted to be, not on any night in fact, but getting out of there quickly was a different matter. The streets were clogged with drunken people lurching from pub to pub to the kebab shop and burger bars. The heat wave London was in the middle of was showing no signs of abating, and the world and his wife seemed to be taking their pleasures al fresco.

Bonner cranked the window handle on his door to let a bit of breeze in, and looked over at Delaney, whose dark eyes glittered with the yellow flash of the passing street lights. Christ, he looks like a wolf, he thought, and shuddered it away.

"Where you been, Cowboy?"

"Here and there. You know . . ."

"No."

"What happened to Jackie Malone?"

Bonner shrugged. "Just got the call."

Delaney nodded and looked away. Bonner kept his eyes on him. "It wasn't just her. Wendy was looking for you too. And Siobhan."

"I had things on my mind."

Bonner nodded sympathetically. "She told me it was your anniversary."

Delaney flashed him an angry look. "Would have been. It would have been our anniversary. Four years and they're still walking around somewhere with blood pumping in their hearts while she rots to bones in her grave."

"You can't blame yourself."

"If I wanted to talk about it I would have gone to confession, Sergeant."

"Yeah. You'd go to confession and I'd cut my penis off and call myself Madeline."

"Could get yourself promoted that way."

Bonner slammed the palm of his hand hard on the horn as a couple of women stumbled in front of the car. A blonde and a brunette, pissed. The women peered through the windscreen and cracked their lipstick in seductive appreciation, the blonde raising a bottle of strong cider in a toast.

"You boys want to party?" Irish accent.

"One of yours, Cowboy. From the land of Sodom and Begorrah. Want to stop and play with the colleens?"

Delaney looked across at him without answering.

"That's right, you're wanted in a murder investigation. Murder, another thing your countrymen specialise in." He edged the car forward, spilling the blonde to a laughing heap on the pavement. The brunette helped her up and, slack-kneed and laughing like donkeys, they linked arms and headed into the nearest pub.

"Murder and prostitution. The Emerald Isle's most popular exports . . . short of the black stuff, of course."

"One of these days, Sergeant Bonner, someone is going to shut your mouth permanently."

Bonner laughed, genuinely amused. "I know plenty of people would like to, and frankly I can't say I blame them, but if you don't have a sense of humour, how are you going to survive in this wicked world?"

"Maybe you aren't going to."

"Oh, I'm a born survivor, me. The original cat with nine lives."

"Jackie Malone thought she was indestructible too."

Bonner looked at him shrewdly. "She tell you that, did she? In an intimate moment."

Delaney ignored him, yawned and looked out of the window as the Porsche picked up speed and headed west. Bonner flicked another sideways glance at him, trying to read him. Failing. He carried on anyway.

"Of course death can be an intimate moment, can't it, Cowboy? She breathes out, you breathe in. But she doesn't. Again. Ever. And that last breath of hers . . . you can almost taste the departing life. The smell of her. The heat leaving her body. Her muscles relaxing."

He shook his head and looked across again with a dry smile.

"What do you reckon, Cowboy? Almost better than sex?"

CHAPTER
FOUR

Ladbroke Grove. West London. Parts of it were pleasant; upmarket professionals who couldn't quite make Holland Park lived there. Tall Victorian townhouses stocked with Jennifers and Nigels. Vivaldi and Bruckner floating through the still air on hot summer nights, with talk of options and opera and immigration laws. Parts of it weren't so pleasant. Flats and houses stocked with students, drug-dealers, prostitutes, and script editors who worked at the BBC's Television Centre up the road in Shepherd's Bush. Delaney got out of the car and wondered which of them was worse.

Across the road the entrance to a large townhouse converted to a block of flats was sealed with yellow tape and guarded by uniformed police. A young female constable with honey-blonde hair stood more upright, flexing her spine with an almost feline sensuality, and smiled as Delaney approached. Her last day in uniform; she was due to transfer to CID soon as part of her graduate fast-tracking and was keen to impress.

"Good evening, Inspector."

"Sally." Delaney gave her a nod and a quick smile. Time was he'd have stopped and chatted with her. She was an attractive young woman and he'd have flirted with her, as sure as sin, even as a married man. Harmlessly of course; he'd loved his wife. Before he was married, however, it would have been an entirely different matter. A lot of people on the force thought it a bad idea to dip the pen in company ink. Delaney hadn't been one of them. His pen had written far, far more than custody reports over the years. But that was then. Delaney was now in a world that had no joy in flirting. He walked up to the front door, letting out a long breath.

Time to go to work.

He put his hands in his pockets and walked into the hallway, barely registering the curious gazes and nods from the uniformed police who guarded the crime scene.

"Upstairs, guv."

"I know where she lives."

"Bit of a nasty one."

"They're all nasty, Constable. People are nasty."

Delaney looked down at the geometrically patterned mosaic on the floor. Reds and yellows. Late Victorian, the only original feature left of what would have been a beautiful townhouse. We get what we are given, he thought, and then we screw it all to hell. He walked up the stairs, stairs he'd been up a lot of times before, stairs that had seen thousands of people come and go over the years, and the odds were that more than one of those people were murderers. The last person, or persons, to see Jackie Malone alive definitely was. That was a stone-cold fact.

He paused at the landing and wondered what the one-bedroomed flat had originally been. A nursery, perhaps? A master bedroom? Had children through the years played and laughed and fallen asleep here to bedtime stories and nursery rhymes played on musical boxes? Had they looked out of the high Victorian window longing for Peter Pan to fly in and whisk them off to Never-Never-Land.

Whatever it had been, it was a murder scene now, and Jack Delaney wasn't about to start clapping his hands. Truth was, he never believed in fairies, but he knew evil existed, and he could feel its presence hanging in the air like the cold, damp touch of a corpse.

The burly constable stood aside deferentially and let Delaney pass into the room, where his practised eye immediately started looking for what was familiar, what was out of place.

It was small. A sofa, a sink with a hot plate beside it. An electric kettle, once white, now yellowing with grease and use. A TV and DVD player on a brown cabinet. Some DVDs on the shelf beneath them. He flicked through the titles: *Head Girl, Sin Sisters, Crime and Punishment, Spunk Junkies*. They hadn't come from Blockbuster. Some cupboards. On the floor a faded imitation Persian rug sitting on top of a light oatmeal carpet. A telephone and an appointments book. A basket with a couple of apples and a thick rubber band in it, some magazines. It was clean, tidy. Nothing out of order. Nothing out of place.

Except the smell.

Delaney looked across at the other door and knew what lay beyond. Had he not been told, he'd have known. The smell was unmistakable to him. Death.

Death was particulate and it reached out to him, assaulting his nostrils, invading his lungs. Her life might have fled quickly, but her body was giving up its essence slowly, and as Delaney stood in her living room and inhaled Jackie Malone into his soul, he felt a calm come over him. Displacement activity, they called it. He couldn't bring the dead back to life, but he could do what he could; he could find those responsible and make them suffer.

"Guv." Snapping him out of his reverie.

Delaney nodded at the large uniformed officer who stood by the door and went through to the bedroom. Jackie Malone's office, her factory floor, her operating theatre.

He quickly looked around. A medieval torture chamber in black and red, with satin sheets and a champagne cooler. The pain and the pleasure. The agony and the ecstasy. Scene of Crime Officers, SOCO, or whatever they were called nowadays — Delaney could never keep up with the ever-changing acronyms of the Met — white-plastic-suited like very poor astronauts, were dusting and photographing. One of them gave him a pair of light blue latex gloves. He snapped them on with a grimace. Jackie Malone kept a box of the same on a cabinet by the door for examinations of a thoroughly different nature. The officer moved aside and Delaney looked down, seeing the corpse for the first time, face up, arms cruelly tied, lying on the floor like a broken and discarded doll.

Corpse: such a cold word for such a warm-blooded woman. Except her blood wasn't warm any more. It was cold and still, scored in brown lines on her ivory face and puddled about her mutilated body.

Delaney took a swallow as the acrid taste of whiskey rose in his throat. As he remembered her.

Irish, of course. With those thick black curly locks and bright blue eyes, she had to be. A distant descendant of a lucky sailor who was washed up from the wreck of the Armada on to the rain-soaked fields of southern Ireland. Stumbling into Cork or Waterford, and there, from the eye of the storm and the lash of the rain-filled wind, finding comfort in the welcoming arms of an Irish girl. Love was, after all, a universal language. Just like lust, the commodity that Jackie Malone dealt in. Or loneliness. She always did know how to make Delaney laugh, mind, make him forget himself. He looked at her eyes now. Lifeless, flat, and he remembered them twinkling, remembered them flashing angrily, full of life, just like herself. Thirty-two years old. Several hours dead.

He looked across her ravaged body.

Naked. Hands and feet tied with coat-hanger wire. Her body covered with knife cuts. With stabbing punctures. Her sweet face slashed from forehead to chin. A smile by Bosch carved into her throat. The wound gaping, black-edged and raw. Delaney swallowed again and looked across as Bonner came into the room.

"You okay, guv?"

"Yeah," Delaney lied. He was good at lying. He looked away to Sally Cartwright, the young constable, who had followed him into the building. Her face was almost as pale as the body on the floor. She had a notebook open and was concentrating on that. Looking away from the horror of it all.

"You've spoken to the neighbours?"

"Sir."

"And?"

"Nothing. Across the way is empty and downstairs is an old couple. They keep themselves to themselves."

"And they say there's no such thing as society."

"Margaret Thatcher did, sir, but then her dad was a grocer. The old folks downstairs know she was a tom. They got used to people walking up and down all hours of the day. They turned a blind eye."

"And a deaf ear."

"Have their hearing aids turned off unless they're watching *EastEnders*, apparently."

Delaney grunted. They had that the wrong way round. He pointed a finger at the young PC. "I want a full statement nonetheless. People see things. They might not want to get involved, but they see things." He looked down at Jackie Malone. "Even when they don't want to. Even if they don't know they have, people see things."

"Guv."

Delaney stood aside as the crime-scene photographer moved in to take shots of the body. Across the bed a forensic officer dusted a large rubber phallus. Bonner nodded at Delaney.

"You think that's the murder weapon?"

Delaney turned expressionless eyes on him and Bonner grinned, unabashed.

"What is it they say? When you've eliminated the impossible, what's left, however improbable, is the whatever. That thing looks damn improbable to me, and I grew up on a farm."

Delaney turned to Sally Cartwright.

"Why hasn't she been covered up?"

"We're waiting for the pathologist, sir."

"Where the bloody hell is he?"

"She, sir. Dr Walker's attending."

Delaney grimaced. "What's the hold-up, then? She waiting for the second act of *Rigoletto* to finish?"

"I didn't know you were a fan of opera, Detective."

Delaney turned round as Kate Walker approached. A tall, slim woman in her early thirties, dressed more for fine dining than forensics. Jet-black hair and a feral tint of green in her eyes. Unamused eyes.

"Oh yeah. Opera and colonoscopies. Top of my list."

Bonner smirked. "Ah yes, 'The Ring Cycle'."

"Shut it, Bonner." He turned back to Kate Walker. "Sorry to spoil your supper party, but there's a woman here needs our help."

Kate flicked a cursory glance at the dead body of Jackie Malone. "I'd say she was beyond that."

Delaney held her angry gaze, meeting her fire with his own. "I think we can assume that this wasn't a suicide. I want to know what happened."

Kate smiled disarmingly. "I can tell you when she died. I can tell you how she died and I can tell you what she had for dinner. You know why?"

"Why?"

"Because that's my fucking job. Now why don't you give me a break with the attitude and let me do it?"

Delaney dug in his pocket, fishing out a packet of cigarettes, and flicked one into his mouth.

"You got a great sense of respect for the dead, lady."

"What is it with you, Delaney? You don't like a woman doing a man's job? Or you just don't like women?"

Delaney held her gaze for a moment and took the cigarette out of his mouth.

"I just don't like you, Dr Walker."

Bonner flashed Kate a sympathetic smile, but it slid off her as smoothly as rainwater off a Chelsea girl's gumboot. She looked down at the body on the floor, her eyebrow lifting slightly. Delaney picked up on it. "Something?"

Kate shrugged. "Something not quite right."

"That an expert opinion, is it?"

Kate ignored him and bent down to examine the body, pulling on a pair of latex gloves. "Let's see if the vitreous fluid can give us a rough time of death." She pulled out a syringe, attached a large-gauge needle and carefully stabbed it into Jackie Malone's lifeless right eye.

Delaney had already turned away. Outside in the corridor he opened the sash window at the end of the hall, swearing as it stuck and grunting as he forced it

19

further open. He palmed the cigarette back into his mouth, flaring a match and drawing a long, abrasive cloud into his lungs. He tensed his lips and let it flow back out in a long-drawn-out sigh. Bonner shook his head as he approached.

"What is it with you and her?"

"Your point?"

"Come off it, Cowboy. You can't stand the woman, or she you for that matter. Why is that? She knock you back on the old Hampstead hayride?"

"I don't like what she stands for."

"Which is?"

"The Establishment."

Bonner flashed his warrant card. "I've got news for you, guv. You're a fully paid-up member too."

"And you're a fully paid-up prick."

"I do my best."

Delaney shrugged as Bonner put his warrant card away. "You and me, we live in a different world, Eddie, my old son. That's a licence to catch rats, is all. To pick your knees up, stick your elbows out and dance to the tune of the likes of her frigging uncle."

The penny dropped with Bonner. "Not a big fan of the superintendent, then?"

"One of these days you'll make a great detective." Delaney threw his cigarette out of the window and walked back into the front room, watching as the forensics crew dusted a small cabinet that stood beside the sofa. He turned back to Bonner.

"Any word on Jackie's boy . . . Andy?"

Bonner shook his head. "He's not been living with her for some months."

"Is he with his uncle?"

"Yeah, according to the neighbours. He's off travelling."

"That's something, I suppose."

The forensics crew moved through to the bedroom, and Delaney walked across and opened the drawer of the small cabinet. He emptied the contents and put them on top. Condoms. A squeezed tube of lubricant. Cards with a phone number and a cartoon picture of a rubber-clad dominatrix. "No Pain. No Gain." A packet of rubber bands. A box of brass drawing pins. At the back of the drawer was a small black notebook. Delaney took it out and flicked through. A diary. Jackie Malone's spidery handwriting noting names, numbers. He turned to the latest entry. His own name, DELANEY, spelled out in capitals with his work number below it.

Bonner called across. "Anything?"

Delaney moved the diary out of sight and looked over at the sergeant. "You said she was calling for me?"

"A lot of times."

"And?"

Bonner shrugged. "Nothing. She only wanted to talk to you. They assumed it was personal." He paused, licked a hint of his tongue on the top of his lip. "You know?"

Delaney held his gaze. "No."

"So you've no idea what she wanted?"

"How could I? I never spoke to her."

"Maybe she was worried about something?"

"Looks like she had good reason." Delaney glanced through the open door, watching as Kate tilted Jackie's head slightly to one side, examining the clogged blood that had seeped thickly from each nostril. She gently laid her head down, picked up a micro-cassette recorder and clicked it to record.

Delaney turned away and walked across to the open window. Ignoring the unspoken criticism as he fired up another cigarette, exhaling lazy smoke into the hot night, the nicotine spiking into his blood and sparking pictures in his mind.

A woman in her early thirties sprawled on the hard floor of a petrol station. Her dark hair matted with blood. Blood trickling from both nostrils. A shotgun blast, shattering the plate-glass window. Delaney started as Bonner spoke.

"Those things can kill you, you know?"

Delaney took a long pull and exhaled. "Good." He flicked the fag end through the window, watching it spiral down and bounce on the pavement below in a tiny shower of sparks. He turned back to Bonner. "Get on the phone. I want Billy Martin found and brought in."

"Who's he? Her pimp?"

"Yes, he's her pimp. Or was her pimp, sometimes. Billy Martin . . . he's her brother."

"The boy's uncle you were talking about?"

"Not the one he's with, no. That's Russell Martin. He's just a drug-dealer."

"Nice family."

Delaney gave him a sharp look. "You don't know anything about her, Bonner."

"You do, though?"

"I'm going to find out. I can promise you that."

Kate Walker came through from the bedroom and Delaney turned to her. "Anything?"

"Early days, I need to do the post."

Delaney picked up on her hesitant manner. "Something, though?"

"I'd say she died somewhere between twelve o'clock this afternoon and say four o'clock."

Bonner laughed drily. "She could have had twenty punters in that time. Can't you be a bit more specific?"

Kate turned cold eyes on him. "Not unless you see a grandfather clock stopped somewhere round here giving us a big clue."

Delaney glared at her. "Why don't you save the attitude and just tell us what we want to know when we want to know it for a change?"

"Like?"

"Like how she died."

"I won't know for sure till the post. But I'd say asphyxiation."

"How?"

"She was gagged. The sex toy. Her nostrils were clotted with blood. She couldn't breathe. She would have been in great pain."

Delaney looked over at the window.

"She was tied up. She was badly beaten and she was scared. Terrified for her life, most likely."

Delaney looked back at her.

"And she vomited. She couldn't clear her mouth and choked to death on it."

"She drowned in her own vomit. You're saying that's what killed her?"

"I'm saying that's what I think she died from."

Delaney nodded, conceding. "And the cuts, the mutilation? Was that before or after she died?"

"My opinion?"

"Your opinion."

"She was dead before she was cut or stabbed. If her heart was still pumping when she was cut, that room back there would have looked like a charnel house."

"It looked pretty unpleasant."

"Trust me, if she was alive when she was cut, her blood would have literally sprayed the walls."

Delaney nodded, relieved in some way. "That's something, I guess."

"It's not much, but yes, it is something."

Bonner shook his head. "What's the point, then? What kind of sick guy —"

Kate cut him off. "I don't think it was just one guy."

Delaney looked at her. "Go on?"

"I think there were at least two of them."

"I think you're right."

"You know what, Delaney? That's made my day."

Bonner looked at them both. "Am I missing something here?"

Kate looked at Bonner, unimpressed. "She was tied up with coat-hanger wire, Sergeant. I can't see one man being strong enough to do that on his own. The wire is too stiff. He'd have needed help to hold her down."

"But if she was into bondage? That kind of kinky play."

"These guys weren't playing at anything. She's dead. That's how serious they were."

"But if she was already dead when they tied her up? Like when they cut her."

"No. The ligatures on her wrists and ankles indicate that she was still alive. The blood was still pumping."

Delaney looked at her, his own blood pumping in his ears now.

"You think they meant to kill her?"

"Who knows? I guess that's your job to find out."

Bonner shook his head. "So we've got a pair of fucking sex freaks out there?"

Delaney nodded towards Kate, a sardonic smile twitching the corner of his mouth. "Watch your language, Bonner, there's a lady present. But I don't think so anyway. Not in the normal sense."

"What's normal to you, Inspector?"

Delaney looked into her cool green eyes. "Sexual sadists. Killers with this kind of twist. They don't usually mutilate the face. You ever seen that before?"

Kate's eyes gave nothing away. "People are capable of absolutely anything. You should have learned that by now, Detective Inspector, if nothing else."

CHAPTER
FIVE

If an Englishman's home was his castle, what was an Irishman's? Delaney's was no castle, that was for sure. A scruffy studio flat in Tufnell Park. A small kitchen and sitting room with a bedroom to one side. The place hadn't been decorated for twenty years. A brown sofa, a G-Plan sideboard, a dusty carpet of faded red and green swirls. In the corner a TV and DVD player. A shelf with a few old, well-thumbed paperbacks. He closed the door behind him, contemplating the difference between where he lived and where Jackie Malone had died. Not a great deal. Jackie Malone had a different house somewhere, of course; she had a whole other life. She came home from her two-room working flat to a life. At least she used to. Delaney looked around at what he came home to and almost envied her her cold shelf in the morgue. A flashing light on his answering machine caught his attention. He looked at it for a moment or two and crossed to the sideboard.

He flipped over a glass, picked up a bottle of whiskey and poured himself a shot. Desperate measures. Desperate times. He toasted himself mentally and slid the burning shot down his throat. Then took another.

Some people drink to forget. Some people drink to be funnier, to be more confident, to socialise. Delaney drank to kill the fluttering butterflies of thought that exploded into his brain every morning when he woke up. Every day for the last four years. Since he cradled his wife's head in his useless arms and watched the light die in her eyes. The light die in his whole world.

He poured himself another measure and looked again at the flashing light on his answering machine.

He pushed the button and listened as the machine rewound to the voice of the dead.

"Delaney, it's Jackie Malone. I need to speak to you. Call me. You've got my number."

Click. Swallow.

"Delaney, it's Jackie again. I really need to speak to you. Just call me."

Click.

"It's me. Where are you, Delaney?"

Delaney took another swallow as he listened to the desperation in her voice. Not a question he was sure he could have answered. *What have you done, Jackie? What have you let them do?*

Click.

Delaney was reaching forward to turn the machine off when another voice spoke and he held his hand back. The voice of a seven-year-old girl with just a hint of Irish in it, enough of a familiar hint to break his heart all over again.

"Daddy, it's Siobhan. When are you going to come round? We miss you. Bye."

He ran a hand through his hair and sighed as the machine clicked again. "It's Jackie again, Cowboy. Don't tell me you've gone all bashful on me? We need to speak. This concerns you. I'll be in all day. Call me or come round. You know where."

Click. Click. Click.

The machine clunked to a stop. It was an antique now and he knew he should have replaced it, but it had his wife's voice on it and Delaney called himself daily just to hear it. He pushed the message button and another dead woman's voice filled the room, filled his life all over again, but it would never fill the hole right in the middle of him.

"This is Sinead. Jack and I aren't here right now. This is an answerphone and I'm sure you know by now what to do when you hear the beep, so go ahead and do it."

Delaney sat back on the sofa and shook his head gently. She was wrong. He had absolutely no idea what to do. He tipped the bottle and poured himself half a tumbler. Some memories he wanted to keep, no matter how much whiskey he drank, and some he wanted to destroy. These images he used alcohol to try and kill, but it only helped fuel his nightmares. A petrol station at night, the cold striplights spilling across the forecourt. The transit van, its back doors open like the maw of an evil creature. A man running, dressed in black, leaping in as the van pulled away. The faint smoke leaking from the barrels of the shotgun, sulphurous and yellow.

Delaney stood up and lurched to the sink in the corner of the room and threw up, the sour whiskey burning his throat as he gasped for breath. He ran cold water, cupping it in his hand and splashing it over his head. He filled a glass and drained it, then picked up a mouthwash bottle from the shelf above the sink and gargled. He looked up into the mirror but couldn't meet his own gaze; he walked to the cabinet by the door and picked up the keys to his old Saab.

The night was still warm and Delaney kept his window open as he drove, the thick air blowing his hair flat to his head and slapping him awake. The white lines in the middle of the road and the fat, jaundiced street lights flashed past him as in a dream, and Delaney had to shake his head now and again to clear his thoughts, to focus on the road. The wail of a horn and the screech of brakes barely registered as he swerved to avoid an oncoming taxi and continued to drive.

He pulled the car to an untidy stop in a pleasant suburban street north of Hampstead station. A few miles from Delaney's impersonal little flat and a million light years from his own world.

He looked at his eyes in the rear-view mirror and ran the back of his hand over them, as though to squeeze the hurt from them. He shook his head sharply and combed his fingers through his tangled hair, took a swallow from a bottle of water tossed earlier on to the passenger seat and opened the car door.

He looked up at the house for a long moment. A bay-fronted Victorian terrace, set back from the road, with a neat front lawn and a gravel path leading up to the oak door with stained-glass panels. Thin tendrils of honeyed light spilled from the gaps in the curtains.

Delaney closed the slightly creaking wooden gate behind him and walked along the path, stepped into the narrow porch and rang the bell. Musical chimes filled the warm air, and from somewhere Delaney dug up a smile as the door was opened. The light spilled out and caught his eyes, revealing a warmth beyond the door that lay hidden like bluebells under a foot of snow.

"Hello, Wendy."

"Jack. Have you any idea what the time is?"

"None at all."

"It's gone midnight! We've been worried about you. Come on, come in." Delaney nodded gratefully and followed her through the door. Following like Alice down a rabbit hole into a whole different world.

Wendy closed the door behind him. Thirty-seven, six inches shorter than Delaney. Attractive, polished, dirty-blonde hair and pale blue eyes. Worried eyes. She moved forward and stood on tiptoe to kiss Delaney on the cheek and then held her palm to where her lips had been.

"You need a shave."

Delaney nodded, and Wendy took her hand away, suddenly self-conscious. "Come through to the lounge."

Delaney followed her, his heavy feet soundless on the plush carpeting. It was a family home. Pictures on the wall, a faint smell of polish in the air, photographs, a cluttered piano, thick, comfortable furniture, a worn but expensive rug on the floor. Delaney sat on the edge of a fashionably battered leather sofa and smiled apologetically. "I didn't want to be a nuisance . . ."

"It's all right, Jack. Really it is. Especially today, your wedding anniversary. We've been really worried about you."

"I meant to call, you know."

Wendy looked at him, the sympathy a physical presence in her eyes. "Where've you been?"

Delaney considered the question, not sure he had an answer, and just shrugged.

"God, you look terrible. Can I get you a drink?"

"Not for me. Where's Roger?"

A moment's pause and a flicker of something replacing the sympathy in her eyes.

"He's gone to Dublin for the weekend. Golf trip with the lads."

"Is Siobhan in bed?"

"And where else would she be at this time of night?" Wendy laughed suddenly. A silky laugh, rich, a purr in there somewhere. "God, Jack, what are we going to do with you?"

"If I was a horse you could probably shoot me." He smiled up at her. "You're a good woman, Wendy."

"Why don't you go up and see her?"

"She'll be asleep."

Wendy shook her head. "She'll have heard the car. She's been just as worried about you as I have. More. She's been waiting all day to see you, desperate to show you her First Holy Communion dress."

"God, her First Communion. When is that?"

"Saturday. It's a lovely dress."

"I bet she looks a picture in it."

"A princess."

"I'll go up and see her then." He stood up and Wendy put her palm against his cheek again.

"We all miss her."

He nodded and looked at a silver-framed photo that stood on the mantelpiece. His wife's eyes smiling at a future she couldn't see.

Delaney pushed his daughter's bedroom door open. It was another world again to him, a different universe. A world of pastel lights and pastel colours. A kingdom of teddy bears and soft dolls. The world of his dark-haired, bright-eyed seven-year-old daughter. She had her mother's blue eyes, like parts of her soul gifted. She smiled up at him as he came into the room.

"Hello, Cowboy."

"Hello, Partner. Give me a kiss." He swooped her up in his arms as she launched herself from the trampoline of her bed.

"I want a story."

Delaney put her back on the bed with another kiss. "It's very late, poppet."

"Please."

He couldn't resist those eyes. "All right. Just a quick one."

"With guns and drugs and murdered women."

"Not tonight."

"All right then. One of your fairy stories." Siobhan smiled grudgingly, pretending to be disappointed.

Delaney laughed for the first time in that terrible day and sat down beside her on the bed as she snuggled into the warmth of its cartooned covers.

"Once upon a very long time ago, in the year of our lunch of green cabbage and bacon, lived a humble woodcutter's son. He lived deep, deep in the ancient forest and had been born with a curse. He was a great artist. That is, he would have been if it hadn't been for his hands. His mind was filled with many beautiful pictures that he longed to paint, but whenever he put his simple brush to canvas his hand twitched and went out of control."

"Why?"

"Why indeed? That's the question of all questions, and if we can answer that then we can answer everything."

"But why did his hands twitch?"

"Ah, you see, a wicked witch had cursed him at birth. So whenever he tried to paint a picture, the result was quite diabolical and everyone laughed at him. One day he became so despondent that he decided to set out and find a cure for his problem. Now everybody in the ancient forest knew that the only person able to solve such a problem for him was the old hermit who lived on top of the hill in a cave. And so the humble woodcutter's son went to visit him."

"What did he say?"

"Well, the old hermit was very sympathetic. Which made a pleasant change and soon gave him hope. In fact he gave him a strange mushroom, telling him to eat it and gaze into his pond. This the woodcutter's son

33

did, and as he looked, the vision of a beautiful girl appeared to him. The hermit told him that all he had to do was make the girl fall in love with him and the curse would be lifted."

"What was her name? The beautiful girl?"

"Her name was Estrella, the Princess Estrella, and she was quite the most beautiful girl he had ever seen."

"And did he marry her?"

"Well, he set off to the castle singing with joy and expectation. When he arrived and was shown in to the princess, he could hardly contain his happiness. The princess, though, when she heard of his mission, well, she burst into silver peals of laughter, and waved her hands as she cast a spell and shrank him to the dimensions of a frog. She then placed him in his own little glass jar on a shelf next to all the other young men who had had similar ideas and were similarly contained."

Siobhan blinked her eyes sleepily.

"Why did she do that?"

"Well you see, the princess was really the wicked witch's daughter all along. The humble woodcutter's son still loved her, though, and wasn't altogether too unhappy because he could still look at her through the jar."

Siobhan couldn't keep her eyes open and mumbled as she turned her head on the pillow, "What a nasty thing to do."

Delaney stroked a soothing hand on her hair. His other hand holding her tiny one, gripping tight.

"And anyway, that wasn't a very good story. What about the happy ending? What about his pictures?"

"They can't all have happy endings."

"Why not?"

"It's time you went to sleep, young lady. We can't have princesses with bags under their eyes, can we?"

"I'm not sure I want to be a princess any more."

"We don't get to choose who we are, darling."

He kissed her gently on the forehead as she closed her eyes and drifted into sleep. He watched her for a moment or two longer, for as long as he could bear, and then closed her bedroom door behind him and went downstairs.

"How is she?"

Delaney smiled sadly at Wendy. "She's fine. She looks more like her mother every day."

"Is she asleep?"

"Dropped off like a log."

"I'm glad you came by. She'd have been really disappointed if you hadn't."

"It's the job, Wendy. You know how it is."

"I know how you are. You don't have to do it all on your own, Jack."

"I guess we all do what we can."

"She misses you."

"I'll get the flat soon and she can come and live with me when I do. You know that."

"It's not a house she needs. It's a home."

"I know."

"It's time to move on."

"Don't, Wendy. Please . . . just don't."

"It's been four years."

"So people keep telling me." It was true, but it was just numbers, it didn't mean anything to him.

"It's what she would have wanted."

Delaney shook his head.

"You've got to put it behind you, Jack. For her sake. For Siobhan's sake. For your sake."

Delaney stood up. "It's late, Wendy. I'd better get home."

"Why don't you stay over?"

Delaney looked at the slight flush that had crept over her cheek like she'd just been softly kissed, and the wetness in her eyes that came from more than grief.

"I can't."

"Siobhan would love to see you in the morning."

"I've got things I need to do."

"You're welcome any time, you know that?" He met her gaze, and she could not hold it, her eyes sliding away.

"It means a lot to me, Wendy."

She looked up and smiled, the moment passed, shaking her head at him. "Jack, you look like shit. Get some sleep. Get some decent food. Take care of yourself, for Christ's sake."

Delaney laughed again. The blasphemy sat as prettily on her lips as a robin perched on a statue of the Pope.

"You're a good woman, Wendy."

"Not always."

And Delaney pulled her into a hug. The kind of hug that a man gives his wife's sister.

CHAPTER
SIX

Tuesday morning. The sun was still low in the sky but it was hot. Hot enough to put a shimmer in the air and raise tempers to boiling point.

The Waterhill estate was less of a carbuncle and more of an open sore on the architectural face of north London. Urban decay as installation art writ large. A breeding ground for fear, for degradation and for violence. Where hope was a word that had no meaning whatsoever and murder was as familiar as the rain, the graffiti and the burnt-out wrecks of cars that dotted the estate like the statuary of stately homes. It was not an attractive place.

Howard Morgan had never been mistaken for attractive either, even before the burn scar running from neck to eye and forehead that had so disfigured one side of his face. He was in his forties, heavily built and heavily muscled. His dark hair was greasy and long to his collar, his jeans were oil-stained and filthy from working in his garage. There was a brute, animal intelligence in his eyes, eyes that flickered like sparking coals in a kicked-over fire, and there was intent also. Murderous intent.

Morgan had his thick arm wrapped around the pale and slender neck of a terrified, bespectacled man in his late thirties, and was bellowing into his face.

"You tell me where she is!"

The man could barely manage a gurgle, his consciousness slipping from him like thick blood oozing from a slow wound.

"Get off him."

Sally Cartwright came running up the road and flicked out her asp, the twenty-first century's telescopic version of the truncheon. She wielded it with poorly disguised pleasure as she shouted at Howard Morgan. Morgan released his grip long enough to push Sally away, and as he did so, the bespectacled man tried to escape, but Morgan was too quick, ramming the man's head hard against the brick wall behind him. He stepped back and the man slumped to his knees with a low gurgle and then fell to the ground unconscious. Sally caught her balance and moved forward holding her asp high, ready to strike.

Sally's colleague PC Bob Wilkinson came gasping up to join her. He was in his early fifties and had several thousand more miles on the beat behind him, and it showed. It was clear in the shortness of his breath and the cynicism in his eyes. He held his asp warily forward, and moved to block Morgan's getaway. But Morgan, breathing as heavy as Bob Wilkinson, backed into the wall, making no move to run.

Sally thumbed the send button on her police radio.

"Foxtrot Alpha from forty-eight."

Bob Wilkinson meanwhile stared at Howard Morgan, the asp in his hand twitching like a hazel rod finding water.

"What's your name?"

Confusion rippled across Morgan's face as he stood against the wall, trembling, though not with anger any more.

"Is he going to be all right?"

Bob knelt and put his hand to the injured man's neck as Sally's radio crackled.

"Go ahead, Sally."

"Ambulance urgently, please. Waterhill estate. IC1 male. Head injuries." She thumbed the radio off and glared at Morgan. "What's your name, sir!"

Morgan snapped his head back to meet Sally's focused stare as the unconscious man groaned slightly and moved. Bob held his arm.

"Please try not to move. You may have concussion."

Morgan looked at Sally, taking in her presence for the first time. "My name's Morgan."

"Morgan who?"

"Howard Morgan."

"Howard Morgan, I am arresting you . . ."

She stopped as Bob stood up and pulled her to one side.

"Hang on a minute, Sally."

"What's up?"

"You know who that is." He nodded at the prostrate man, the distaste sitting on his lips like sour wine.

"No. What difference does it make?"

"That's Philip Greville."

Sally's radio crackled again, "Forty-eight from Foxtrot Alpha. Ambulance on way."

Sally shook her head, puzzled. "Who's Philip Greville?"

"The worst kind of slag, that's who."

"Meaning?"

"Meaning he's on the sex offenders list. Kids."

Sally nodded, taking it in.

"He was outed last week in the local papers. People know who he is. They know *what* he is."

Sally nodded over to Morgan. "Doesn't give them the right to assault him. Are you saying we shouldn't arrest Morgan?"

"Of course I'm not. I'm just saying we should find out what's going on first."

Morgan came to life again, pointing at Greville and shouting at Sally.

"He's got my daughter."

Sally held up a soothing hand. "All right, sir. Try and keep calm."

"Make him say where my Jenny is." Morgan couldn't hold back the tears and he didn't even try. "You make him tell."

South-west of the Waterhill estate, the White City police station squatted powerfully under the Westway flyover, sprawling in every direction like a concrete fortress. Crime didn't pay, unless you were an architect, it seemed.

Delaney turned in to the car park and pulled his ageing Saab 900 to a halt, the handbrake creaking as he levered it upwards. His knees creaked in almost harmonic sympathy as he levered himself out of the car. He yawned expansively. Too many late nights were writing cheques his body could no longer cash. He'd been up since five thirty this morning but he might as well have stayed in bed for all the progress he had made on Jackie Malone's murder. They were no further forward and he wasn't relishing the thought of Kate Walker's uncle, the superintendent, demanding an update, demanding progress. As soon as he heard the dead woman had been asking for Delaney he'd be on his back, no doubt getting him taken off the case, and Delaney didn't want that. Superintendent Walker had made it quite clear he had little time for Delaney and would be quite happy to see him bounced out of the force.

The trouble was, Delaney didn't have anything to give him, Jackie Malone was part of the criminal underworld and people like Jack Delaney just weren't welcome there, even when they were trying to find the killer of one of their own. He had spent the best part of the morning talking to the streetwalkers who worked the area near Jackie Malone's flat. Not too pleased to be roused from sleep and letting him know it. No one knew a thing. No one heard a thing. No one saw a thing. Life on Mars, Jack thought ironically; what about life on fucking Earth?

He walked through the entrance doors and sketched a wave at the desk sergeant, Dave "Slimline" Patterson, a five-foot-ten rugby-playing barrel of a man in his late thirties who, rumour had it, lived in fear of his wife, who was five foot nothing but came from Aberystwyth.

Patterson grimaced sympathetically at Delaney. "Thought you weren't due in till this afternoon?"

"So did I. Walker wants all noses to the grindstone."

"Up his arse more like."

Delaney laughed in agreement and keyed the numbers into the security pad, then walked through the doors and headed up the stairs to the CID briefing room. He groaned inwardly as he looked up to see the man he had just been cursing coming down them.

Superintendent Charles Walker was a handsome man in his early fifties. A hard face made interesting by a jagged scar on his left cheek. He wore the scar like he wore his full dress uniform, with pride stepping over into arrogance. He claimed it came from his early days in the army, though Delaney had his doubts; there were any number of coppers he knew who'd like to meet the man in a dark alley some night, but not to give him a blow job.

"Delaney. Any word on this murdered prostitute?"

Delaney shook his head. "I think the preferred media-friendly term is sex worker, sir."

"The media can kiss my backside, Delaney."

"Sir." Delaney nodded drily, all too aware that the superintendent courted the media like a C-list celebrity. Charles Walker was a political copper and always had been; crime statistics were stepping stones to promotion for him, nothing more, nothing less. And he did everything he could to put himself in a good light with the media.

"I want all eyes on this missing girl. It's why you've been called back in. The dead tart is not priority. We clear on that?"

"Sir."

"Seems you had some kind of history with the woman."

"Professional, sir."

Walker looked at him, the doubt and distaste all too clear in his expression. "Your reputation is well known, Detective Inspector; let's not enhance it any. Just focus on the missing girl."

"Sir."

"And do that goddam tie up. You look a disgrace, man."

The superintendent gave a dismissive flick of his head and carried on down the stairs. Delaney momentarily considered giving him what Dirty Harry would have called a five-point suppository, but unfortunately they didn't have metal badges in the Met, and he wouldn't want to give Walker the pleasure. Instead he curled his lip, kept his counsel and headed up to the briefing room, where the sound of laughter and loud chat did nothing to improve his mood or the state of his aching head.

Mornings in police briefing rooms were pretty much the same the world over, and this one could just as easily have been a staff room in a school, or a conference room in a big department store, or a hotel where sales executives had been summoned for a training session. The same amount of boredom, ego, petty jostling, cheap jokes, flirtations and bad coffee. The only thing different with the police was the stakes.

Jackie Malone's picture was pinned to the left of the noticeboard, but taking centre stage was Jenny Morgan. Live kids in jeopardy clearly took precedence over dead prostitutes; fact of life — and death. Delaney could see the sense but couldn't drag his gaze away from Jackie's photo. Her eyes seemed to look straight at him like Kitchener's finger, unremitting with blame. He finally looked across to the photo of the young girl.

Jenny Morgan's photo showed the face of a pretty, if solemn, twelve-year-old. Her hair and eyes were as dark as her father's and she stared out defiantly at the world.

Delaney couldn't stop himself from yawning, and covered his mouth as he watched Bonner speaking with DC Sally Cartwright, who had finished her morning's beat in uniform and was now officially on her first day with CID. She had changed into a smart charcoal-grey suit and wouldn't have looked out of place in an estate agent's. He was not at all surprised that Bonner was paying her far more attention than her older ex-colleague. Bob Wilkinson could be a regal pain in the backside, Delaney knew that, but he liked his honesty and his straightforwardness, and most important of all he trusted his instincts. An old-fashioned copper. If Bob Wilkinson said someone was dodgy then you could bet your defunct Irish punt that they were.

The whisper of bored conversation came to a halt as Delaney's immediate boss walked into the room. Chief Inspector Diane Campbell was in her forties, she wore her bobbed hair like a helmet and her make-up like an act of war. She snapped a critical look at Bonner, whose schoolboy smile slid quickly off his face like a fried egg off a greasy plate.

"What have we got, Bonner?"

"Jenny Morgan, ma'am. She's been missing since after school yesterday. That's nineteen hours."

"And it's only just been reported?"

"That's right, ma'am. This morning. Her father. Single parent."

"Why did he take so long?"

"We're looking into it. But from what the relief told me, he's not the sharpest pencil in the case."

Campbell looked across at Delaney. "So I gather. The father, Howard Morgan. Has he been charged for the assault on Greville?"

Bonner shook his head. "Not yet."

"Good. Because there are potential political implications here."

"Ma'am?"

"Somebody leaked the information about Greville to the press; we're all being looked at here."

"Maybe it's not us that should be looked at."

"Try and persuade Greville not to pursue, for the moment at least. I gather he wasn't seriously injured?"

Delaney coughed and spoke up, his voice hoarse. "No. And to be honest, he's not my top priority at the moment."

"If we do have a top priority, it's what I tell you it is. We all clear on that?"

Bonner smiled. "Pellucid, ma'am."

"Shut it, Sergeant."

"Ma'am."

"Delaney. I want the father, Howard Morgan, on TV as soon as possible, and I don't want any confusion over the issues involved here. We clear?"

Delaney nodded. "Pellucid, ma'am."

A hint of a smile almost twitched Campbell's lips but she managed to contain it.

"Apologies to those of you who were about to go off shift. But the super wants all hands to the pump until that little girl is found. Anyone got a problem with that?"

No one did. She looked over at Delaney again. "Keep me posted." She moved briskly from the room and Delaney moved to the front, taking charge of the meeting.

"You heard what she said. Time is critical here. We've already lost nearly a day because of her father; let's not lose any more. I'm going to talk to Morgan. Meanwhile, I want background checks. I want to know everything about him, and I want to know everything about his daughter. School friends, boyfriends, hobbies, clubs, the lot. DC Cartwright, you're with me."

"Sir."

Her face lit up a little at being called DC for the first time. Delaney pointed at DI Jimmy Skinner, a tall, thin, pale-faced man in his thirties who spent every hour he could find playing internet poker. "Jimmy, I want you to speak to Greville."

"Is that to be a polite conversation?"

"You heard what the boss said?"

"I did."

Delaney turned to Inspector Audrey Hobb, early fifties, two years off her thirty and looking forward to retirement.

"Audrey, I want all your available uniforms out on the street with pictures of Jenny. Young girls don't just disappear in broad daylight; somebody must have seen something."

"Let's hope so."

The group got to their feet as though dismissed, but Delaney held his hand up.

"Hang on a minute. There's one more thing." He pointed to the picture on the left of the noticeboard. "Jackie Malone. Some of you are familiar with the case. She had a boy sometimes in her care, Andy. We think he's with his uncle, Russell Martin, but we want to make sure. DS Bonner will organise some photos. When you're out on the street, I want you to show his photo too. Okay, Audrey?"

"Fine by me."

Bonner leaned in. "You think the chief will like it, sir?"

Delaney ignored him. "Okay, that's it. But one last thing. We all know how these cases sometimes turn out, and we all know how critical time is. The longer we take, the less chance we have of finding her alive. But this isn't going to be one of those cases. We're going to find that girl. We're going to do everything to make that happen, and we are going to take her out of harm's way. We clear?"

"Sir." The response was immediate, and, galvanised, the briefing room emptied. Delaney fumbled a couple of painkillers from a small bottle he kept in his pocket and sighed. It was going to be another long day.

CHAPTER
SEVEN

Delaney stopped at the water cooler in the corridor outside the briefing room and poured himself a clear plastic cup's worth. The gurgling of the cooler as it dispensed the water matched the gurgling in his stomach. Whiskey and late-night kebabs, not a good combination. He looked out of the window up at the massive flyover that poured traffic into the city like a Roman aqueduct sluicing sewage. The water was cool at least and did something to ease the throbbing in his forehead. Bob Wilkinson joined him at the cooler, pouring himself a cup.

"You look like shit, boss," he said.

Delaney winced. "Everyone's a detective."

"I'll stick with the uniform, thanks. Leave the glory-hunting to the likes of you and young Sally Cartwright."

Delaney snorted. "Glory. Right."

"Any word on Jackie Malone?"

Delaney shook his head. "The post-mortem's tomorrow. Might give us something to go on, but I doubt it."

"It's not like the books."

"Rarely."

Bob Wilkinson moved as if to leave, then hesitated, looking back at Delaney.

"What is it?"

"Just thought you ought to know . . ."

"Go on."

"There's a bit of gossip going round."

"About?"

"About you and Jackie Malone."

"What about her?"

"That you might have been too friendly with her. Maybe you're not the best man to be looking into her murder."

"And what do you think?"

"I think if I were Jackie Malone I wouldn't want anyone else on it."

"Thanks, Bob."

Wilkinson scowled. "Yeah, well. I'm off to St Mary's to sweet-talk a paedophile."

Delaney dropped his cup into the bin as the sound of purposeful feet clacking on the hard floor behind made him turn round. Sally Cartwright approached eagerly. She was joining him in interviewing Morgan and was clearly relishing her first day as a detective constable. As they walked along the corridor towards the interview room, he recognised the all-too-youthful enthusiasm that shone from her eyes and felt sorry for her. People came on the job for all kinds of reasons, and the ones who wanted to do good, who wanted to help people, who wanted to put something back into the community were the ones who suffered most. There might at one time have been a place for idealism in the

Girl Guides, but not any more, and certainly not in the Metropolitan Police. Pest control, Delaney thought, that's all we are, glorified pest control, but at least stamping on bugs was something he liked to do.

Interview room number one was on the ground floor near the entrance. Usually used for talking to members of the public, taking witness statements and so on. For the serious villains the room at the back of the station near the custody cells was used. Windowless and soulless. Interview room number one at least had a window; even though it just showed the car park beyond, it let sunlight in and that made all the difference. Otherwise it was a bland square room with a mirror on the wall opposite the window, and a rectangular table with two plastic moulded chairs either side, in unapologetically seventies orange. Morgan sat with his back to the window and Delaney pulled out a chair for Sally and sat down beside her, giving Morgan an appraising look. Estate agents reckoned prospective buyers made their minds up about a property within minutes; it took Delaney a lot less than that with people. This guy had *bent* tattooed all over him. He could see it in the way he sat restless in the chair. His fingers mobile, rubbing his arms or smoothing the fabric of his oil-stained jeans. He was as comfortable in a police station as a pig in a slaughterhouse.

Morgan rubbed his thigh again and looked up at Delaney, the hope hungry in his hangdog eyes. "Is there any news? Have you found her?"

"We've only just found out that your daughter has been missing overnight, haven't we?" Delaney's tone was far from sympathetic and Sally, taking out her notebook, watched puzzled as he leaned in angrily, getting into Morgan's face.

"And those hours could have been vital!"

Morgan blinked, clearly unnerved by Delaney's proximity.

"What are you saying?"

Delaney slammed his hand down hard on the table, "I'm saying we need to know exactly what you know and we need to know it now."

"Guv . . ."

Delaney flashed a look at Sally. "Shut it." He looked back at Morgan. "You do understand what I'm saying?"

"Of course I do. I want her found."

"Why did you attack Philip Greville?"

"He brought his car to my garage last week."

"And?"

"And afterwards some people told me he'd been in the paper. He'd taken some girl and been in the paper for it. And prison . . ."

"Go on?"

"And then . . . and then when my Jenny didn't come home . . ."

"You thought it was him?"

Morgan looked up. "Wasn't it?"

"See, what I don't understand is, why . . . If you knew there was a known child offender in your area, and your daughter didn't come home from school, or at any time during the night, why did you leave it to this morning till you did something about it?"

Morgan shook his head. "I didn't know."

"You didn't know what?"

"I didn't know she was missing. I was working late on a job. I came in, I assumed she'd put herself to bed. She takes care of herself."

"She's twelve years old, for Christ's sake."

Morgan shook his head again, remorsefully, and Sally gave him a reassuring smile as she looked up from her note-taking.

"It's all right, Howard, just tell us what you know. Anything you tell us could be important. When did you last see her?"

Morgan shifted awkwardly in his chair, his eyes not meeting hers. "I work late sometimes. Since her mother died she's been good at taking care of herself."

Sally nodded sympathetically. "When did her mother die?"

"Two years ago."

Delaney sat back in his chair, crossing his arms. "How did she die, Mr Morgan?"

"Cancer. They couldn't do anything. Too late, they said. We never did hold with doctors. They said if we'd been earlier, but we weren't. Too late, that's what they said."

Sally wrote in her notebook. "So it's just the two of you?"

"That's right. Just the two of us. And Jake."

Delaney sighed angrily. "Who's Jake?"

"He's my brother. My older brother. He works with me at the garage. There's no one else."

"Do you have any other relations? Anyone she might have gone to see?"

Morgan shook his head. "No, it's just us. We've got each other."

"Okay, Mr Morgan. Think carefully: did either you or your brother see Philip Greville after you had fixed his car?"

Morgan's brow furrowed, as if trying to squeeze some juice of memory from his troubled mind. His eyes had the look of a hurt and hunted animal as he tried to remember.

"I can't see him."

Delaney cursed under his breath and fumbled in his pocket again for his bottle of painkillers.

St Mary's Hospital is a sprawling Victorian complex on Praed Street in Paddington. The old and the modern rose-coloured cheek by pierced jowl. Where Princess Diana once came to have her babies, and where the punched and the battered drunks of a Friday and Saturday night clog up the rooms and try the patience of the night staff working A&E as regularly as a Swiss clock.

Bob Wilkinson was standing at the vending machine squashing a thin paper cup between his bony, nicotine-stained fingers, scowling as he drank the bitter fluid contained within and hoping to Christ the thing wasn't swimming with the MRSA bug. He hated hospitals almost as much as he hated people. He looked further up the corridor where Bonner was finishing talking to Greville, who was laid out on a bed; the DS was smiling at him, treating him like he was a normal human being, not kiddie-fiddling pond scum. Bonner was the future of the Met as far as Wilkinson could tell, just like Superintendent Walker. More spin doctor than thief-taker; the kind of shiny-suited, even-teethed bastards who danced around to a political agenda, letting the paedophiles fiddle while Rome burned.

The object of his scrutiny, Bonner, smiled a final time at Greville and walked back up the corridor to join Wilkinson at the vending machine, fishing in his pocket for some change and wrinkling his nose. "What is it with the smell in this place?"

Wilkinson shrugged. "Hospitals are all the same, boss. Nothing about them is pleasant."

Bonner chunked the coins into the machine. "Including the coffee."

"Especially the coffee."

Bonner jerked his head back to the room where Greville lay on top of the bed, still clothed, his nose now taped. "What do you reckon to twinkletoes?"

Bob scowled. "He'll live. Unfortunately."

"He had it coming, I guess. Sooner or later on that estate he was going to get a kicking when word got round what he was."

"You ask me, he deserves a lot more than he got."

"Just as well our job is just to catch them, then."

"Maybe."

Bonner gave him a shrewd look. "Someone leaked his name to the press."

Wilkinson laughed. Short, dismissive. "Don't look at me. I'm coming up to my thirty."

"You reckon he's involved with this missing girl?"

Wilkinson shook his head regretfully. "His alibi stands up."

"An entire orchestra saying he was in rehearsal all day and in concert all evening. I'd say that stands up."

"He's probably clean on this, but he's involved in something. Take it to the bank. It's not just his wand he's been wagging."

"That would be a baton."

"Call it what you like. Slags like him don't change, they never do. You ask me, we should be leaning on him. And leaning on him hard. Not tiptoeing around like a pair of fucking ballerinas so he doesn't press charges."

"Times have moved on, Constable."

Wilkinson crumpled his plastic coffee cup and threw it into the bin. "You might look good in a tutu, boss, but I'm too old for this crap. We should be out looking for that little girl, not covering the suits' blue-nosed arses."

"I reckon you and Delaney would make a good team."

"That's because he's a proper cop."

"What's that mean?"

Wilkinson gave him a flat look. "Someone who knows that the end always justifies the means, Sergeant Bonner."

Bonner gave a short laugh. "Jack Delaney. Last of the midnight cowboys." He threw his own coffee cup into the bin and jerked his thumb at Bob Wilkinson. "Come on then, Tonto. Time to see what scum has washed up on the morning tide."

Morgan's Garage was about half a mile from the Waterhill estate in a run-down stretch of mainly commercial real estate, a no-man's-land of lockups and storage facilities within a brick's throw of the Harrow Road. Wire fences protected weed-polluted tarmac and graffiti-sprayed warehouses. At the end of the street stood a few houses that had been built in the fifties in the hope of an urban renewal for the area that never came. Morgan's workshop was an extended garage that his father had fitted out sometime in the early sixties and that hadn't been touched since. Red bricks and a concrete floor. A bare bulb overhead, a 1972 Ford Escort stripped back beneath it, yellow, rusting and in need of serious loving attention.

Inside the garage Delaney moved a grease-covered spanner to one side of the cluttered worktop as Morgan picked up a photo frame and carefully replaced the original of the photo that was now pinned to the briefing room wall back at White City police station. Jenny still looked out at the camera, her eyes giving nothing away. Sally took the frame from his callused, stained and shaking hands.

"This is definitely the most recent photo you have of her?"

"She don't like having her picture taken."

Delaney held his gaze. "Why's that?"

Morgan shrugged and looked off to the side. "She just don't."

Sally smiled sympathetically. "What about boyfriends?"

"What do you mean?"

"Does she have a boyfriend?"

Morgan shook his head angrily. "Of course she doesn't."

Sally continued gently. "It's possible. Someone from school, perhaps?"

"I would know!"

"She's a very pretty girl."

"She's my girl. I would know!"

Delaney considered the fury that shone in the man's eyes with an almost religious fervour. He listened to the body language and met Morgan's defiant gaze with a look that held as much anger, and more, in check.

"You didn't know she was missing for nineteen hours, though, did you?"

Sally flinched, startled at the aggression in his voice, as Delaney stepped forward, getting into Morgan's space.

"What else don't you know?"

Morgan rubbed his left arm, up and down, as he stepped back a pace. "I didn't know she was gone. I look after her."

Delaney snorted. "You do a great job. Does she have a computer?"

Morgan didn't answer, and Sally prompted him gently. "Does she have her own computer, for schoolwork?"

"In her bedroom. She has one in her bedroom. I don't know how to use it."

For the first time, maybe, Delaney felt a twinge of sympathy for the man.

Sally continued to smile encouragingly at Morgan, good cop to Delaney's bad. "Do you mind if we take the computer, Mr Morgan?"

"Why would you do that? She needs that. She told me she needs it for her homework. All the kids have got them."

"I know."

"When she comes home, she'll want to know where it is. She'll be home soon, won't she?"

"We hope so." Sally had a soothing voice, like soft honey. Delaney found himself thinking that she'd probably make a good mother some day; Howard Morgan was just like a child in a lot of ways.

"Sometimes people use their computers like diaries, Mr Morgan," she said. "They write things in them."

"I don't know. She never showed me."

"It might help us find her."

"Take it then. I just want her home. She should be home."

Delaney considered Morgan for a moment or two but could see nothing in his eyes that he hadn't already seen in his own. The thought didn't reassure him.

There are all sorts of places where the dispossessed and the helpless of London gather. Abandoned warehouses, filthy underpasses, old churchyards tucked away in shameful Victorian decay right in the heart of the city, although the city, of course, has no heart. Bob Wilkinson knew that for a fact. This was a city that killed people. Literally. You could kill a person with a building as easily as you could with an axe — he didn't know who said that, but he agreed with the sentiment. Bob would have liked to take an axe to some of the people he had to deal with in his job on a daily basis. He watched as Bonner sniffed disdainfully and looked down at the inert body of a young girl. They were in an underpass, a late-night drop-in for the substance- and alcohol-abusers who had nowhere else to go. In the winter it would probably kill them, but in the summer it kept them out of the rain and out of the noses of late-night theatre-goers on Shaftesbury Avenue. Didn't keep them out of Bonner's nose, though, and it was a smell he clearly didn't much care for.

He toed the young girl roughly with his shoe, looking at the picture of Jenny Morgan that he held in his hand.

"Easy, Sergeant." Bob's disapproval was clear in his voice, but Bonner ignored him and kicked the sleeping girl again.

"Wakey, wakey."

The young girl turned her head and blinked angrily up at Bonner.

"Why don't you fuck off?"

It wasn't Jenny. Bonner nodded at her and put the photo back in his pocket.

"All right, princess. Back to your beauty sleep."

Bonner and Wilkinson walked on through the subway that led from the hospital to where their car was parked. The girl called after them.

"Hang on, copper, you got any change?"

"Yeah," Bonner called back and carried on walking.

Bob looked at him and shook his head. "You're a piece of work, you know that."

"That's a piece of work, Sergeant, to you." Bonner grinned.

"And you can kiss my arse," Wilkinson muttered, not quietly.

Bonner pretended he hadn't heard it. "We haven't got time to fuck about, Bob. That little girl needs to be found; it's about getting the job done quickly."

"I bet your girlfriend loves that approach."

"My women love everything about me."

"Course they do, sir."

Bonner strode quickly up the subway stairs as Wilkinson followed behind, thanking Christ on a bicycle that he was getting out of the job soon.

Delaney looked around Jenny Morgan's room. It was sparse, neat. No posters of boy bands on the wall. No pink furry ponies or glittering costume jewellery. No Keep Out signs. No notebooks with doodles on the cover and I heart this or I heart that. No photos of horses, or best mates hugging each other in photo booths designed for passport pictures. No jewellery boxes or musical boxes or clothes strewn on the floor. No books lined up carefully or artlessly on shelves, no CD player or DVD player. Just a bed, a couple of cupboards and a rug arranged neatly on the floor. It could have been a hostel room, or a nun's room. Nothing to show it was the bedroom of a twelve-year-old girl. On a desk that stood in front of a small window overlooking her father's yard was a small laptop computer.

Delaney opened the cupboards and looked through the drawers. Clothes, old birthday cards. Project folders from school. But no letters, no diaries, no real clue to the missing girl's personality. Maybe she didn't have one. Maybe she was as blank a canvas as her bedroom seemed to be.

He turned on the computer. As he expected, her desktop was clear. No documents or pictures left carelessly, everything ordered into its proper folder, its proper file. He heard voices from downstairs, switched the computer off and picked it up, looking around the room to see if he had missed anything.

He hadn't.

Downstairs, Sally was talking to Jake Morgan, Howard Morgan's older brother. He was in his late forties, as heavily built and dark-browed as his sibling but a few inches taller, and the oil stains on his face looked as ingrained as a tattoo. He was wearing a filthy T-shirt under a pair of dungarees, his massive arms hung loosely by his sides, and as Delaney looked at the slack expression on his face, the tune of duelling banjos ran unavoidably through his mind.

Jake frowned as he looked at what Delaney was holding. "What you got there? That's Jenny's." His voice was slow, as if framing the simple words was an effort for him, but Delaney could hear the menace in it.

"We need to find Jenny, Jake. You know that's why we're here." Sally smiled pleasantly at the large man. "This is Detective Inspector Delaney. We need to take her computer to see if it can help us find her."

Jake turned nervously to his brother. "We didn't steal it, did we, Howard?"

Morgan looked guiltily at Delaney. "We didn't steal it."

"We're not bothered where the computer came from originally, just what Jenny might have written in there."

"Someone gave it us for a job."

"It's okay, Howard." Sally smiled again and Delaney found himself thinking she should get a job as a model: the smiling face of the Metropolitan Police. Something he'd certainly never qualify for.

"I need you and your brother to go over everything you remember, Jake," he said. "Everything about yesterday, about the last time you saw Jenny."

Jake nodded, his agitation showing in the way he clenched his fists. The cloth of the T-shirt straining at the biceps and making the tattoos on his forearms bulge. Forearms like industrial diggers, Delaney thought. A man could do a lot of damage with arms like that.

"I live up the road." Jake's voice was as slow as tar.

"And?"

"I live up the road. So I didn't see her. Not yesterday."

Delaney looked over at Howard. "Someone must have seen her."

Morgan shifted uncomfortably. Delaney looked at him steadily. "We're going to hold a press conference later. Television. I want you to be there."

Morgan shook his head, distressed. "I can't do that."

"If she has run away, then an appeal from you might just bring her home."

"She didn't run away." Morgan shook his head again, as if the action would make it so. "She loves her dad."

Sally stepped in before Delaney could respond. "It would be a big help. And don't worry, we would prepare a statement for you. All you'd have to do is read it."

"No! I can't do it."

Delaney looked at Morgan's darting eyes and his trembling fingers. A chill settling in his heart.

"What do you want to tell us, Howard?"

Jake stepped forward. "We can't read, see? Just boxes. For parts and that. Jenny did our reading and writing for us. Since . . ."

Morgan grunted. "Since my wife died, Inspector."

Delaney nodded. "Okay."

Morgan looked to the side again, the hurt clear in his eyes. "She never kissed me."

"I'm sorry?"

"Jenny. She never kissed me."

"What do you mean?"

"She never kissed me goodbye before going to school. She always kissed me goodbye. What if she never comes back?"

But Delaney didn't reply. Some questions you just couldn't answer.

The Pig and Whistle was the aptly named pub a short staggering distance from White City police station. It had been used by the boys and girls in blue for over a hundred years, and Sally Cartwright, a sparkle in her eyes, was basking in the noisy hubbub and savouring her first day out of uniform. Opposite her sat Bob Wilkinson, the sparkle, had there ever been one, long since gone from his eyes.

"The way I see it, Sally, there's only one thing you need to know as a detective, and that is . . . once a slag, always a slag." Everyone was a slag to Bob. Young, poor, rich, old . . . if they were a criminal, or a suspected criminal, they were a slag. It kept matters simple.

"And the way to deal with slags . . ."

But DC Cartwright didn't get to benefit from her older colleague's wisdom, as Delaney approached carrying a couple of drinks.

"Come on, Bob. She's off the clock. The slags'll keep till tomorrow, eh?" He handed Sally her drink. "Here's to you. First day on the job."

Sally nodded reflectively. "Not the best of days, boss."

"The way it goes sometimes."

"Don't like to think that girl's still out there somewhere, on her own."

Bonner, with DI Skinner and Dave "Slimline" Patterson, joined them, handing round drinks and crisps and packets of nuts.

Bonner smiled at Sally. "We'll find her."

Delaney raised his glass. "Here's to DC Sally Cartwright. The future of the Met, God help us."

The drinks were drained and another round ordered, and another.

Many hours later Delaney stumbled into his flat, lay back exhausted on his bed and fired up a cigarette. Like Sally, he was disappointed they hadn't found Jenny Morgan, but it was Jackie Malone's ravaged body that haunted him, and he hoped her cold, naked corpse wouldn't join him in his dreams again, her mouth wet with blood on his lips, his hands finding openings that nature had never intended.

As Delaney laid his head back on his pillow, and drifted into troubled sleep, across town in a back alley of Soho a young girl lay huddled in the doorway to an accountancy office. The moon in the cloudless sky gave her skin a ghostly-pale look. Two officers on night patrol looked down at her motionless body; one hooked off his police radio and made the call.

Another child dead on the streets of London.

CHAPTER
EIGHT

Kate Walker turned the thermostat on the shower as high as she dared and waited a moment before stepping under the scalding water. She closed her eyes as the jets pummelled her tired muscles. She'd been up since six o'clock, not just because of the bright sunlight spilling in through her bedroom window, but because, as she always did, she'd spent a restless night. Night horrors, they called it, and the term always made her laugh. After the horrors she saw on a day-to-day basis, dreams shouldn't have had any hold over her. But they did. They always had. Since she was a little girl she would wake early, and when she drifted back into sleep the dreams would start. Dreams that would leave her muscles locked and a penetrating sadness that took a while to shake off. The hot water helped. She rubbed the exfoliating scrub over her body as if to wash away the lingering emotions of her nightmares, watching the soapy water puddle around her feet and swirl soundlessly down the drain. After a few minutes she put the sponge aside and just stood under the water. Letting it pool through her hair and spatter against her glowing skin. She stood there for at least five minutes, breathing deeply, her eyes closed, her heartbeat slowing to a normal pace.

Delaney woke with a painful start, the ringing phone clattering into his consciousness like a dental drill set on kill. He picked it up, grunted a few words and hung up. He looked at the clock on his bedside table and cursed under his breath, then stood up unsteadily and stumbled through to the bathroom, wincing at the blinding sun as it spiked in at him through the Venetian blinds.

He dragged an electric razor across the resisting planes and angles of his face and looked at himself in the mirror. His eyes still looked as if they had seen too many things they no longer wished to see and the cold water he splashed into them couldn't wash the hardness away. The muscles of his cheeks sagged and the puffiness around his eyes spoke as much of alcohol as sleeplessness. He splashed more water into his bloodshot eyes and rubbed a towel roughly across to dry his face. Then he pulled on his jacket and yawned. Another day.

Outside, the sun cooked the fractured pavements of the city. Everywhere signs of life stirred. People thronged and bustled, humanity busy with purpose. Thrusting like beetles into the underground stations that swallowed them whole to vomit them out again throughout the metropolis. The oxygen particles in the blood of the metropolis, making it pump, making it breathe.

But death in London was also as regular as a heartbeat. Death from old age, from cancer, from heart attacks when playing squash or having energetic sex, from pneumonia and exposure, from automotive accident, from desperation and loneliness, and from murder. On a daily basis the bodies mounted up and were brought to Kate Walker and her colleagues for examination, for analysis.

This Wednesday morning, while the sun shone bright, she had five cold bodies on the slate, including Jackie Malone, and one young child jumping to the head of the queue. Another statistic on the slab. Another job to do.

Kate snapped the latex gloves tight to her fingers and looked down at the mortuary table. The young girl's body lay ready for her examination. Kate put her at about eleven . . . maybe twelve, maybe ten. Life hadn't been kind to her in that short span. That was evidenced by the scars on her lifeless skin and the fractures that were revealed in the X-rays hanging on light boxes at the back of the room. Kate wished she could shine a light into the dead girl's brain and see what had happened in her life. But nothing was ever that simple. Certainly nothing in Kate's life. She picked up a scalpel, knowing that the little girl had already been through a world of hurt, but taking comfort in the knowledge that she was beyond pain now. She flicked the switch on the recording machine and began dictating as she went to work.

Delaney hurried along the corridors and into interview room one. If anything, it was hotter than it had been yesterday, but he made no move to open the windows. He took off his jacket and hung it on the back of a chair next to Bonner, who was sitting across the table from Terry Collier, a slight ginger-haired man in his late twenties. Collier was about five-foot-nine tall and as thin as a fishing rod; dressed in an avocado-green moleskin suit, he held a pair of round rimless glasses which he was polishing nervously.

Delaney smiled at him, but it didn't reach anywhere near his eyes. "Sorry to keep you waiting."

Collier put his glasses back on and ran a finger under his shirt collar and loosened his tie. "I don't understand why I am still here."

"You're still here, Mr Collier, because I want to talk to you."

"You can't hold me here. This is England, not Iran. I can leave any time I want to."

Delaney stared at him, letting the words hang in the air until Collier looked away.

"You came in earlier to amend your statement, I believe," Delaney prompted him.

"That's right."

"We need to talk about that."

Collier hunched defensively and looked pointedly at his watch. "Yes, I came in first thing. I told the woman at your front desk everything. She has all the details."

"People say God is in the details, Mr Collier. But I don't believe them. See, in our line of work the Devil is in the details. We get all the details and we always ferret the bastard out."

"I don't understand what you're talking about."

"You're an English teacher, aren't you?"

"Yes."

"So I am sure you know what a metaphor is." Delaney pulled the chair from under the table, the legs scratching loudly on the floor. He banged it into position and sat down heavily. Collier flinched instinctively back as Delaney leaned forward.

"Tell us again, for my benefit."

"Tell you what?"

Bonner smiled encouragingly, "You were on playground duty at end of school Monday?"

"It's all in my statement."

"Nobody's accusing you of anything, we just need to know all the facts."

"You could have fooled me."

The petulance in Collier's voice made Delaney want to reach across the table and slap him hard in the face, but he clenched and unclenched his fist under the table and let the moment pass.

"You could have been the last person to see Jenny Morgan alive, you do understand that, Mr Collier?"

Collier looked shocked. "Are you saying she's dead?"

"I didn't say that. Do you think she's dead?"

"How would I know that? What are you implying?"

Delaney let the words hang again, and looked down at Collier's statement. "You were on your own. No other teachers were with you?"

"Just me."

"And earlier you told our uniformed officers that you didn't see Jenny Morgan leaving?"

"That's right."

"But now you remember that you did?" Delaney kept his anger in check. Either the man was a liar and worse, or he was a bloody idiot.

"It came to me later. She left with a friend. Carol Parks."

"And you've only just remembered that!" Delaney couldn't stop his voice rising or his hand slapping hard on the table again.

Collier jumped back in his chair. "There are hundreds of children at that school. Am I supposed to remember every one?"

Delaney pushed a picture of Jenny Morgan across the table to him. "Just her."

"I know what you're trying to do here."

"We're trying to find a little girl who's missing, that's what we're trying to do."

"You're saying that I was the last person to see her alive. I know what that means. You've got me down as your prime suspect. You think I did it!"

"Did what, exactly?" Bonner leaned forward, any friendliness long since drained from his eyes.

"I just meant . . ." Collier shook his head, flustered, and Delaney brought his cold eyes to bear on him.

Collier swallowed nervously, running his finger under his collar once again.

Delaney stood up and pulled his jacket off the chair. He looked at Bonner. "I'm going to see the girl."

Collier stood up. "What about me?"

"We haven't finished with you yet. Sit down and the sergeant will organise you a cup of tea."

"You don't want me with you, guv?"

"I'll take Cartwright," said Delaney. "The feminine touch."

Kate Walker pulled off her blood-stained latex gloves and dropped them in the stainless-steel swing bin. She nodded to her assistant, who wheeled the remains of the young girl away. In life the child had suffered all sorts of indignities, and in death she had fared no better. Sharp steel was no friend to human skin or internal organs, and although in most cases Kate managed to do her job in a professional manner, in a disconnected way, to work on someone so young and so fragile and who had been so obviously in pain was hard. She ran a hand through her hair and composed herself. The morgue was no place for emotions, and for Kate that was a good thing. She picked up her schedule for the day and tried to put the image of the pretty, dark-haired, little girl out of her mind. They didn't even have a name for her yet.

Primrose Avenue was the kind of name, Delaney thought, that belonged in Surbiton or Chelsea, or else some suburb that wasn't dominated by the high-rise reality of a Waterhill estate casting a shadow all over it. But Primrose Avenue was where Carol Parks' family lived, and if there was a smell hanging on the hot still air, it wasn't the sweet smell of spring.

Abigail Parks, a modestly if smartly dressed woman, had been startled at first to find two detectives on the front doorstep of her small but immaculately kept home. She regained her composure quickly, though, and took them both through to the back garden, where her daughter, brought home from school to be interviewed, was waiting.

Out in the sunshine Delaney smiled reassuringly at Carol Parks, who took hold of her mother's hand like a lifeline. She was a quiet, brown-eyed girl of twelve, with mousy blonde hair and crooked teeth being set straight with National Health metal braces. Delaney had brought Sally Cartwright with him, but her youthful, cheerful presence had done little to calm the young girl's obvious nerves.

"You're not in any trouble."

"I haven't done anything."

"We know that. We just need to talk to you about Jenny. Your friend Jenny Morgan."

Carol shook her head, leaning into her mother. "I don't know anything."

Her mother squeezed her hand. "It's all right, nobody is accusing you of anything."

Sally crouched down a little, bringing herself to Carol's level. "She's your special friend, isn't she?"

Carol nodded.

"What do you remember of the day before yesterday, when you left school?"

"I didn't see her after school."

"Mr Collier said he saw you two together, leaving."

"After that. I left her at the gate."

"But you normally walk home together, don't you?"

Carol didn't answer, and Delaney looked at her mother, the question in a bent eyebrow. Abigail Parks put an arm, defensively, around her daughter's shoulder.

"It's not far. They walk together. The school is only around the corner."

Sally smiled at Carol again. "But you didn't walk home together on Monday?"

Carol considered for a moment and then looked down at the ground, shaking her head.

"Why not?"

"She wanted to wait behind."

"In the playground?"

Carol slid her eyes off to the left, not looking at Sally. "Yes."

Delaney stepped closer. "Why, Carol? Why would she do that? What aren't you telling us?"

"Nothing. I told you, I don't know anything!"

She burst into tears and Delaney sighed. Kids were born liars, every single one of them. But they weren't very good at it.

Sally knelt down and took her hand.

"It's okay, Carol. It's just very urgent we find Jenny. We need to find her quickly and make sure she's safe. You do understand that, don't you?"

Carol nodded, but still wouldn't look at Sally, shaking her head as she gazed at the floor. "I don't know where she is."

Her mother patted her on the head. "It's okay, poppet." She nodded apologetically to Delaney. "I'm sorry we couldn't be of any help."

Delaney nodded back, frustrated, and handed her a card. "Speak to her; if there's anything she can tell you, get in touch as soon as you can."

"Of course."

Delaney pulled the door behind him as he left and strode angrily to his car. DC Cartwright, following behind, knew better than to try and engage him in conversation. As he opened his car door he looked across at her. "She was lying to us, Sally."

"I think so too, sir."

"About what, though?"

Sally shrugged. Delaney sighed and got into his car. If people just told them what they needed to know, their jobs would be a whole lot easier. Then again, if people just told the truth they would all be out of a job. A whole lot of people would be.

A short while later, Delaney pulled his car to a stop back in the White City police station car park and looked across to see Bonner watching Collier walk away from the building. He locked the door behind him and crossed angrily over to the sergeant.

"I thought I told you to hold him."

"He insisted, guv. There was nothing we could do."

"For now, maybe."

"Did you get anything from the girl?"

"She said she left Jenny at the school. They didn't walk home together."

"So our English teacher has been telling porkies?"

Delaney shrugged. "Maybe."

"Something else?"

Sally nodded. "We got the impression that there was something Carol Parks wasn't telling us."

Delaney watched as Collier walked through the front gates and out of sight.

Bonner shrugged apologetically. "We had nothing to hold him on. Uniform have been all over his house."

"And?"

"Like I say. Nothing."

Delaney scowled. His instincts had Collier in the frame somehow but he couldn't pursue the thought further as Morgan walked up to the entrance with his brother Jake.

Sally gestured to the building. "You coming in?"

Delaney looked across through the clear glass of the entrance doors to see Superintendent Walker plastering a look of concern and solicitude on his smooth face and shaking hands with the Morgan brothers with as much sincerity as a second-hand car salesman. His scowl deepened. "I've got to be somewhere. Bonner, you're with me."

Sally nodded and would have asked more, but Delaney had already turned and was striding purposefully away from the building.

CHAPTER
NINE

There was something fitting, Delaney thought, about a pathology lab being housed in the basement of a large Victorian building. The Victorians' twin fascinations with death and science going together like a horse and carriage. A black horse, obviously, with black feathers dancing from its head, pulling in its wake a black hearse with a black coffin inside.

Delaney ran his hands along the cold surface of the original white tiles and seemed to draw some strange comfort from them. He looked across at the mortuary table. A place of steel and blood, a place of obscene evisceration and exposure. The human Rubik's cube of a body snapped apart and disassembled to discover its secrets.

Jackie Malone was laid out on the table. Her body violated in life on a voluntary basis was about to be violated in death. A penetration by steel that she neither profited from nor had any choice over.

Kate Walker picked up an electric rotary saw and nodded as Delaney and Bonner approached.

"Sorry to keep you waiting."

"She's not going anywhere." Kate flicked the switch and the loud burr of the saw filled the room, bouncing off its antique tiles and setting a resonant tremor in Delaney's bones. He threw a sardonic look at Bonner.

"You wondered what kind of twist likes to cut dead people up, Eddie."

Kate fixed him with a defiant stare. "I guess that's why you and me are different, Cowboy. I like to do things, you just like to watch." She cut short any reply from Delaney by flipping down her goggles and lowering the blade of the saw. The throaty whine replaced by a keening whistle as it tore through flesh and sinew and bit into the bone of Jackie Malone's ribcage.

Delaney looked away. He'd been to hundreds of post-mortems but never to one where he had known the victim. Not like he had known Jackie Malone.

Time passed. Organs were removed, weighed, examined. The host structure that had once held Jackie Malone was rendered to its component parts. Flesh, blood, bone and sinew. If there was a soul once attached it wasn't there now, at least not one visible to scientific eyes.

Delaney looked across as Kate snapped off her latex gloves and dropped them in the bin. He didn't have to ask the question.

"Pretty much as I suspected at the murder scene. Death due to asphyxiation. She choked on her own vomit."

Bonner cracked a cold smile. "Whose elses would it be?"

"Give it a rest, Bonner." Delaney was in no mood for graveside humour any more.

"Her injuries were received post-mortem in the main. The serious ones at least."

Delaney nodded, the relief palpable. "Any useful semen?"

Kate paused for a moment at his choice of words but let it pass; she didn't joke in front of the dead. "Traces of lubricant in both the vaginal and anal passages. A lubricant consistent with those used in standard condoms, a hundred varieties."

"Not unusual, then?" Bonner asked.

"No. Especially not given the nature of her occupation."

Bonner shook his head, puzzled. "Sex crime. All that passion, rage . . . yet they still have the control to put a condom on."

Delaney frowned. "I blame television."

Kate looked across at him, but he wasn't joking.

"Everybody knows too much these days, don't they?"

Kate agreed. "About everything."

Howard Morgan's face filled the TV screen. The livid scar running from neck to eyeline on his left side made more lurid by the leaking colours of the old television set.

Abigail Parks thumbed the remote control so that she could hear his words.

"We just want you to come home. You're not in any trouble." His voice was stiff, halting, his eyes skittering nervously to the left, where unseen by the camera DC Sally Cartwright mouthed the words to him.

Abigail looked across at her daughter, who was watching the television with restrained nervous tension.

"If you are watching this. Just call us. Please."

Morgan's ravaged face was rendered both wide-and-small-screen in department stores throughout the capital. But few people stopped to hear what the scarred man was saying. Few people cared.

Outside, people went about their everyday business. Summer in the city and everything looked bright, everything looked cheerful, even the Japanese tourists. At Piccadilly Circus young lovers had their photos taken on the steps beneath Eros, red buses swung round the roundabout and underneath the large neon advertisements, giving snap-happy visitors the perfect photo opportunity. A London as far removed from Delaney and Jackie Malone and Howard Morgan and his daughter as the moon.

And along the Mall, heading towards Westminster, a sleek black car, its occupant another space traveller, but then all worlds collided sooner or later in the metropolis.

Superintendent Walker, fresh from the press conference, held a mobile phone to his ear and looked out at the passing tourists, making little attempt to hide the boredom in his voice.

"I have a meeting with the Home Secretary in half an hour." He listened impatiently. "I'm sure you do have your difficulties, my dear, but I have had problems with your people in the past. Problems I don't need right now." The hardness slipping into his voice now like cold steel unsheathed. "If he's not up to the job, we can always have him shipped back to Belfast . . . or wherever the black bog is that he crawled from."

He clicked the phone off and examined his nails.

Under the surface of the teeming streets, Kate rubbed moisturising cream into her hands and checked her own blood-red nails, clipped short. Delaney crossed to stand in front of her, watching as she massaged one hand with the strong fingers of the other. Hands, Delaney couldn't help but think, that should have been caressing the neck of a cello, or holding a paintbrush, not a scalpel. She looked up and caught his gaze, thrusting her hands into the pockets of her green trousers.

Delaney gestured at the inert body of Jackie Malone.

"Could you tell if intercourse took place at the time, thereabouts, of the murder?"

Kate gestured at Jackie's ravaged body. "I don't think this was sexually motivated."

"They wanted her dead."

"They succeeded."

"You saying she wasn't raped?"

Kate considered and shook her head. "I'm not saying that. I'm just saying I can't give you a definite answer on it."

"Meaning?"

"Meaning that intercourse had certainly taken place. Given the nature of her chosen profession, it's hard to tell if it involved her killer, or killers. Whether it was a voluntary or involuntary act."

"Any indications?"

Kate walked over to the instrument table and picked up another pair of latex gloves, easing her fingers into them as she talked, flexing her hands and looking back at Delaney.

"There was quite severe bruising around both the rectal and vaginal orifices. This would indicate a high level of resistance consistent with rape prior to the murder. And it does fit into the time pattern."

"You can't be definite?"

"Like I said, her job involved a certain amount of specialised activity."

Bonner laughed. "Stick and stones may break my bones, but whips and chains . . ."

Kate flicked a look at Bonner. "As you delicately put it, Sergeant, she did work in a . . ." she paused to find the right word, "niche market. S and M. Sadomasochism. There is scarring and bruising on her body that pre-dates the fatal assault."

Kate pointed to areas of bruising still visible on Jackie Malone's body, made more distinct by the cold whiteness of her skin.

Bonner grimaced. "She was into being beaten up?"

"I don't suppose she was into it, Sergeant, although who knows? But I guess that was how she paid the rent and put food on the table."

"So the rough sex could have been part of a sexual fantasy enacted by a client prior to her being murdered?"

Kate gave Delaney an appraising look. "Some men like that sort of thing, Jack. Don't they?"

Delaney smiled back, a smile as cold and thin-lipped as Jackie Malone on the mortuary table. "Why don't you just stick to looking inside her head?"

Kate broke the look first. She picked up the circular saw again and lowered its screaming blade on to the dead woman's skull. The saw growled as it struggled through bone, the dust flecking Kate's green top and spotting it red with tiny bits of matter.

Delaney turned away. "I've got an appointment."

Kate watched him as he walked away and turned to Bonner. "What is it with him?"

"I don't think he likes your uncle."

She looked after Delaney thoughtfully for a second and then turned her attentions back to Jackie Malone.

Outside in the cool corridor Delaney leant against the wall to stop the earth sliding from his tilting feet, laying both hands against the cool tiles and sucking air into his lungs like a drowning man rescued.

Gradually the pounding of blood in his ears lessened and the world shifted back on its proper axis. His breathing steadied, and straightening up, he stumbled for the bright sunshine outside. Hot enough to warm a planet but not hot enough to burn the memories clean.

He looked across the road, through the crowds of walkers and the slow flash of cars, to the kind of modern bar he really disliked, all white wood and chrome behind a big plate of clear glass. A goldfish bowl with alcohol. And visible behind the broad sweep of the counter, shiny steel pipes and amber-coloured bottles that delivered oblivion by the half-pint or shot.

He looked at the people standing there drinking, laughing, living in a world removed from pain. And wanted to join them. He wanted to throw down his badge on the dusty tarmac like a sheriff in an old western and leave the suffering and the responsibility behind. He considered it for a long moment, tasting the whiskey on his tongue, feeling the cold Guinness anaesthetising not just his throat but also his mind. The sensation almost willing his legs to step out into the road, but a passing woman stumbled suddenly into him. Slurring an apology, she knocked him back from the road, back from the bar, back to a missing girl and a murdered prostitute. He stood thinking about Jackie Malone for a moment, remembering her laugh. A deep, throaty, entirely infectious laugh. The only woman who ever made him forget his dead wife, if only for a brief while. Then he walked across the road for just one cold beer.

One and done.

CHAPTER
TEN

Delaney nodded at Dave Patterson as he walked back into police headquarters. "Slimline."

"Cowboy."

Patterson looked like he was going to say more, but Delaney quickly tapped in the security code, opened the door and walked up the stairs, not wanting to get caught up in idle chat.

The CID office was deserted. He hurried across to his desk and sat quickly behind it, looking around to see he wasn't being observed. He reached down and opened the lowest drawer; rummaging under the cluttered paperwork and case files, he found the small black book he was looking for. Jackie Malone's diary. He glanced around again, making sure he was still alone and flicked through the pages, looking for any other mention of his name. He tore out the last ten pages, flicked his cigarette lighter and set light to them, watching the flames lick greedily up the pages, devouring the writing on them. He held them for a second or two and then dropped them into his metal waste bin, watching until nothing was left but feathery ash. Then he put the diary into his pocket and threw some more papers into the bin to cover up the ash.

He put the bin back in place and looked up at the clock on the wall. Eight thirty in the evening, and not a single response to Morgan's televised appeal. Not one that checked out, anyway. He despaired for the sad lives of people sick enough to prey on other people's misery by making bogus confessions and giving false sightings. As he looked at the second hand of the clock sweep around the dial, he knew that as every hour passed the chances of finding Jenny Morgan alive diminished. It had already been far too long, and Delaney couldn't help wondering if she was soon to be another candidate for Kate Walker's clinical attention. And that was another mystery. Why a woman like Kate Walker should be doing the job she was. She'd had a privileged education, old money behind her; she could have done anything she wanted to do. What made a woman like her choose to dissect people for a living? He stood up and shrugged into his jacket. People like her came from a different place to the likes of him. He'd never understand them and he wasn't going to waste any time trying to change that. Not valuable drinking time anyway.

Howard Morgan sat alone in his front room. A bottle of cheap rum stood on the low formica-topped table in front of his chair, a glass full of the coarse liquid gripped in his immense fist. He raised the glass and swallowed half of it in one gulp, the amber liquid trickling from one corner of his mouth as it burned its way down his throat, a tear leaking slowly from his scarred eye. He looked at the photo of his young daughter that he had placed on the table and swallowed hard. His broken voice a croak. A valediction.

"I'm sorry."

He downed the rest of the rum and poured the glass full again.

"I'm so sorry."

Night-time again on the river. The heat still hung heavy in the air, like a blanket. The moon, covered with a few shreds of clouds, threw a cold, hard light on the ground below and bounced off the water.

In the silt-covered reeds a lap of water swelled, sucking the mud from the banks with a wet gurgle and rolling a head that half floated and banged against the bank. The lifeless eyes seemed devoid of colour, the moon reflected in miniature in each iris, the skin white with the texture of rain-soaked cardboard. The mouth pulled back in a rictus of death, the hands held with twisted-coat hanger wire. Darkness fell across the river as the moon was covered.

A girl's scream hung on the air and was muffled suddenly. A few moments later the moon slid clear of a tangle of clouds and lit the path by the river once more.

"Come on, love, I've got to get the car back. Move your bloody arse." The words of young love, post-coitus. A man in his early twenties picked his way along the water's edge.

"Hold on a minute. I'm trying to find my knickers." She was young too, pretty and teetering on heels built more for display than pedestrian use. "I can't bloody find them."

"Come on. It's not the first time, is it?"

And then another scream, of terror now, as Billy Martin leered up at the young woman from the water's edge, like a grey voyeur trying to peep up her all-too-flimsy skirt. The tilting, water-soaked head of Billy Martin. Ex of the parish.

She ran, still screaming, into the arms of her impatient boyfriend. Gasping for breath, she tried to describe what she had seen, but words failed her. She dragged him back to show him, but by then Billy Martin had gone again. Dragged under once more by the tidal flow, sucked back into the cold and silent embrace of the water's depths.

CHAPTER
ELEVEN

Thursday morning. Tempers soared on the Western Avenue as the rush-hour traffic crawled coughing and rasping to a virtual stop, the air thick with fumes and noisy with the angry honk of horns. In the winter the roads were choked badly enough with commuters, but in the summer months, with the added tourist traffic, a journey by car into the capital was made a far from pleasant thing. Ken Livingstone and his congestion charges were as much use in dealing with the problem as a sticking plaster on a dismembered limb.

The heat was already climbing well into the eighties as Delaney came into the office, yawning and scowling at the traffic noise that sounded through the open windows. He threw his jacket over the back of his chair, ran his fingers through his straggly hair and squeezed his knuckles into his bloodshot eyes. Fishing a couple of painkillers from his desk drawer, he swallowed them dry and grimaced as they stuck in his throat. He poured a long dash of cold coffee from the filter pot into a stained mug and groaned as he took a swallow. It had been sitting there since yesterday, and unlike fine wines and handsome women, the ageing process hadn't improved its appeal. He set about making a fresh pot as

Bonner sauntered in, fresher than a Swiss daisy. The DS watched amused as Delaney squinted against the bright sunlight splashing in through the windows.

"Heavy night, boss?"

Delaney grunted a monosyllabic reply; truth to tell, he couldn't remember the last time he had woken up without a hangover. He waited for the coffee to percolate through the machine, then poured himself a cup and walked across to Bonner, who was working on Jenny Morgan's laptop computer.

"Anything back from the techies?"

Bonner shook his head. "Nothing new, but I thought it was worth going through it again."

"Anything new?"

"Loads of e-mails to her school friends. Nothing very recent. Nothing very useful."

"Chat rooms?"

"Not that I can see. Certainly nothing from her mails."

"Check them all out. One of those school friends might not be."

"Might not be what?"

"A school kid, Bonner. Keep with the programme." Delaney winced, regretting raising his voice.

"You think somebody might have been grooming her?"

"The internet. It's a paedophile's paradise, isn't it?"

"It's every sick fucker's paradise, sir. Tell you what, if porn was petroleum, we'd have engines running on tap water by now."

But Delaney was distracted, hooding a hand over his eyes and looking out of the window, watching as a familiar thin red-haired figure walked briskly up to the police station entrance.

"What's he want?"

"Who?"

Delaney pointed out of the window. "The ginger-haired streak of piss. Jenny's English teacher."

Bonner shrugged. "Maybe he bonded with you, boss."

Delaney approached the front desk, nodding at Ellen, the young woman who was manning it that morning, and turned to Terry Collier, who was sitting patiently opposite.

"Mr Collier. Something else you remembered that you neglected to tell us earlier?"

"Yes. There's something you need to know."

Delaney looked at him for a hard moment. "You'd better come through then."

Delaney ushered Collier into the front interview room and shut the door firmly behind him.

"If this is something you should have told us earlier and we find her dead, I am going to come looking for you."

Collier was flustered. "You can't speak to me like that. I have rights."

Delaney's voice was a whisper. "You don't know anything about me. You don't know what I am capable of doing. But believe me, if you have fucked us around, I will make sure that you do."

Collier blinked and held up his hands apologetically. "We're on the same side here. We both just want to find the girl."

Delaney kept his voice level. "What do you want to tell me?"

"Jenny Morgan. She was a member of our computer club. At the school."

"And?"

"And I run the club."

Delaney couldn't hide his frustration. "Make your point."

"She had her own e-mail account that she ran from the school. I found it this morning on the computer she used. I came here straight away."

"Good."

Collier fished in his pocket and produced a piece of paper.

"I was able to get her log-in details. I'm what you call a super-user. We need to monitor what sites the kids are on. You wouldn't believe what is available on the internet these days."

"I think you'll find we know very well."

Collier's pale skin reddened under Delaney's gaze. "We're not supposed to access their private e-mail . . . but under the circumstances . . ." He handed Delaney the slip of paper. "I came in straight away."

Delaney gave him a long, cool look. "Then you've got nothing to worry about."

Collier smiled nervously.

"For now."

Bonner propped the piece of paper on the keyboard in front of him and typed the letters and numbers written on it into the computer. A mailbox appeared and Bonner opened it and clicked on the icon showing the latest e-mail. He scanned a line or two and smiled widely, his advert-bright teeth flashing with pleasure as he read the recent contents of her inbox.

"Come in, number ten!"

Delaney leaned forward to look at the monitor. "What have you got?"

"Seems like Jenny did make a new friend on the internet."

"Who?"

"Someone calling himself Angel." He pointed at the screen. "And she arranged to meet him at Baker Street tube station on the day she disappeared."

"What time?"

"Three forty-five."

"Right after school."

"Looks that way."

"If that's where she actually went, we should be able to get CCTV footage."

"Definitely." Bonner cracked a smile. "One thing we can thank the terrorists for. So the streak of ginger is off the hook?"

"Maybe, for now. But he's still wriggling. And that worries me."

"Always late remembering things. Telling us stuff bit by bit. Parcelling it out like a soap opera."

"More than just that. Seems our English teacher has a bit of history. This isn't his first time in the frame with a young girl. Four years ago he was accused of molesting one of his female pupils. Thirteen years old."

"And he's still teaching?"

"The charges were dropped. The parents' call apparently. But he changed schools anyway. Moved right out of the area."

"You think this internet stuff he brought in might be some kind of cover-up?"

"It's all a bit convenient, isn't it? He tells us he didn't see her leave and then later he remembers he did. And later still he brings us this."

"True."

"I don't want to let him go just yet. I want you to have a gentle word with him. Keep the pressure on."

"Boss."

"I'll get down to Baker Street, see what the cameras tell us."

Baker Street station was one of the first underground stations built in the capital. Beautiful Victorian architecture that served to lift the spirits of the travellers using it. Delaney walked into the main concourse and looked around, the building tugging nostalgically at his memories. Some things had changed, of course; most memorably and most sadly, a fast-food sandwich and fizzy-drink store now inhabited the space that was once taken up by a pub. Many a time Delaney had grabbed a quick pint or two, a pie and a takeaway can before catching the last Metropolitan train heading west.

"See that, Sally?" He pointed out the brightly lit shop at the end of the concourse.

"Sir?"

"Used to be one of the finest boozers in London."

"Before my time, sir."

Delaney nodded sadly. "Yeah." A long way before her time, and the truth was, it was a dive of a bar, but there was no better way to wait for a train on a cold winter's night, or a hot summer's one come to that. He wasn't even going to bother mentioning Ward's Irish tavern that once used to be under Piccadilly Circus, in the tunnels that originally housed lavatories. Even more of a dive than the Baker Street bar, the name of which he couldn't remember, but it served a half-decent pint of Guinness and Delaney used to feel right at home there; a whole other world hidden beneath one of the most famous locations in England. A working-class, beer-drinker's haven amidst the horror of Regent Street.

Delaney snapped out of his reverie. "Get us a couple of large coffees, Sally, and I'll meet you inside."

DC Cartwright nodded and headed off to a coffee shop at the base of the steps leading down into the station.

Opposite the ticket offices were large, dark mirrored windows with a bench in front of them and behind them a British Transport Police station. Delaney was expected. At one time there might have been some, not always friendly, rivalry between the two police forces, but the terrorists had put an end to any of that.

He was shown through to a viewing room where a computer and monitor had been set up so he could watch the digital footage from the CCTV cameras.

A short while later Sally joined him and handed across a large cup of coffee. She sat beside him as he selected the footage from one of the cameras. Baker Street, like all major underground stations, had CCTV cameras recording every square inch of it. They started with the main entrance on Marylebone Road and watched Monday's foot traffic from half three onwards. Delaney stretched the muscles in his back and sat back uncomfortably in the plastic chair, all too aware that they could be there for some time.

Terry Collier also shifted in his chair, as uncomfortable as Delaney but for very different reasons.

"For God's sake, you're treating me like I'm a suspect here. I've been helpful. I've done my civic duty."

"Civic duty. Do you think that's what this is all about?"

"Isn't it?"

"It's about a twelve-year-old girl who's missing from home."

"I know that. That's why I came in. I'm her teacher, for Christ's sake. Don't you think I care?"

"I'm sure you do, Mr Collier."

"Of course I bloody do."

"And did you care for Angela Carter?"

Collier sat back in his chair, the red flush that had risen to his neck and cheeks draining as he shook his head.

"I don't believe this."

Bonner smiled. "You recognise the name, then?"

"You know damn well I do."

"Then you can understand our concerns."

"Is this what it's going to be like from now on? For the rest of my life? Any child goes AWOL, because she's missed a bus or gone off with her friends or any reason at all . . . and you lot are going to be after me?"

Bonner leaned in hard. "Jenny Morgan's been missing for three days."

"I know that! It's this Angel you should be looking at. You read the e-mails."

Bonner looked at him for a moment and then said softly, "You didn't say *you'd* read them."

Collier coloured and shook his head. "No. I'm not playing this game." He rubbed the palm of his hand. "Out damned spot, is that it? Why can't you people understand? I haven't done anything. I didn't do anything then, and I haven't done anything now."

Bonner leaned forward and shouted into his face: "Shut up!"

Collier sat back, shocked into silence, nervousness creeping across his face like a sudden palsy.

"See, the thing is, we don't care whether you think you are innocent or not. All we care about is the fact that a twelve-year-old girl has been missing from home for three days. That's our priority. And if you know anything more about her disappearance then you sure as hell better tell me now."

Collier seemed to crumple in his chair. He shook his head, his voice tremulous. "I've told you everything I know. I swear to you. I don't know where she is."

Bonner wanted to stand him up and punch him hard in the face. Getting information from a suspect was a lot easier in the old days, he thought. Before his time, of course. That kind of interrogation had to take place outside of a police station nowadays. He looked at Collier and decided he'd ask him some questions later. In an informal setting. He smiled coldly at him, and was pleased to see that Collier looked very far from reassured by it.

Delaney leaned forward, and stopped the footage. "Five o'clock. If she was going to be there she'd have shown up by now." He crumpled his paper cup and threw it in the bin. "Give us the side entrance."

Sally moved the mouse and clicked on the next icon in the list that Delaney had drawn up.

The grainy black-and-white image leapt to life on the monitor screen. People walking slowly in and out of the side entrance. At three ten a thin man approached the entrance but rather than going in stood to one side and looked deliberately at his watch.

Sally leaned forward excitedly. "This could be him." Delaney nodded, his eyes impassive as he watched. If he felt a small spark of optimism he didn't show it in his expression.

The man reached into his pocket and pulled out a cigarette; he snapped open a Zippo lighter and sparked it alight, drawing on his cigarette like a man heading for the gallows and wanting to savour every moment of pleasure left.

"Could be he just wants a smoke before going down to the tube; figures he's got time before his train."

Delaney fast-forwarded the image until the man had sucked the cigarette clean and thrown it on the pavement. He turned and walked into the station, disappearing from view.

"False alarm."

"Looks that way."

There were a few things more boring than watching CCTV footage, but offhand Delaney couldn't think of any. At three forty-three on the screen, however, a young girl walked into shot and Delaney felt a jolt of adrenalin kick into his jaundiced veins. It was Jenny Morgan, and she was glancing around, as if she was waiting for someone.

Sally held her breath. "Looks like Collier's come good for us."

Delaney leaned forward, watching the screen. "Maybe."

Jenny walked into the station and out of view and Delaney pointed to the tapes, "Get the inside footage," but as Sally reached over to find it, Delaney held his hand up. "Don't worry she's back."

Jenny came out of the station and stood where the smoker had stood earlier, looking at her watch and swivelling her head to look up and down the street.

"She's definitely waiting for someone, boss."

Jenny suddenly smiled and waved as someone in a long overcoat and a hat approached her. Her face lit up in a big smile as the figure gave her a quick hug, back to the camera.

They stood still for a few moments. Sally drummed her finger on the tabletop impatiently.

"Turn round. Come on, you bastard, show us your face."

As if on command, the person turned around, the camera capturing both of them perfectly. Delaney arched an eyebrow, surprised.

Sally blinked. "I wasn't expecting that."

"No."

Delaney leaned forward and paused the film footage.

"Let's get back to the station. We'll get the picture blown up, put it on leaflets, get it on the television."

"This changes everything, doesn't it?"

Delaney looked at her for a moment. "Yeah, it does."

CHAPTER
TWELVE

Kate Walker sat at her desk typing up the notes from the autopsy on Jackie Malone. Her delicate fingers flashed over the keyboard with staccato precision and a professional rhythm. She finished the last paragraph, summing up, and saved the document. Her main conclusion was that the world was a sick and dangerous place and Jackie Malone had done little to put herself out of harm's way. But then sometimes women didn't have a choice. Something she herself knew all too well.

She took a long drink from a cold glass of water and pulled across some papers she had printed off from the internet earlier. She was due to give a speech soon to a group of undergraduates at her old university and teaching hospital. Jane Harrington, a lecturer from her days as a medical student with whom she had become friendly, was now head of her faculty and was constantly trying to persuade Kate to join her staff, both to teach and as a practising doctor at the university health centre. Kate had always refused the overtures, but was persuaded every now and then to give a talk or a seminar, one of many alumni strong-armed in to talk to the students about the real world outside the metaphorical cloisters of the college.

The real world of work mainly, and in Kate's case the real world of danger to women. She wanted to put her work into context. She dealt with the outcome, the final chapter of the story, but there was always a genesis, a cause, and they usually followed a pattern. Violence didn't exist in a vacuum, particularly violence against women and children. She wanted as much as anything to be reassured that the work she was doing was having some effect. That by helping to catch the murderers, the rapists, the child abductors and abusers, the statistics would be going down. That the Metropolitan and national police services were winning the battle, turning the tide, killing the virus source by source, stopping the spread and starving the madness of oxygen. But as her eyes flicked down the lines of statistics she had printed off, she felt worse than Sisyphus pushing his stone. At least one out of every three women had been beaten, coerced into sex, or otherwise abused. One in four would be a victim of domestic violence in her lifetime. On average, two women per week were killed by a male partner or former partner. One hundred and sixty-seven were raped every day and at best only one in five attacks was reported to the police.

Kate collected her papers. People wondered why she did the job she did, and there was the answer. She wondered how many of her audience would understand. They didn't live in her world and if they were lucky none of them ever would. But you couldn't beat statistics, and she knew that many of the young women listening to her speech would, if they hadn't been already, sometime in the future be beaten, abused, terrified, hurt, raped or murdered and there was nothing she could do about it. Nothing she could ever do about it. Because when Kate was called in to help, it was already far, far too late for them.

Kate put the papers aside and rubbed a hand across her forehead. Her hand came away damp. As she looked at her finger, she picked at a minuscule fibre that stuck to the pad of her thumb, the sort of fibre that a forensic pathologist would be delighted to discover on a dead body. She brushed it off and then rubbed her hand harder, her nails almost breaking the skin.

She picked up an overnight bag that she kept in her office and walked out and down to a shower that was made available for her exclusive use.

She always showered between each autopsy. A habit picked up in her days working as a police surgeon before she specialised. Often she would give a physical examination to a rape victim and then do the same to the accused rapist. A shower between examinations was mandatory to prevent cross-contamination of evidence, but Kate was glad of the excuse.

She stood in the small cubicle and closed the curtains around her. She cranked the handle until it was almost too hot to bear and made herself stand under the jets of near-scalding water.

CHAPTER
THIRTEEN

Superintendent Charles Walker smoothed his hair back with a manicured hand and smiled at Melanie Jones, the pretty young reporter from Sky Television News. There were other press gathered around, but he focused his attention mainly on her as he read out the prepared statement.

"The search for Jenny Morgan continues round the clock. At this time we are following several leads but urge any members of the public with information to come forward."

Diane Campbell looked down from her window at the press who gathered around the front of the building like a pack of baying wolves at a kill. And at the epicentre of it all, Superintendent Charles Walker remained the face of calm authority, of concern and reassurance.

"Prick," she muttered under her breath, and put a cigarette in her mouth, lighting it up. She didn't get any argument from Delaney, who was standing beside her also watching the circus unfold below. Twenty-four-hour news meant that someone's private tragedy could be played out round the clock for the entertainment of millions. He knew the coverage meant more chance of information coming forward, more chance of them finding Jenny before it was too late, but the slickness of it, the show-business of it all, disgusted him.

Chief Inspector Campbell looked at the photo that Delaney had just handed to her, the photo he had blown up from the CCTV footage taken from Baker Street station, and drew deep on her cigarette, blowing out a long, sinuous kiss of smoke which was taken away by the light breeze.

"Bonner tells me those things can kill you, Diane."

She turned her eyes in a lazy smile back on Delaney. "We're all going to die, Jack."

"When?" He pulled a cigarette from his own pack and stuck it into his mouth. "Smoking in a public building. We could get fired for this."

"You could, Jack. I'm not dispensable."

"Dispensable? I guess that's the best thing you can say about me."

"Oh, I don't know. You've got a nice arse."

Delaney laughed despite himself. "See, now if I said that to you, I probably would get fired."

"You know what the difference is, Jack?"

"No."

"The difference is, if you had said it, it would have been true."

Delaney nodded and drew deep on his cigarette. "Facts. You can't argue with them."

Diane held the photo up. A woman in her thirties. Blonde hair, dark, haunted eyes.

"Do we know who she is?"

Delaney shook his head. "Not yet."

"We should get this down to the media. Out on the news, on the web. Someone will know her."

"Not just yet. Let's find out what we can first. We don't want to spook her."

"So the girl's teacher, Collier, he's in the clear on this?"

"Not necessarily. You know how often women are involved in child abductions, recruiting runaways from railways stations and the like."

"He's hardly likely to lead us to her if he's involved."

"People do stupid things, boss. It's what pays our wages."

"We'd have got round to looking at station footage sooner or later. Maybe he's being clever."

"Maybe."

"Keep me posted."

"Boss."

Delaney flicked his cigarette out of the window and left.

Sally Cartwright waited by her car, watching as Delaney strode quickly over to her. He opened the door and handed her another copy of the blown-up photo of the mystery woman.

Melanie Jones came hurrying over. "Detective Inspector. Can I have a word?"

Delaney opened the passenger door. "Get in the car, Sally, I'm driving."

Melanie picked up on the urgency in his voice. "Have there been any developments, Inspector?"

"Your friend with the scar on his face and a five-hundred-pound suit should keep you posted." Delaney got in the car, turning the photo face down on the dashboard, and slammed the door on the reporter.

He pulled the car away, leaving Melanie Jones frustrated in his wake. "Where are we going, guv?"

"To have another chat with Jenny's friend."

"You think she knows who the woman is?"

"Yeah. I think she does."

"At least if Jenny's with a woman she's probably safe."

"Doesn't work that way, Sally."

Sally looked across at him as he pulled out into the traffic, cranking his window right down to let some air in. "You think she's in danger?"

"Who knows? If we panic the woman who's taken her, she might be."

"She's not going to physically hurt her, is she?"

"That's probably not why she took her. That's very rare for a woman. Especially a woman on her own."

"Which of course she may not be."

"She probably isn't. She groomed her on the internet, made her feel safe."

"Meaning she's got a partner."

Delaney shrugged. "We don't know. But the sooner we find out, the better."

The loop of the thick iron chain screeched a little as it rubbed against the hook it was hung from. It was an old, heavy chain, pitted with rust, and the noise it made as it scraped metal on metal would have put the Devil's teeth on edge.

Below it, kicking her legs sullenly, sat Carol Parks, swinging herself backwards and forwards.

Delaney and Sally Cartwright were back in Primrose Avenue, standing at the bottom of the garden watching as the young girl sat on her old swing and squinted sullenly up at them.

Delaney rested his hand on the chain, stopping the movement and the noise, and smiled at Carol. He would have liked to kick her backside off the thing but didn't think the tactic would be helpful, so he smiled instead, bringing the full brilliance of his Irish eyes to bear.

"I used to have a swing when I was a kid."

Carol shrugged, not at all impressed. "Really?"

"Yeah. Back in Ballydehob. Do you know where that is?"

"Essex?"

"Close enough." Delaney smiled at her again. "One time I swung so high and so hard I went right over the top, flew out of the seat and smashed my head on the ground."

He had her attention now, the frown easing off her lips slightly. "Honest?"

"Oh yeah. Right on the noggin. Knocked all the brains out of me. I reckon that's why I ended up joining the police."

A slight smile.

"Did you swing here with Jenny?"

"Sometimes. We're not little kids, you know."

"Of course not. I suppose it's all boys and bands, eh?"

"No."

Delaney nodded. "Not bands?"

"Not boys."

Delaney smiled again, trying to work his charm; failing.

"Come on, I bet you and Jenny had a queue of boys pestering you at school. Couple of pretty girls like you."

"Jenny isn't interested in boys."

Delaney looked at her for a moment. "You don't seem to be too worried about her."

She shrugged again: whatever.

"Only we've got half the Metropolitan Police out looking for her. Her father is in pieces. But you don't seem to be too troubled at all. And she's your best friend."

"She'll be all right."

Carol kicked her feet again, setting the swing in creaking motion once more.

Sally stepped forward and put her hand on the girl's shoulder to stop her. "You know something, don't you?"

"I don't know anything."

Delaney shook his head. "See, I reckon that bump on the head gave me psychic powers as well, and I don't think you're telling us everything."

Carol looked away. Delaney looked at the girl's mother, who nodded and knelt down in front of her daughter.

"Tell them, Carol; if you know anything you have to tell them."

110

Sally smiled again, reassuring. "You're not going to be in any trouble. But if you know anything, you have to tell us. We need to know she's all right."

"She is."

"How do you know?"

"I promised I wouldn't tell. She made me promise."

Delaney stooped down to bring his face level with Carol's, his voice soft and soothing. "I know you made a promise, but things have gone too far now, haven't they?"

Carol looked at him for a moment, worrying her lower lip between her teeth.

"She's gone to be with her aunt."

Delaney looked across surprised to Sally, then back at Carol.

"She doesn't have an aunt."

"Yes she does."

Sally crouched beside her. "She doesn't. If she had we would have spoken to her. Maybe she just called herself an aunt, like family friends sometimes do?"

Carol shook her head. "No. She's her real aunt. She told me. She didn't think she had a real auntie either, until she met her."

"Met her where, Carol?"

"On the internet. At school."

"Do you know what her name is? Did she tell you that?"

Carol nodded.

"What is it? You have to tell us."

And she did.

CHAPTER
FOURTEEN

"Do you know what I hate about people?" Delaney asked Sally as he shifted into a lower gear and blasted his horn as he overtook an elderly woman who in his opinion shouldn't be allowed to be in charge of a bicycle, let alone a Mercedes with God knows how many horsepower under the bonnet. Sally wasn't happy with the way he was treating her car, but he was the boss so she kept her own counsel.

"No, sir?"

"Everything." Delaney stepped on the accelerator. "Because people lie, Sally. They do bad things to each other and they look you in the face and they lie about it."

"Maybe it's your upbringing, sir."

"Meaning?"

"All that Catholicism, confessions and all that."

"I wasn't brought up among priests and nuns, Sally."

"You weren't?"

"I was brought up by wolves."

He flashed a humourless grin at her as he brought the car to a screeching halt outside Morgan's workshop.

"Let's go and talk to the liar. See if he's ready to make his confession."

Inside his workshop, Morgan watched as Delaney and Sally approached. He wiped the back of his greasy hand across his mouth and a flicker of something shifted in his eyes.

"Have you found her?"

Delaney shook his head, and the hope in Morgan's eyes died.

"Mr Morgan. Is there something you forgot to tell us?"

"No." He looked puzzled as Delaney leaned angrily in.

"You told us earlier that Jenny didn't have any other relatives?"

"That's right, just Jake and me."

Delaney leaned in even closer and held a photo in front of Morgan's face.

"So who's this then, the sugar plum fucking fairy?"

Morgan blinked, confused, and took the photo off him, his face filling with blood as he looked at it, his scar pulsing and his eyes darting like cold water on hot coals.

"Do you know this woman?"

"No."

Delaney turned to Sally. "Liars, you see, Sally. Every damn fucking one of them."

Sally looked at Morgan; you didn't need a detector to tell he was lying. "She's your sister, isn't she?"

Morgan shook his head, fear in his eyes.

"Why the hell didn't you tell us you had a sister?"

Morgan backed away from Delaney. "Where did you get this? Why are you asking about her?"

"You admit you do have a sister then?"

"Not any more! I haven't seen her in fourteen years."

Sally stepped forward. "What happened between you?"

Morgan pulled his shirt open to reveal the extent of his scarring, across his chest, up his shoulder, up to his pain-filled eyes and forehead. "This is what happened. She did this to me with a steam hose. She's not right in the head."

"What are you saying?"

Morgan looked at her for a moment. "Where did you get this photo? What's it got to do with my Jenny?"

Delaney held up another photo of the pair of them together. "We think she's with her."

"She can't be." His eyes were wild now.

"We think she made contact over the internet."

Morgan grabbed Sally by the arm. "You've got to find her."

Delaney would have stepped in but Sally held her hand up. "Try and stay calm, Mr Morgan. We know Jenny's all right now. She's safe. She's with a relative."

"What are you talking about . . . safe? She's not safe. You have to find her."

Delaney barely kept his temper in check. "Then maybe it's about time you started telling us the truth."

"I don't know any more. I told you, I haven't seen her in fourteen years."

Delaney shared a look with Sally. The trouble was, he believed Morgan. He jerked his head for them to go outside, and Sally followed him out as he put a fag in his mouth and fumbled angrily for his matches.

114

Outside in the yard, Delaney blew a short burst of smoke as he watched Jake Morgan operate a jack to lift a minivan off the ground. His back and shoulders were burned by the glaring heat of the sun but if he felt any discomfort he wasn't showing it. His muscles were bunched and straining and Delaney sensed that he could probably have lifted the van up with his bare hands.

Sally looked back at Delaney. "Jenny's with a relative. I guess that changes everything."

Delaney nodded thoughtfully. "Maybe."

"We can stand down the media circus."

"This is a relative she hasn't ever met before, who hasn't been involved with her family for fourteen years if Morgan is telling the truth."

"And you think he is?"

"Yeah. I do. He hasn't got the brains to lie to us."

"He lied about his sister."

"Not really. As far as he was concerned, she doesn't exist any more."

"Can't say I blame him, seeing what she did to him."

"If she is as unstable as he claims she is, then it's just as urgent we find Jenny quickly. She's still been abducted, that's what we need to focus on."

"She wasn't abducted. She went voluntarily."

"She's twelve years old, Sally. She was taken without her father's consent; he didn't even know she was missing till the next day."

"Exactly. Maybe she's better off with her aunt."

Sally looked across at Delaney, biting her lips but the words were out.

"Sorry."

"Don't apologise. My daughter's definitely better off with *her* aunt."

Delaney pulled out his mobile and punched in a quick sequence of numbers, listening impatiently as the phone rang. "Bonner, where have you been?"

"Doing what I was told. Looking into Howard Morgan's sister, Candy Morgan."

"You've found her?"

"No. Just found out about her."

"And . . .?"

"And it's not good news."

"Go on."

"She's been in the system."

"Prison?"

"Off and on. She's twenty-eight now and has spent a lot of her life behind bars of one kind or another."

"Go on."

"She turned a steam hose on her older brother for a joke when she was fourteen years old."

"Some joke. We've seen what it did to him."

"She's not a nice person."

"What else?"

"You name it. She was taken into care after putting her brother in hospital. Three months later she burned the house down."

"She's got a thing with heat, obviously."

"And knives. We've got paper on her for most things you can think of. Theft. Aggravated assault, mainly on

116

women. Drug-dealing. Prostitution. She just got out of Holloway five days ago after serving eight years."

"Eight years! What did she do, murder someone?"

"Seems like some girl came down from Birmingham and started working her patch. She cut one of her ears off and fed it to her."

Delaney flicked another cigarette into his mouth and, crooking his phone on his shoulder, managed to flare a match and light it. "Nice."

"This woman is very far from nice. She served her full term because she took a razor blade set in a toothbrush and sliced a female guard's cheek open."

"You think she's got issues?"

Bonner laughed drily. "Yeah. Like Myra Hindley had issues."

"I meant mental health issues."

"She was never hospitalised, if that's what you mean. But this woman obviously gets off on violence. Particularly against other women. Not only that, but she attempted suicide twice whilst in custody. This is far from a healthy bunny here. I'd say we'd best find her quickly, because she ain't where she's supposed to be. Picked up, moved out, no forwarding address."

Delaney went to hang up but a thought occurred. "Any word on Billy Martin or Jackie Malone's boy?"

"Nothing yet, boss. This case has taken priority."

"I want you to keep going on Jackie Malone. And you report anything you find directly back to me. We clear on that?"

"You got it."

"Just to me." Delaney clicked his phone shut and ground out his cigarette with a sharp twist of his ankle. He looked over to where Jake was lifting off the nearside front wheel of the van, complete with tyre. He tossed it to one side as though it weighed as much as an empty carton of milk.

Sally saw the concern in Delaney's face. "Not good news from Sergeant Bonner, then?"

"Seems like Morgan was right about not seeing his sister for fourteen years. And he was right about something else too: she's a very nasty piece of work by all accounts."

"Maybe some girls aren't better off with their aunts."

Delaney gave her a flat look. "Time will tell. Always does." He walked across to where Jake was working. "Jake."

The mechanic stood up, squinting in the bright sunlight and shielding his eyes with his hand.

"Yes, sir."

"You don't have to call me sir."

"I haven't done anything wrong." His eyes flicked nervously.

Sally held her hand up reassuringly. "Nobody is saying you have."

"Have you found her then?"

"Not yet. Apparently she's with your younger sister."

Jake blinked. On a face not normally articulate with comprehension, he looked even more confused.

"I don't understand."

"Candy."

Jake backed away. "She's not coming here. I don't want her here."

Sally held her hands out. "We don't know where she is. We need to speak to her."

"I don't want her coming here. She hurts people."

"Have you spoken to her recently?"

Jake shook his head, terrified.

"Did she hurt you in the past?"

"She set light to Susie."

"Who's Susie?"

"She was our dog. She set light to her tail and then she burned my brother with the steam hose. She likes to break things. Hurt people."

"Have you any idea where she might be?"

"I haven't seen her since she burned Howard with the steam."

"You haven't spoken to her on the telephone?"

"I don't use the telephone."

"It's important if you know anything to tell us."

Jake nodded, his worried eyes darting to left and right. "I do know something."

"What's that, Jake?" Delaney gave him a supportive smile.

"I know she's bad, I know she likes to hear people screaming. You've got to save Jenny."

Delaney nodded. "We're going to do the best we can."

Jake grabbed his arm and Delaney was all too aware of the power in his grip. "Don't let her hurt her."

Delaney nodded again and Jake released his hold. Delaney gestured to Sally, and as they walked back towards the car, he had to make a conscious effort not to rub his arm.

"You think she's going to hurt the girl?" asked Sally as they moved out of earshot.

Delaney opened the car door without answering.

"What are we going to do, sir?"

Delaney could hear the frustration and concern in her voice, and understood it all too well. "We're going to go to prison."

"Sir?"

"Holloway. The university of hurting people. Find out why she got a distinction."

Holloway prison lies north of King's Cross. If you were a hooker working the area round the station, you could probably walk there. If the crack cocaine hadn't rendered you unfit for the journey, of course. The only way a crack whore could make that journey, Delaney thought as he crunched through the gears, was in the back of a police wagon. Knick-knack, paddy whack, give a dog a bone.

Sally was chatting away next to him but Delaney was only partly paying attention. He had made the mistake of asking her what she knew about Holloway, unaware that as part of her degree in criminology she had written a thesis on the role of the prison as a force for the social control of women, particularly as it had notably been used to house the suffragettes. Now she was practically repeating it verbatim.

Sally had got up to about 1903, talking about when the prison was solely designated for the housing of

120

female offenders, when Delaney thankfully pulled up to the imposing-looking modern building and parked the car.

As they got out once more into the glaring heat of the sun, Delaney looked up at the blank-faced walls. It was a far cry from the gothic beauty of the original building. This could have been anywhere, Los Angeles, Sydney, Bradford. But behind the modern facade there still lingered a sense of its past. It wasn't hard to imagine ghosts walking at night, and the screams sounding in the darkness, he was sure, would be real enough.

Sally looked down at the plaque that had been laid in the original Holloway prison in 1852. It read: "May God preserve the city of London and make this place a terror to evil doers." Delaney followed her gaze. "Sometimes the terror in here is better than what waits for them outside."

The doors were opened and closed behind them. Nothing much had changed with that over the years. The doors might not be thick studded oak any more, and there might not have been electronic seals and cameras following their movements from every angle in years gone by, but the principle was the same. Once you were inside the prison you only got out when those inside said so. If it was an hour later, or sixteen years later, once the doors had closed behind you, you had no control over the matter.

Delaney and Sally waited at the reception area until a uniformed guard came to take them to the governor's office. He had kept them waiting for over fifteen

121

minutes but Delaney didn't let it anger him. He knew the governor's job was all about keeping control. Exerting authority and keeping control. They may well have worked in associated jobs, but once that first gate had closed behind them they were in the governor's world now, and if he wanted to make a point then Delaney wasn't bothered. Besides, it was far, far, cooler inside the prison than in the blistering heat outside.

It was certainly cool in the governor's office. Air-conditioning saw to that, and it was as far removed from its Edwardian counterpart as a century of thinking allowed. The glass in the windows might have been toughened to withstand serious assault but the light they threw into the room was warm and pleasant. The whole room was pleasant, in fact: bright colours in prints and original paintings, a comfortable rug on the floor, modern books lining the shelves that made up one wall of the office.

Delaney swept his eyes around the furnishings as he sat in the comfortably cushioned chair that the governor had gestured him towards. Alan Bannister was a thin man of six foot four, with receding grey hair and rimless spectacles. Delaney put him in his mid-fifties and figured that he'd struggle to stay upright in a stiff breeze.

"Are you sure I can't order you some coffee? It really is no trouble."

His voice was soft, educated. Delaney couldn't imagine him coping too well if an inmate got violent, but he guessed that was what his staff were for. And some of the lady officers he had seen on the way up here could have scared most of the inmates at Parkhurst.

"We don't want to take up too much of your time, Mr Bannister."

"What can I do for you specifically, Inspector?"

"Anything you can tell us about Candy Morgan will be useful. What state of mind was she in?"

"State of mind?" He shrugged. "She was glad to be leaving. That's for sure."

"After eight years, I imagine she would be."

"It's not always the case. A lot of our inmates don't want to be released, even if they won't admit as such to themselves."

"Institutionalised?"

"Partly."

Sally nodded. "And partly the friendships, relationships they have built? It's like a family for some of them in here."

Alan Bannister shrugged. "Sometimes it's that. Or it's just because what waits for them outside is a lot worse than the life they have in here."

"Sounds like you think it's a good thing for them to be incarcerated?"

Bannister shook his head, the passion ringing in his voice. "I don't think that. The fact that they are here, however, is an indication that society has failed them, and by releasing them back to that society we are more often than not sending them into a vicious cycle of abuse and neglect."

Delaney held up his hand dismissively. "Yeah, all the women here are Girl Guides and society has let them down. Which brings us back to the biggest cookie-baker of them all. Candy Morgan."

"So you said on the phone."

"Was she one of those likely to reoffend? Institutionalised? She was here a long time."

"Like I said earlier, the women in here all have issues," said the governor. "But Candy Morgan was a particularly troubled soul."

"I'd say that was an understatement."

"But I had the sense she was hopeful about her future."

"Hopeful?"

"Like she was looking forward to it. Not just because she would be getting out of prison, but because she had a sense of purpose. That's not often the case."

"What kind of purpose?"

"Nothing specific. Nothing she spoke to me or my staff about anyway. But there was a new sense of excitement about what lay ahead for her in her closing days here. That much was clear. She wasn't looking backwards literally or figuratively when she walked out the door."

"Did she ever mention her niece?"

"Not to me."

Delaney was disappointed, but it was not entirely unexpected. "I understand she had counselling?"

"It was part of her parole conditions. She served her full, original sentence, but she would have been here a lot longer had she refused it."

"Because of the attack on the prison officer?"

"As you can well understand, we take that kind of thing very seriously."

"What provoked the assault?"

"According to Ella Stafford, the officer involved, there was no provocation at all."

"Can we speak to Ella Stafford?"

"I fail to see how that can help you find the missing girl."

"I don't know either, if I'm honest. That's what police work is." Delaney shrugged. "Turning over stones. You turn over enough . . ."

"And soon enough something unpleasant will come crawling forth."

"About the size of it. So can we speak to her?"

"She retired shortly after the incident and moved to New Zealand."

"Can you get me her contact details there?"

"I'm sure we'll have a record. For her pension if nothing else."

"We'd be grateful. What about Candy Morgan's counsellor?"

"What about her?"

"Can we speak to her? I presume she still works here."

"She does, but she won't be able to tell you anything. The women who speak to counsellors have to know that whatever they say is entirely confidential. You can understand that?"

Delaney let a little anger slip into his voice. "I understand that a little girl is missing from her family, is in the care of a very dangerous and disturbed woman and we all have very serious fears for her safety."

The governor considered for a moment and then nodded, conceding. "I'll see what I can do."

"Thank you."

Sally flipped the page on her notebook. "Can you tell us who she shared cells with whilst she was here?"

"Of course." He picked up the phone and pushed a button. "Louise, could you dig up Candy Morgan's file again for me? Thanks."

"We appreciate the help."

Alan Bannister looked at Delaney thoughtfully. "I know it sometimes doesn't look that way, but I hope we're both on the same side."

"I hope so too."

A short while later the governor's PA had returned with the name of Candy Morgan's cellmates written on a piece of paper. Delaney read quickly through the list, stood up and thanked the governor, gesturing to Sally that it was time to leave.

Outside, as they walked back to the car, Sally had to lengthen her stride to keep up with Delaney's fast pace.

"Not much to go on." He held up the piece of paper. "I know Stella Trant. Her last cellmate."

"How come?"

"She was a sex worker. Probably still is." He pushed the button on Sally's key ring to open the locks.

"Why don't I drive, sir?"

Delaney didn't answer for a moment as he looked further down the list, then he turned to Sally, tossing her the keys. "I won't be long." He walked back towards the entrance.

"Sir?"

"Just wait in the car. There's something I forgot to ask the governor."

Alan Bannister looked a little surprised to see his assistant Louise showing Delaney back into his office.

"Inspector. Something else I can help you with?"

Delaney picked up on the hint of irritation in the man's voice, but ignored it and leant back against the door frame. "It's about Jackie Malone. She was an inmate here a couple of years ago. I see she shared a cell with Candy Morgan."

Bannister considered for a moment, looking off to the side.

"I remember her. What about her?"

"She was murdered a few days ago."

"I'm sorry to hear that."

"A particularly brutal murder."

"Do you know who did it?"

"Not yet."

"And this has something to do with Candy Morgan?"

"Maybe nothing."

"But . . .?"

"But Jackie's son is missing too. Well, not missing exactly, but we can't locate him."

"You think there's a connection?"

"I don't know. I just wondered if you knew how close they were? Candy and Jackie."

"I can't help you on that. Sorry, but it was a long while ago they shared a cell."

"If anything occurs, you'll call me?"

"Of course."

Delaney stood up and walked to the door.

"Inspector?"

Delaney stopped and looked back at him.

"May I ask why you didn't mention this earlier when you were here with your constable?"

Delaney didn't have a problem with lying. "I hadn't remembered the connection."

CHAPTER
FIFTEEN

Delaney looked out of the passenger window as the car passed St Pancras station on his right and turned left past an Irish pub that stood on the corner. A pub he'd spent many a Saturday afternoon in watching rugby and drinking poteen from the hip flask of a septuagenarian regular. Just the thing on a cold winter's day, but too much even for Delaney in the blaze of the summer heat. Sally made a couple more turns and parked outside a row of mid-Victorian terraced houses. Delaney opened his door and got out, his knees still a little stiff, one of these days he was going to get down to the police gym and start exercising again. He walked up to a yellow door that desperately needed a new coat of paint and leant on the doorbell. After a short wait and no response he leant on the doorbell again.

"All right, all right give us a bleeding chance." The voice was muffled but the Irish accent was clear. The door cracked open and a woman peered out, her hair flashing amber gold in the bright sunlight and her frown deepening as she took in Delaney and Sally Cartwright, recognising them immediately for what they were.

"Shit."

Delaney held up his warrant card to her. "Yeah, it's the filth, Stella. We'd like a word."

Stella turned back resigned into the flat, slouching down on the threadbare sofa with barely disguised boredom. Delaney and Sally followed her in. Sally stood by the door and Delaney sat in the faded yellow armchair opposite the sofa. Stella Trant was a flame-haired woman in her late twenties. Medium height and pencil thin, she wore blue jeans that clung to her body like the skin of a snake with a pale shirt and a green striped tank top. It was pushing thirty-five degrees outside but she wasn't even breaking a sweat. She reached down to pick a can of Special Brew off the floor and took a swig. She had startlingly green eyes and a smoky southern Irish lilt in her voice. "I'd offer you one, but I know you're on duty."

"Right." Delaney looked about the shabby flat and smiled, sliding a bit of charm into it. "I guess anywhere is better than your last accommodation."

Stella laughed, a dry, rasping sound, as she flicked a roll-up between her finger and thumb. "I wouldn't bet on it."

"No."

"This is about Candy, right? I had a call."

Delaney was annoyed at that; he'd speak to the governor later, but let it pass for the moment. "You were cellmates for how long?"

"The last six months."

"And you got out when?"

"Two weeks ago."

"Planning to go back?"

Stella fixed him with a flat look. "What do you think?"

"You're aware of the conditions of your parole?"

"Yeah. And I'm doing nothing to jeopardise it."

"That's good."

"What's this all about?"

"Candy has disappeared. She's moved from where she's supposed to be."

"She'll show up."

"She's taken a twelve-year-old girl with her."

Stella looked up, surprised.

"Have you spoken to her since she got out, Stella?"

"I haven't heard from her and I don't expect to."

"You were quite close on the inside?"

"Yeah, well the inside is the other side of the world and another century ago, if you know what I mean."

"You mean things are different now?"

"You'll make commissioner yet, Sherlock."

"Yeah, I'll be made commissioner and you'll be made a Dame of the British Empire."

"Nah. We Irish . . . we're citizens of the world, isn't that right?"

Sally smiled tolerantly from the door. "Tell us about your relationship with Candy?"

Stella reacted. "Relationship? You implying something by that?"

"Just asking questions. That's what we do."

"Yeah, you ask questions and answer them yourselves. And innocent people end up in prison."

Delaney flashed some teeth at her. "You innocent then, Stella?"

Stella smiled slowly. "I've had my moments."

Sally sighed. "Just tell us about your relationship with Candy Morgan."

"I didn't swing that way. Besides, I wasn't her type."

"Are you saying she's a lesbian?"

"I'm not saying anything. She was in there for eight years. She slept with women." She shrugged. "If that makes her a dyke and not a lonely, scared woman looking out for some comfort, then yeah . . . I guess you could call her that."

"She was scared?"

"Not in that sense. Candy could take care of herself."

"That much we gather."

Stella looked at him. "You can believe it too."

"So what was she scared of?"

Stella shrugged. "Maybe of the things she might do."

Delaney smiled. "Bit of a philosopher on the side, are you, Stella?"

"I'm all kinds of things on the side."

"See, from what we hear about Candy Morgan, there's not a lot that would have scared her."

"I'd say you heard right again."

"And you definitely haven't spoken to her since she got out?"

Stella shook her head and looked to the side.

"I told you."

Sally walked around to face her. "It's all right if *you're* scared, though, Stella. We know what she's capable of."

"I doubt that you do."

"What's that supposed to mean?"

"Who ever really knows what other people are capable of, given the right circumstances?"

Delaney smiled coldly. "We do, Stella. We get to clean up afterwards."

"My heart bleeds."

"Only this time there's a little girl involved. So we don't want to be doing any cleaning up. You see what I'm saying to you here?"

"You think she might hurt the girl?"

"What do you think?"

Stella shook her head angrily. "I don't know. I told you I don't know, all right?"

"No, Stella, it's not all right!"

Sally uncrossed her arms. "We can protect you, Stella."

Stella snorted with laughter. "What? You two? You're going to be my bodyguards?"

"The police. The police can protect you if you help us."

Stella suddenly gave Delaney a hard, flat look as the penny of memory dropped. "Like you protected Jackie Malone."

Delaney stood up angrily and crossed to her, grabbing her wrist. "What's this got to do with her?"

Stella flinched backwards, out of his grasp, taken aback by the anger in his voice. She rubbed her wrist, passively dismissive. "It's got nothing to do with her as far as I know."

"So why mention her?"

"Because she's dead, Inspector Delaney. She was supposed to be your friend. And now she's dead."

The anger in Delaney's eyes was replaced momentarily with something else, something guarded. "What did she tell you about me?"

"Come off it, Inspector. You think we don't talk to each other? You think I don't know what was going on?"

"I looked out for her, that's all."

Stella let his statement hang for a moment, then smiled at him. "And you did a real good job."

Sally looked over at Delaney, puzzled. "Guv?"

Delaney shook his head. "It's got nothing to do with this."

Stella nodded. "Like I say, the police's assurances of protection don't exactly count for a great deal. You've worked the streets as long as I have, you learn that pretty fast."

"If you know something about where Candy Morgan is, Stella, you damn well better tell me what it is."

Stella met his gaze, almost sympathetic. "I know she was planning to get back at her family."

"Get back how?"

"I don't know. She didn't tell me everything. It was something she was going to do. That's all she said. She was going to get back at them big time. Hurt them in the worst way possible."

Delaney looked hard into her eyes; she didn't flinch or look away. "She gets in touch with you, you call me, okay?"

Stella gave the slightest of nods, and Delaney gestured to Sally to join him. He looked back at Stella as they walked to the door. "You'd do well to remember it's not just losing your parole that you've got to be scared of."

CHAPTER
SIXTEEN

Delaney pulled his seatbelt with an angry tug around his shoulder and snapped it into place.

"Guv. About what she was saying?"

"Just leave it, Sally."

"I was just going to say, if Jackie Malone was a friend of yours then I'm sorry. And if I can help . . ."

Delaney looked at her and sighed, shaking his head.

"I just want you to know I've got your back."

"I appreciate it." Delaney flipped the radio on. A group of teenage boys were singing close harmony in a language Delaney didn't understand even though it was English. He pushed the tuning button and Johnny Cash came on the air; he was going to walk the line apparently. Something Delaney had stopped doing a long time ago.

Kate sat back down at her desk. Collecting together the glossy photos of Jackie Malone pre- and post-post-mortem. In two dimensions the wounds looked worse somehow. Kate knew that they were inflicted after she had died, but laid out like that on her desk they seemed too graphic, too manufactured. Somebody turning mutilation into an art form, making a statement out of the slashes and cuts in Jackie Malone's naked body like the symbols of a grotesque new language. What was it they were trying to say? she wondered.

Her job was to deconstruct the manner of death, not the meaning of it, and yet as she looked at the black-and-white photos she found herself thinking that she could identify the killer's signature if only she could understand the language he was speaking. She could almost hear Delaney's mocking voice in her head. Could she do her bloody job or not?

She shivered, despite the heat, and scooped the photos up, sliding them into a large white envelope and put them into her desk drawer, slamming it shut. *Damn the man. Damn him straight to Irish hell!*

She ran the back of her hand across her forehead, swallowing; her throat had gone suddenly dry. She looked at her watch and decided to break for lunch. Something she rarely did, usually just grabbing a sandwich at her desk. But she needed some air. She needed to get out.

She left the building, stopping to draw in a lungful of the hot, dry air, and then walked away, leaving the morgue behind. She felt a slight prickling in her back and looked over her shoulder; no one was there, but as she continued to walk she couldn't quite throw away the feeling of disquiet. She shook the thoughts away again. Whoever had done what they did to Jackie Malone hadn't done it to leave Kate Walker a personal message, and thinking that they had was plainly ridiculous. So why did the skin on her back still crawl?

Delaney looked at his watch, running his sleeve over his sweating forehead. It had been a long day but it was still only two o'clock. The sun riding high in the sky burned hotter than ever. Bonner carried two large Styrofoam cups of coffee up to Delaney as he leaned back against his car talking on his mobile phone.

Sally Cartwright was still waiting at the serving hatch of Bab's Kebabs, a burger van that to her knowledge had never sold kebabs, and that was permanently stationed conveniently close to the White City nick, in a little industrial park. Roy, the man who owned and ran the van, was a big fan of science fiction, apparently, but if there was a connection Sally wasn't a good enough detective to find it. Roy was unimpressed as he dangled the herbal tea bag that Sally had provided into a cup of hot water.

"You drink this shit and you're never going to make detective inspector. Black coffee and doughnuts, that's what you should be having."

"And you watch too much American television."

Roy scowled. "What television should I be watching? British?"

Sally considered. He had a point.

"Best shows in recent years. *Battlestar Galactica, Heroes, A Town Called Eureka*. All American."

"Right," said Sally, not really listening; she hadn't seen any of them.

"And look at the garbage we put out. *Cape Wrath*? Do me a favour." Roy flipped the bacon sizzling on his grill, warming to his theme. "And don't get me started

138

on *Doctor Who*." He glared back at her with the impassioned eyes of a zealot. "Should have stopped with Tom Baker."

"Not my thing."

"Yeah, well." Roy flicked the herbal tea bag into the bin. "What would you know anyway? You're only just out of school uniform yourself. But if Doctor Who was supposed to be a grinning idiot then he would have been written that way from the start. He's not a bloody *Blue Peter* presenter, is he?"

"I think he's quite sexy."

"Sexy! He's Scottish!"

Sally didn't have an answer for that so stayed silent as she watched Roy spear the bacon from the griddle and lay it across some thick slices of white bread.

"I suppose next you'll be telling me you want red sauce with these."

Sally jerked her thumb backwards at Delaney and Bonner. "They're for them. I don't eat bacon sandwiches."

"Maybe you should."

"Why?"

"What is it they say? You are what you eat. And this is pig, isn't it?"

"Good one, Roy. Tell it to Delaney."

Roy shrugged. "Nah. He's a miserable fucker. Am I right?"

Sally laughed, despite herself. "You're not wrong."

"Never am, me."

Sally collected the sandwiches and walked away before he could get started on *Red Dwarf*.

Across at the car, Delaney was finishing his call. "He can't have just vanished off the face of the planet. Look harder."

He folded his phone as Bonner handed him one of the coffees. "Billy Martin?"

"Nobody's seen him. Nobody's heard anything about him. For days now."

Bonner shrugged. "He'll turn up, boss. He's a regular turd. Flush the cistern round the sewer a few times and he's bound to come floating up sooner or later, smelling of shit and talking the same."

"Later might be too late." Delaney saw Sally approaching and changed the subject. "What have you got for me on Candy Morgan?"

Bonner looked puzzled. "Nothing. You told me to —"

Delaney held up his hand to cut him off as Sally joined them, holding out the sandwiches.

"Didn't know if you wanted sauce but he put it on anyway."

Delaney took a sandwich and nodded at Bonner. "You hear anything, call me first." He turned back to Sally as he opened the passenger side of the car. "You can drive."

"Where are we going?"

"Candy Morgan's counsellor. She poked around in her head for long enough, apparently; let's see if she found anything useful in there."

"Guv."

Sally got into the car as Delaney took a bite of his sandwich and chewed happily. In his opinion Roy, the science-fiction-obsessed burger boy, was an irritating feck. But he could cook a bacon sandwich.

He swallowed the mouthful, but as he thought about where Billy Martin might be, his hunger was suddenly gone. He thought about Jackie Malone lying on the morgue table, and then guiltily he thought about Kate Walker too. Thought about her long, shapely legs. Thought about her dark, luxuriant hair, the way she tossed it angrily back, the flash of her eyes and the soft curve of her blood-red lips. And despite himself he smiled.

Kate felt rather than saw the movement. She spun around, her arm flying up, palm forward, instinctively defensive. The blow glanced off her forearm, sliding painfully across her elbow. She gasped but didn't let the pain stop her from completing her spin, taking her out of harm's way. She centred herself and lashed out with her right foot, the kick reaching high to slam into her assailant's head.

The other woman was tall — at five ten she had a good couple of inches on Kate — but years of yoga had made Kate more than flexible, and there was anger behind the kick. The taller woman grunted, taken unawares, and dropped to her knees. Kate pulled back her hand, making an upside-down fist, her other hand held palm down to the side of her waist, and stepped up as her opponent fought to catch her breath. Their eyes locked as Kate readied herself.

"Enough." The woman held up a hand. "For Christ's sake, Kate, that felt like you meant it."

Kate grimaced apologetically and held out a hand to help her up. "Sorry, Jane. Didn't mean to knock you over."

Jane laughed, wincing with pain. "I'd hate to be here when you did."

"Want to call it a draw?"

"I want to call it a day. This body is getting too old for this kind of abuse."

Kate slapped her on the back. "Rubbish." At forty-five, Dr Jane Harrington still had the kind of body a lot of twenty-two-year-olds would envy. And as they walked off the exercise mats across the gym towards the showers, Kate could see that they were both getting a fair number of admiring glances. Some of them almost welcome.

In the shower block, Kate turned the dial medium high and stood under the fierce jets of steaming water. Her body ached all over, but it was a pleasant ache, the kind that only came from hard exercise, exercise that took her off into a different space and flooded her body with endorphins. She had always been sporty, even as a girl, but in martial arts she had really found her element. The discipline, the focus, the toughness of mind and body. And she was good at it. That was important to Kate; she didn't like to be second best at anything. And the confidence the training gave her was more than just a bonus. She liked to be in control of her life, and if somebody meant to hurt her, then they would find out just how in control she was. The hot water hammered her skin and she felt glowing, vibrant. She didn't know why she let that arrogant prick

Delaney get under her skin, but he did, he always had. She smiled, a little guiltily, remembering how hard she had kicked her friend. She was sure that subconsciously it was Jack Delaney she wanted to be kicking. It was certainly him who had made her call Jane and suggest a workout. Sometimes you just had to burn the negative energy away, and the dojo was the best place Kate knew to do that. As a doctor she could see comic irony in violence as therapy, but it was controlled violence and Kate was all for it.

Jane held out a glass of orange juice as Kate walked up to join her at the sports club bar, dropping her holdall to the floor and taking the drink gratefully.

"I was beginning to think you'd drowned in that shower."

"Was I long?"

"Kate, you are always long. But today I think you set a new record."

"Sorry." Kate clinked her glass against Jane's and took a long swallow, finishing half of it.

"So what's going on?"

Kate sat on the tall stool beside her and put her glass on the marble bar counter. "What do you mean?"

"You seemed a bit distracted earlier."

"Distracted?"

"Tense. Preoccupied. You don't usually knock seven bells out of me. Six maybe; not usually seven."

"Just work."

"Oh?"

Kate shook her head dismissively. "Nothing specific, just a couple of cases."

"Not like you to bring your work away from the office."

"It's pretty nasty. A prostitute. She was cut up really badly."

Jane looked at her closely as she took a deep swallow of her own drink.

"You know what I think you should do?"

Kate laughed. "Come and work with you, I suppose?"

"I know your job isn't doing you any good."

"I make a difference, Jane."

"You took a Hippocratic oath to save lives. How is cutting up dead people doing that?"

"Because when I help catch a murderer and put them away, it stops them from killing again."

Jane was unconvinced. "Killing again? How many victims that you deal with are murdered by a serial killer?"

Kate didn't answer and Jane nodded smugly. "Exactly. You know as well as I do that ninety-nine-point-something of all murders are committed by family members or friends or criminal associates. The serial killer is a myth for all practical purposes outside of American films and novels."

"Not true. Serial killing has increased enormously in America. And what they have in America always ends up here a few years later."

"Yeah. McDonald's maybe. And indoor bowling alleys and nude beach volleyball. But the Fred Wests and the Nilsens and the Shipmans, they're rare. They're nothing to do with some fashion from America. They make up a tiny fraction of your work and you know it."

Kate laughed and shook her head. "It's the same old story, Jane. I'm not going to change. I love what I do. The dead deserve justice just as much as the living."

"Justice? You're a doctor, Kate, not a lawyer."

"Either way, I'm not going to change my job. I love what I do."

Jane laughed ironically. "I hope you make a better forensic pathologist than you do an actress."

"Why don't we change the subject?"

Jane fixed her with a look. "Okay. How's the love life?"

"What love life?"

"Something has got you coiled up like a jungle cat stuck in a bathtub of soapy water, and if it isn't work . . . it's got to be a man."

Kate shook her head. "What is it they say? A woman needs a man like a fish needs a deep fat fryer."

Jane leaned in and looked her in the eye. "Yeah. Definitely a man. You going to tell me about it?"

Kate stood up and finished her drink. "I have to get back to work."

Jane called after her. "Just tell me it's not one of your clients."

Elaine Simmons was in her early fifties. Dressed conservatively in a thick woollen skirt and jacket, despite the heat. Delaney was used to judging people by appearances, and he knew Ms Simmons was aware of it. After all, they both played the same kind of game.

Delaney was used to reading people so he could help put them behind bars. Ms Simmons was used to reading people to keep them out. If asked for his views on the role counsellors played in keeping crime statistics down, he wasn't usually complimentary.

"The point is, Ms Simmons, you recommended Candy Morgan for release."

Elaine Simmons smiled at him in a neutral kind of way. "I'm guessing here that you don't usually have much time for the likes of me, Inspector."

"You'd be guessing right."

"Wishy-washy liberals, holding the criminals' hands and treating them with more respect than their victims."

"Sounds about the right description."

"We all have a job to do."

"If you kept on holding their hands, maybe that would work."

"What do you mean?"

"See, if you held on to them, then those hands couldn't be put to use again, could they? Strangling people. Stabbing or glassing people. Raping. Sodomising. Old ladies, young children."

"You're not a fan of probation and rehabilitation, I take it?"

"Are you?"

"I wouldn't be in this job if I wasn't."

"Every single week someone is murdered or raped by an offender on parole. Let out early on the recommendation of yourself or one of your colleagues."

"We're not the bad guys, Inspector. These statistics should be put into context. Last year only point six per cent of offenders assessed as high risk reoffended."

Delaney could feel a throbbing in his temples and a red mist building up behind his eyes. "I was just putting matters into the context, Ms Simmons, of the fact that career criminals are let out after serving only half their time. Let out on probation due to the fact that the government reckons it is more cost-effective to let murderers loose on the street than to build the prisons needed to house them all."

Elaine smiled sympathetically. "I'm sorry you see it that way."

"Save your apologies for Jenny Morgan's father."

"I don't feel he has cause for alarm."

Delaney couldn't believe what he was hearing. "His psychotic sister has kidnapped his daughter, for Christ's sake. I should think he has every good reason to be alarmed."

"Candy Morgan was assessed very thoroughly before she was released. I really don't think she poses a threat to anyone, least of all her niece."

"She cut somebody's ear off. She sliced a guard's face open with a razor."

"She changed."

"They all change when parole comes up."

"Candy was different."

Delaney laughed dismissively. "They're all different, they're all innocent."

"Have you spoken to her, Inspector?"

"Obviously not. That's why we're here."

"When you speak to her, you'll see what I mean."

"You have nothing to give us that will help us find her?"

"I've no idea where she is. But I can assure you that the girl is in no danger."

"How can you be so sure?"

Elaine hesitated, then shook her head. "You'll just have to take my word for it."

Delaney looked at her, realisation dawning. "You know something, don't you?"

"No. I have no idea where she is."

"But you know something. She has told you something?"

"Anything we ever spoke about is confidential. You know that, Inspector."

"I know that a twelve-year-old girl is missing."

"I'm sorry, but I can't help you."

"Bullshit!" Delaney slammed his hand down hard on her desk.

Elaine jumped back, startled.

"You know anything that can help us find that girl then you tell us now. Or so help me I'll make you pay for it if anything happens to her."

Elaine Simmons met his angry look. "Believe it or not, Inspector, you're not the first person to shout at me."

Sally intervened diplomatically. "We just want to find the girl. I'm sure you can see that."

"Of course I can. And if I could help in any way I would. Like I said, I honestly and genuinely believe that Candy Morgan is a changed woman. She has had a horrible, troubled life but she has turned it around. She's turned a corner."

"She's turning a corner straight back to Holloway when we catch up with her."

"And if she hasn't done anything wrong?"

"Of course she's done something wrong."

"She's a relative. It makes a difference."

Delaney leaned in. "You want to help Candy Morgan?"

"Yes, I do."

"Then tell us what you know."

"I'm sorry, there's nothing else to tell."

Delaney's mobile phone rang; he snapped it open, irritated.

"Delaney?"

He listened for a moment or two then thanked the caller and hung up. He stood up and nodded to Sally. "We're out of here."

"Where to?"

"Back to Holloway."

Delaney opened the door for Sally and looked back at Elaine Simmons.

"I hope you sleep well at night."

"As it happens, I don't, Inspector. And you know why?"

"Surprise me."

"Because I actually care about the people I deal with. To you they may be worthless scum. But to me they are victims just as much as the people they have offended against."

"And it's all the fault of society, I suppose?"

"You're carrying a lot of anger around with you, Inspector. It's not healthy."

"You going to offer to counsel me?"

"Not me, but you should get help. That kind of anger. You let that build and someone is going to end up getting hurt."

"Maybe someone already has."

Delaney followed Sally through the door and pulled it firmly shut behind him.

Sally looked at him a little nervously. "What did you mean by somebody already being hurt?"

"Don't worry about it."

He walked ahead, the tension showing in the taut muscles of his shoulders.

A loose tile let a shaft of sunlight poke through the roof, throwing a small spill of speckled gold on to the attic floor. Dust motes danced in the beam of light as a spider crawled out of the eaves and stopped frozen in the centre of the small golden circle.

Across the attic, in the dark, Jenny Morgan's eyes widened and she shrank back against the hard angle of the roof. She hated spiders. Always had. It seemed to her that the spider had stopped because it had seen her. She let out a low whimper and shrank even further back, hunching her shoulders. She cried out a little as the blue nylon cord that was tied to her wrists bit in roughly. The other end of the rope was tied to an iron hoop beyond her reach, so she was trapped. Alone. In the dark, and terrified.

The spider stiffened slightly and then suddenly shot with lightning speed back into the shadows. Jenny let out a small sigh of relief, her young heart pumping blood so fast that she could feel it in her chest and her ears.

Then a sound came and she stiffened again. The sound of footsteps on the ladder that led into the loft. As she looked across, the woman who claimed to be her aunt was coming towards her. In the darkness she couldn't see the expression on her face or the look in her eyes, but what she could see was the spill of sunlight flashing off steel as the woman raised the carving knife that she held in her right hand.

And Jenny screamed.

CHAPTER
SEVENTEEN

Delaney leaned his elbow out of the window as they waited in a long line of traffic queuing up to Archway. Sally glanced across at him. "You think there should be a difference between sentencing men and women, then? That women should be treated differently?"

"We don't make the law, Sally."

"Most female prisoners are in for crimes that don't really pose a risk to society. Theft, handling stolen goods, petty crimes to help feed their family. The children of those women are often then put into care. And that's just seeding crime for the future. We're breeding criminals and the prison system is a large part of it."

"What about Candy Morgan, do you think she should have been released?"

Sally sighed. "She obviously has mental health problems."

She spun the wheel, pulling the car back into the prison car park, and showed her warrant card to the security guard who manned the gate, Delaney did likewise and they were waved through to drive on and find a space.

He stared ahead as he took off his seatbelt. "Elaine Simmons may sit in her ivory tower and make decisions based on political correctness because she doesn't have to deal with the consequences. You and I do. And if she is wrong about Candy Morgan, then it is little Jenny who will pay the price."

Sally undid her belt and Delaney turned to her. "No point us both going in. You wait here. I won't be long."

He got out of the car and shut his door. Sally wound her window down, grateful for a slight breeze that shifted the hot and heavy air a little.

She sat back in her seat and put the radio on. Radio Four. Some sitcom about a care worker and her variably eccentric colleagues dealing with life in modern London. She chuckled a little but the programme was finishing and the next item was the news, which she had heard already that day about ten times. She turned the radio right down and leaned her head back, closing her eyes, enjoying the warmth of the day and falling into a light doze.

The sound of a woman screaming in agony woke her with a start. The screaming rang out again, from a high window in the prison beyond. She was either mad or in labour, Sally reckoned. Maybe both. But weren't pregnant women allowed out to give birth in hospital? She remembered something about a female conservative MP liking to see women in labour handcuffed or some such.

She looked at her watch, wondering where Delaney had got to. Probably arguing with the governor. Delaney reminded her a little of her father; he never liked to be wrong about anything either. And he was her father's age, though she'd never tell him that. Mind you, her father was still an attractive man according to all the women who seemed to flirt with him whenever her mother's back was turned. But there was no way she'd ever think of Delaney in those terms: he was her boss, and besides, he carried more baggage than Paris Hilton on a two-month holiday to the Seychelles. The last thing she needed right now in her career was to have an affair with a senior colleague. She had already decided that. He was very much her senior in both age and rank. Absolutely no way. Don't even go there.

Still, a one-night shag would be fun. Sally laughed out loud and shook the thought quickly out of her head as she watched Delaney striding across the car park and up to the car.

"Something amusing you, Constable?"

"Just the radio."

Delaney grunted and slid himself into the passenger seat as Sally hurriedly turned the radio off. She felt a blush rise from her neck upwards and quickly changed the subject, nodding to the handful of envelopes that Delaney was clutching.

"What have we got?"

"The Royal Mail. It might be slow but it gets there in the end."

"Candy Morgan's?"

"Yeah."

"You going to tell me an admirer has been writing to her and he's arranged for her to come and live with him after she's released, and he's very kindly put his address on the letter?"

"If only."

"What then?"

"Mostly junk. But one letter from a different bank account. One we didn't know about."

"So if she pays by card at a supermarket, or uses a hole in the wall . . ."

"Exactly. Get us out of here."

"Boss."

Sally started the car and made a quick U-turn, heading back towards King's Cross.

Delaney wound his window right down again and looked out. The streets were lively with people. This was always a busy area but the sun brought them out in their hundreds. What tourists wanted to see in King's Cross was beyond him. Maybe King's Cross was going to be the new Covent Garden. The old Covent Garden was a common stamping ground for hookers and florists; maybe there was a theme developing here.

"What do you reckon, Sally?"

"About what?"

"King's Cross becoming the new Covent Garden?"

As they turned left into one of the side streets, Sally looked out of her window at a rail-thin eastern European woman leaning against a wall, her face a map of misery, the tracks of her addiction marked in the blotches on her skin and the soulless hunger in her eyes. A poster girl for consumerism gone very badly wrong.

"I wouldn't invest my pension in it, guv."

Delaney watched a homeless man who looked about seventy, but who was probably much younger, open his trousers and urinate against the graffiti-stained walls that ran north of the station.

"Probably not."

Jenny Morgan rubbed her untied wrists where the nylon cord had chafed them raw. The woman sat not far from her, sawing lumps of bread from an unsliced loaf. The carving knife was ill designed for the task and the woman swore under her breath as she struggled with it. Jenny glanced sideways at the ladder that led down from the attic and considered making a dash for it. But the woman who called herself her aunt turned, looked up and smiled.

"It won't be long, we'll be out of here soon."

Jenny nodded, swallowing drily.

"You understand why I had to tie you up earlier?"

Jenny's mouth twitched, the smile hanging off her lips like a painted grimace.

"They'll be watching for us. We have to be careful. You understand that?"

Jenny nodded again. The woman turned back to sawing at the loaf of bread.

"Angel" had seemed so different when they had spoken on the internet. Carol Parks had warned her, but Jenny knew better. She always knew better. The young girl wrapped her arms around herself, watching the knife in Candy's hand and the mad look dancing in the woman's eyes. And she was scared. Very, very scared.

156

Delaney tossed a couple of the letters to one side and handed the one from the bank over to Sally.

"Get on to them and find us any transactions she's made since she left Holloway."

"Boss."

Sally walked off and Delaney watched her. She had everything he once had. Youth, ambition, intelligence . . . hope. Something that had died in him a long time ago.

He left her to it and walked down the stairs to interview room number one. The brothers Morgan had now had time to think things through, and he hoped something might have surfaced through the quagmire of their hillbilly brains. Some memory, a useful detail. Anything that might help them find Jenny before it was too late.

Jake Morgan had his head down, twisting and turning a napkin, his thick, powerful fingers flexing and tearing the paper. Howard Morgan looked up hopefully as Delaney walked into the room.

"Is there any news?"

"We're pursuing some leads."

"What sort of leads?"

"Nothing certain. We're still trying to pinpoint her location."

"They're still in London?"

"We don't know."

Jake Morgan threw the paper napkin on the floor and stood up, his massive form dwarfing Delaney.

"She's not going to hurt her, is she?"

Delaney kept his voice calm, reassuring. "Not if we've got anything to do with it."

But Jake was not to be so easily mollified. He shook his head, blinking back the tears that were starting in his childlike eyes. "She hurts people. She likes doing it."

Delaney put a hand on his arm, gently. "Tell me about her, Jake."

"She just changed after Ma died, didn't she, Howard?"

Howard nodded, anger bubbling below the surface of his troubled eyes.

"And you have no idea where she might be? Where she might have gone? Any friends. Any relatives?"

"There's no one." Howard's voice was harsh with pain.

There was something, though, Delaney thought; was it regret, was it fear? He looked at him trying to read him. Failing. "You sure you haven't been in contact with her recently, Howard?"

Howard stood up angrily beside his brother. "I told you."

"You told us a lot of things. Not all of them were true, were they?"

"She's not my sister. Not any more."

"You're still pretty angry with her, Howard, even after all these years?"

"Wouldn't you be?"

"She was fourteen years old at the time. She was just a child."

Howard Morgan glared angrily back at him. "She was never a child. She was born evil, that girl. Ma always said that, didn't she, Jake?"

Jake nodded, his skin reddening as he remembered, his eyes sliding back and forth just like his elder brother's. "Born evil. That's what she said. And if evil is on the flesh then shall it be burned clean."

"Shut up, Jake!" Howard glared angrily across at his brother, who was shaking his head slightly, lost in his own dark thoughts.

"If the water does not cleanse then the fire shall. And everlasting shall be the pain."

Delaney watched as Jake Morgan shivered and his eyes seemed to clear. He looked up at Delaney and smiled incongruously. "Have you found Jenny, then? Is that why we're here?"

"No, we haven't found her, Jake. But we need to. So if you have remembered anything at all, anything she might have said to you . . ."

"Tell her to stay away from the steam."

Howard put his arm on his brother's shoulder. "Don't worry, Jake. She's not going to burn her."

"She burned you, though, didn't she?"

Howard nodded, his eyes narrowing at the memory. "But Jenny's going to be all right. The police are going to find her." He looked up at Delaney. Angry, challenging.

"We'll do our best."

"Because if I find Candy first, I'll fucking kill her."

Delaney looked into the hard, cold certainty of those eyes and recognised the truth in them. He'd seen that same cold hate many, many times in the eyes of killers who had sat opposite him across that desk or across others in other cities. He'd seen it in rapists, in wife-beaters, in murderers.

And he'd seen it in his own bloodshot eyes every morning since his wife was killed. If he could stand face to face with her killers they'd see that look and it would be the last thing they ever saw. That much he had promised her cold body.

A loud crack on the door startled Delaney out of his thoughts and he turned to see DC Cartwright coming into the room. She looked nervous.

"What is it, Constable?"

"You'd better come, sir."

CHAPTER
EIGHTEEN

Delaney closed the door behind him. Trapping the foul air and the stale thoughts inside. Sally's youthful eyes sparkled with excitement.

"What have you got?"

"Candy Morgan, sir."

"Go on?"

"She used a cash machine. Took out five hundred pounds."

"When?"

"About an hour ago."

"Could be someone using her card."

Sally shook her head. "We got the bank to check their security footage, it was definitely her."

"Where?"

"King's Cross."

"The apple doesn't fall far from the tree, does it?"

"Doesn't seem to. Stella Trant didn't move too far from Holloway either, did she?"

"Spitting distance from where Candy Morgan just made a cash withdrawal."

"You think Stella lied to us?"

"I think what Bob Wilkinson would no doubt tell you."

"And what's that, sir?"

"That they're all slags. And slags are born lying and slags die lying. Let's go."

Sally reacted a little surprised as Delaney shrugged into his jacket. "Shouldn't we co-ordinate this, boss? We don't want to go rushing in and lose her."

"She's just drawn out five hundred pounds. What does that tell you, Sally?"

Sally shrugged.

"It tells me she's wedged up. She's ready to travel and now she's got the cash to do it."

Delaney barrelled through the front door, Sally hurrying behind him.

Howard Morgan watched through the window as Sally and Delaney hurried towards the car. He could see the purpose in Delaney's long stride and the expectation in Sally Cartwright's nervously excited face. His fist bunched involuntarily and the muscles in his biceps strained, stretching the fabric of his shirt. He turned to his brother. "Wait here, Jake."

"What's going on?"

"You just wait here." He fished his car keys out of his overall pocket and hurried after Delaney.

Delaney's fist landed on Stella's front door like Odin's hammer. Stella opened the door, her wide green eyes startled with fear.

"What do you want?" Her voice was a nervous stutter, her previous arrogance dissipated in the face of his violent glare.

162

Delaney pushed her back into the room and stepped in, Sally following closely behind and shutting the door.

"What the hell is going on?"

Delaney ignored her and swept open the bedroom door and looked around. There was no one there. Unless Candy Morgan was hiding in the kitchen cupboard, they had missed her. Maybe by minutes.

Delaney turned round and glared at Stella Trant, who crossed her thin arms defensively in front of her chest.

"I told you, I haven't seen her. What the hell are you doing here? You've got no right."

Delaney ignored her again, opening the drawers in a small sideboard.

"Where's your warrant?"

"Shut it," Delaney barked at her. He tipped the contents of the drawer on the floor and threw it to one side to smash against the wall.

"Guv."

Delaney flashed Sally a look and she glanced away.

Stella laughed humourlessly. "What is this? Good cop, bad cop?"

Delaney opened the next drawer and smiled at her. "How would you like to go back to taking your showers communally, Stella? The governor told us you were popular with the bull dykes."

Stella shook her head, unfazed. "I doubt he said any such thing, but I was popular with everybody." She smiled. "Including the governor. Why do you think he takes such a special interest in girls like us?"

Delaney carried on searching through the drawer.

"Did you think it was just his good heart?" She cupped her crotch with her right hand. "The truth is, this was just as valuable on the inside as it was on the outside." She winked at Sally. "You know what I mean?"

Delaney tossed the second drawer aside and opened the third. He smiled sourly as he pulled out a small clear plastic bag. "What have we got here?"

"That's not mine."

"Whose is it? Candy Morgan's?"

"No."

"It's yours, then."

Stella shrugged and folded her arms again. "It's a bit of blow. Which is legal now, isn't it? Nothing you can do about it."

"No, it's not legal. And that means it's a violation of your parole."

Stella shook her head, rattled now. "I've done nothing wrong."

"Then tell us where she is."

Stella didn't answer, but she gave a small, almost imperceptible, nod of the head. Most people wouldn't have seen it, but Delaney played poker; he could tell a giveaway sign when he saw one.

He turned round and gestured at Sally. "Wait for me in the car."

"Guv?"

"Just do it, Constable."

Sally looked at her boss but didn't argue. She shut the front door behind her as she left and Delaney focused his attention back on Stella Trant. "We can do this the hard way if you prefer."

"Jackie Malone always said you were a halfway decent cop. Maybe she was wrong."

Delaney leant forward and slammed his large hand round her throat.

"Maybe she was."

Stella's eyes filled, bright with fear. "Don't hurt me."

"You know anything about Jackie, you tell me now!"

Stella shook her head. "I don't know anything. We shared a cell. We talked, that's all."

"You talked about me?"

"She did. I just listened."

"And what did she say?"

"Nothing. Just that she liked you, that's all. I think she had a soft spot for you."

"You swear there's nothing else? She didn't tell you anything else?"

"Like what?"

Delaney let the question hang and Stella shook her head again. "She didn't tell me anything else. It was just that, for the sake of sweet Jesus. Girl talk. You know?"

Delaney released his grip and stepped back. "Where is she, Stella?"

Stella rubbed her neck, confused. "Jackie Malone?"

"I know where Jackie Malone is. Where's Candy Morgan?"

Stella sighed and looked up at the ceiling, speaking in a low voice. "She's upstairs. The owners are away whilst the place is having building work done, and the builders are off on another job." A small worm of fear squirmed again behind her eyes. "You can't tell her I told you."

Delaney nodded and threw the bag of dope to her. Stella's hand flashed out like a cricketer, caught it and stashed it in her jeans pocket. Then her eyes grew harder. "You do tell her, of course . . . and I might have to have a word with your colleagues."

"What are you talking about?"

"Who were we just discussing, Cowboy?"

"Don't call me that."

"It's what Jackie called you, isn't it? How would your bosses feel if I told them what I know? About her? About you?"

Delaney just looked at her without responding.

Stella smiled suddenly, putting more than a hint of invitation into it. "That's all right, Cowboy, I was only messing. I don't talk to the filth." She winked. "I can talk pretty filthy, mind, and I could whisper in your ear some night if you wanted."

Delaney opened her front door and looked back at her. "I'll be seeing you again, Stella. Don't be making any calls on your mobile."

CHAPTER
NINETEEN

Delaney came out of the house, his face impassive. Sally stepped over to him. "Everything all right, sir?"

Delaney took her arm and steered her none too gently towards his car. He stared straight ahead as he spoke. "Don't look at the house. Just get in the motor."

They both got into the car. Delaney pulled out his mobile and called Bonner. He updated him, told him to put the wheels in motion and hung up.

"We wait here?"

"You wait here. I'm going up."

"You can't, boss."

Delaney shook his head. "Stella may have phoned her. She might be spooked. I'm not taking the chance that she might hurt the girl before we get there."

"The girl might already be dead, guv."

"Then I'm not going to let her get away."

"I'm coming with you."

"You're not. You're going to stay here and wait for back-up."

"You can't go in on your own. She's dangerous."

"I can't waste time arguing about this, Sally."

"Let's go then."

Delaney sighed and opened his car door. He hurried back to the house with Sally close on his heels. The door to the upstairs flat was next to Stella Trant's. Delaney pulled a small pick out of his pocket and smiled sideways at Sally. "You didn't see this."

He twisted the pick and the lock clicked open. He opened the door gently just as Howard Morgan came charging up the street towards them.

"Is she in there? Is my Jenny in there?"

Delaney cursed. "Jesus Christ on a fucking bicycle. Keep him down here, Sally."

"Sir, I . . ."

"Just do it."

Delaney hurled the door back — there was no point in stealth now — and ran up the stairs to the first floor. It was deserted and completely barren. He moved from one room to the next. The place had been stripped back to bare wood and the walls were ready for renovation. The floorboards were rotten in places and evidence of water damage was everywhere. No wonder the owners had moved out whilst the builders were in. The place was a death trap.

Delaney moved back into the corridor and walked slowly towards the back of the house.

"Candy, if you're here, we don't mean you any harm. We just want to know that Jenny is all right."

He listened, but there was no response. "Talk to me, Candy. Everything can be sorted out. It's not too late."

He heard something, a rustle, a movement, and edged towards the room at the end of the corridor. The faded green door was closed and Delaney was sure he heard something behind it.

"I'm coming in, Candy. Don't do anything stupid."

Outside, the sounds of police sirens and screeching tyres signalled the arrival of at least one car.

Delaney took a breath and opened the door. Stepping quickly into the room, he pulled the door shut behind him.

Into darkness. The windows had been boarded over and he squinted in the gloom. His eyes, used to the white glare of the sun, needed time to adjust.

As he walked slowly into the room, he could see a woman climbing quickly up a set of steps that descended from a loft hatch in the ceiling. Delaney charged after her. She cleared the ladder and tried to pull it up. Delaney tugged it down, holding it firm as she disappeared into the darkness above. "Don't do anything foolish, Candy. My name is Jack Delaney. I'm here to help." He took a step on the ladder and paused. "We just want to know she's all right."

He took another tentative step up, and then another, raising his head into the loft space above. His eyes had adjusted now as he scanned the space, ready to duck below. His heart was racing but no sign showed in his impassive face. "It's okay, Candy. We're not here to hurt you."

Candy sat in the corner of the room, one arm wrapped around Jenny, the other holding the carving knife forward. Jenny looked at Delaney, her eyes round with fear. Behind them on the floor were a couple of sleeping bags, some bottles of water, a blanket, a child's comic, a half-eaten loaf of bread. Dangling from the rafter was a blue rope.

Candy spoke, her voice a low rasp. "How can I trust you?"

Delaney recognised the panic in her voice and wasn't reassured by it. Frightened people did stupid things. The impulse to self-protect could be the most destructive force on the planet, and Delaney knew that better than anyone.

"We're the police. We're just here to make sure that Jenny is safe. Look." He held out his warrant card. "Are you okay, Jenny?"

"Yes." Her voice was tremulous, unconvincing.

"She hasn't hurt you?"

"She's my aunt. She wouldn't hurt me, she's looking after me."

"Are you going to put the knife down, Candy?"

Candy shook her head, her knuckles paling as she tightened her grip on the knife. "I was only looking after her."

Delaney sighed. She wasn't going to make this easy for any of them. He edged closer, smiling reassuringly at the huddled, frightened little girl. "It's okay, Jenny. There's nothing to be scared of."

He walked forward some more, his foot slipping a little, and a large section of plasterboard and ceiling fell into the room below. Candy moved instinctively back.

"Don't move. You're going to bring the floor down."

Delaney held out his hand in a reassuring gesture. "Just stay calm." He edged around the rotten section of the floor and reached out his arms. "All I want is the girl. Just let me take her and everything is going to be all right."

Downstairs, Bonner burst into the room and looked up at Delaney through the newly made gap in the floor. "Guv?"

"It's okay, Eddie, stay there. We'll be right down." He turned to Candy and smiled, forcing some reassurance into his expression. "Pass her over, Candy."

Candy shook her head, her eyes nervous, her breathing shallow. She clung on to Jenny, who whimpered a little as the floor creaked and sagged.

Delaney moved slowly forward. Candy backed further into the eaves, one hand clutching Jenny protectively to her, the other holding the knife out, her eyes glittering and skittish. "Back off."

But Delaney took another step forward. "I can't do that, Candy. You know that."

"I mean it."

"And so do I. You how these things work."

He moved forward again, and Candy held the knife, straight and unwavering.

Delaney paused for a moment, then calmly stepped forward and put his hand around the blade of the knife. Candy glared at him, rage coming off her like the shimmer of heat on a hot tarmac road. Her grip on the handle tightened and Delaney swallowed, his Adam's apple inches from the tip of the knife. Then, in a heartbeat, the fire died in her eyes, like the sudden cessation of a summer lightning storm, and, as tears formed, Delaney could see the young child Candy had once been, a lifetime of hurt away. She looked down at the floor and then back up at Delaney, letting her hand fall from knife so that he could take it from her.

"I only wanted to take care of her," she said in a whisper.

Delaney fought to keep his voice level. "I know." He threw the knife across the loft and nodded to Candy. "Just pass her to me."

Candy wiped a dusty hand across her eyes and released her hold on the young girl who stood frozen to the spot. "I love you, Jenny."

Delaney held out his hand to the petrified girl, fighting to keep it still. "Come on, Jenny. Take my hand."

Jenny took a step forward, and the rotten plasterboard beneath her collapsed. She screamed as she was pitched towards the gaping hole in the floor, and Delaney, bracing himself against the eave rafters, swung out and caught her. She dangled for a moment or two, still screaming, as Delaney's forearm muscles strained, but he held her tight and swung her back up on to the safe section of the attic floor.

Eddie Bonner came up the steps into the attic and gathered the child safely into his arms.

"It's all right, Jenny. Nobody's going to hurt you now."

"Take her downstairs, Eddie."

Bonner led the terrified girl to the ladder as Delaney turned back to Candy, who was pressed into the eaves space, the rotten joist creaking beneath her feet.

Delaney, still braced against the rafter, held his hand out again. "It's over, Candy. Take my hand."

Candy looked at him for a moment and Delaney could see the defeat in her eyes, eyes that were far, far old beyond their years. Given what had happened to her in the past, he wasn't at all shocked to see the desolation in them. "I'm not here to judge you, Candy."

"You're a policeman, aren't you?"

Delaney gestured with his hand again. "Not much of one."

She stood up carefully and moved slowly around the gaping hole in the floor, then cried out suddenly as the footing gave way beneath her, tilting her forwards. She lurched desperately to clutch Delaney's outstretched hand and, gripping each other tightly, they edged step by step towards the ladder in the corner of the loft.

Delaney held the ladder steady as Candy climbed down. Sally Cartwright waited at the bottom, handcuffs dangling from her hands, a triumphant smile barely held back from her young lips.

Candy looked around, startled at the large number of police in the room. There was no sign of either Jenny or Bonner.

"Jenny!" She tried to push past Sally, but the DC held her arms and a uniformed officer blocked her way.

"You're going nowhere." Sally's voice was heavy with disgust.

Delaney stepped down. "Where's the girl?"

"Bonner's taken her down to her father."

Candy struggled, furious. "You've let him take her? For Christ's sake, what have you done?"

Delaney stepped in front of her. "What are you talking about?"

"Why do you think I took her from him in the first place?"

"You can explain all that down at the station. Candy Morgan, I am arresting you —"

Candy screamed in his face. "I took her away from him because she's not safe with him. He's ill! Don't you understand that? Don't you understand anything? He's going to hurt her."

Delaney looked at the naked pain in her eyes and came to a decision. He nodded to Sally and Candy. "Come on."

He ran down the stairs, followed by the two women. Bonner was talking on his mobile phone.

"Where the hell is she, Eddie?"

Bonner held the phone away from his ear. "Boss?"

"Where's Jenny?"

Bonner shrugged and looked around. "She was with her father."

"You said she was going to be safe!" Candy screamed at Delaney.

Delaney glared at Eddie. "What the bloody hell were you thinking of?"

"He's her father, isn't he? What's the problem?"

But Delaney had pushed past him, and was running out the front door.

CHAPTER
TWENTY

Outside in the empty street, Delaney could feel the heat bunching his shirt uncomfortably under his jacket. He ran the palm of his hand across his forehead, wiping the sweat away, and closed his eyes. He opened them again as Bonner came up to him. "They've gone." He sighed wearily and flicked a cigarette into his mouth.

"Sorry, boss."

Sally Cartwright came out of the house, shutting her mobile. "A squad car is on its way to Morgan's house."

Delaney nodded bleakly. "Time to break out the raincoats."

Bonner squinted up at the clear sky. "Guv?"

"This is going to turn into a real shit storm."

Jenny Morgan sat in the back of her father's car, watching his face in the rear-view mirror. She had never seen him so angry. The vein on the side of his neck was throbbing like a purple worm, and sweat was pouring off his furrowed forehead, staining his shirt. He gripped the steering wheel hard in his massive fists as if he was going to wrench the whole column out. She wanted to know where he was taking her, but she didn't dare ask.

At White City police station, the temperature in interview room one was no less cool. Candy Morgan took the cup of coffee that Sally handed her and smiled nervously as Delaney sat opposite her. She took a sip of the coffee and sat back in the chair, wrapping her arms around herself. She was shivering as though she was cold, but Delaney knew it was just the by-product of adrenalin kicking in. That and her memories. "How long had you been speaking with her on the internet?" he asked gently.

"About two months."

"And how did that happen?"

Candy looked down at the table, tracing her finger in small circles on the smooth wood.

"I'd been getting therapy."

"Go on." Delaney's tone was far from sympathetic.

Candy looked up at him, challenging. "I guess you know my history."

"Some of it. What's written in your records."

"So I had some issues."

"Yeah, I'd say you had some issues."

"And I was dealing with them." She shrugged. "Trying to deal with them."

"What's this got to do with Jenny?"

"It made me remember my childhood, what happened to me. And it made me think of Jenny and what would happen to her, and I wanted to stop it."

Sally leant forward. "So how did you make contact with her on the internet?"

176

"There are sites. Schoolroom contacts. Networking. It's not hard to track down someone if they are using their real name. And Jenny was."

"But you didn't tell her who you were?"

"Not at first, no. I wanted to build her trust."

Delaney loosened his collar. "And what makes you think there was abuse?"

"She told me what was happening. I recognised the signs."

"What signs?"

Candy looked away. "I could see the way things were going. That's why I had to do something. Before it was too late."

"What do you mean by too late, Candy?"

"I told you. He's a sick man."

"You burned him?"

Candy snapped her head back up and met his gaze. "That's right."

"With a steam hose."

"And I'd do it again in a heartbeat."

"He must have really hurt you."

Candy leaned forward. "I tell you this much. If he's hurt that little girl, I'll finish the job. I don't care if you get to him first. He's not safe in prison. Not from me."

Delaney looked at the feral anger in her eyes and didn't doubt it. "Like I said earlier. Nobody's making any judgements here."

Candy slammed her hand down on the table. "I made a judgement!"

"Candy."

"My father abused him and Jake. And because of that I guess Howard felt it was all right to abuse me. An old family tradition." She looked at Sally. "My mother died in a car accident; the brakes failed, they told me. I was twelve and Howard was twenty-four and it started the night of her funeral."

"The abuse?"

"Kissing and cuddling and little games . . ." She broke off, swallowing the disgust that was rising in her throat.

Sally spoke soothingly. "It's all right Candy. You don't have to say any more. Not right now."

"Yes I do."

They waited.

"Kissing and cuddling, just like Jenny told me he had started doing with her. And eventually . . ." She looked up at Delaney and smiled icily. "And eventually he started fucking me. He got me pregnant."

"What did you do?"

"What could I do?"

Delaney shrugged; again he had no answers for her.

"Howard had friends. An older woman. A prostitute." She shook her head at the memory. "She used a coat hanger. Howard reckoned it was just like cleaning a carburettor."

"Do you think he would physically harm Jenny?"

Candy looked at him, her eyes wide. "Haven't you been listening to a fucking word I've been saying?"

"We need to know what he might be capable of."

Candy looked at him for a beat. "I told you his father was physically abusing him."

Delaney nodded for her to continue. "But it wasn't just Howard; it was our mother too, and Jake. Not just sexual abuse. Real physical abuse; I mean, he really hurt them. All of them. Not me. I was too young, I guess, but I saw and I remember. And it didn't stop until I was five years old."

"What happened to make it stop?"

"Howard happened."

"Go on?"

"I guess he was seventeen, been out of school for three years, not that anyone cared, and was working with Dad in the garage."

"And?"

"The police thought it was an accident. The jack slipped and the car came down on his chest, cracked his ribs, slowly crushed him to death."

"But it wasn't an accident?"

"He brought me in and made me watch what he did."

"Howard?"

Candy nodded. "He made me stay in the corner, then called out to Dad. As he slid out from underneath the car, Howard kicked away the jack so that the car slammed down and trapped him like a half-squashed beetle. He screamed and called for help and Howard just laughed at him."

Sally looked at her. "I'm sorry, Candy."

"It took him over two hours to die, and Howard just sat there and watched him the whole time."

"And you didn't tell anyone?"

"I knew what would happen if I did."

"Nobody said anything?"

"Who was there to listen? And then Mum died and it was my turn. He saw nothing wrong in it and he still doesn't. You see why I had to take Jenny?"

"You should have come to us."

"And you would have helped, would you?"

"Yes."

"Stella told me that Jackie Malone's been murdered. You didn't help her, did you?"

Delaney leaned forward angrily. "What do you know about that?"

"Working girls in London. It's a bit like the Masons, isn't it? We both get to wear leather and we all get to know each other's business."

Sally looked at Delaney. "What's she talking about?"

Delaney shook his head dismissively. "They break the law, do nothing to protect themselves, but when one of them gets hurt it's down to the system, it's never their fault."

"It was Jackie Malone's fault she was tied up and murdered, was it? She did that to herself, I suppose."

Delaney looked away angrily. "Let's just concentrate on finding your niece right now, shall we?"

Sally looked at Candy sympathetically. "You showed Howard in the end. You stood up to him; that took a lot of courage."

"I wasn't brave. I was a coward for years. A victim because I didn't know any different. But when I was old enough to fight back, I did. That one time, and I wish to God I'd been brave enough to finish the job. I wish I'd been brave enough to kill him."

180

"Maybe it's better for you that you didn't."

"No, it's not. He's a cancer and you don't fuck about with cancer. You cut it out. You fucking kill it. Because Jenny isn't like me. She's sweet, she's gentle, she's entirely vulnerable. And he's going to put his cancer in her and destroy her just like he destroyed me."

Delaney looked across at her, her arms folded tight against her chest, her nails digging into her biceps.

"Where do you think he would have taken her, Candy?"

"I haven't seen the bastard in fourteen years."

Sally nodded. "I don't blame you but anything you can think of. It's important we find her quickly. Your brother is clearly out of control."

"Speak to his pet monkey."

"I'm sorry."

"Speak to Jake."

Delaney stood up. "Come on, Detective Constable."

They headed for the door. Candy Morgan called after them, "What happens to me?"

Delaney looked back at her for a moment, deciding. "You come with us."

Sally stood in front of him, registering her concern. "Boss?"

"She comes with us."

Sally recognised the tone in his voice. "Sir."

Candy stood and smiled gratefully at Delaney. "Thanks."

"You can thank me when your niece is safe."

Fifteen minutes later, Delaney was pacing angrily across the floor of Morgan's workshop. He stopped and glared at Jake, who sat holding his head in his massive hands, his forehead knotted with concentration.

"Come on, Jake, where is he?"

"I don't know."

Sally walked into the room. "Her clothes are gone."

Delaney frowned. "He was already prepared, then." He turned back to Jake and put both hands on his shoulders. "When did he leave, Jake? Did he have Jenny with him?"

Jake stood up. "I haven't seen Jenny."

Delaney stepped forward and grabbed his shoulders again. "Where is he?"

Jake jerked backwards, knocking Delaney's hands away. He was shaking like a frightened child, the fear throbbing in his voice. "I don't know."

"He doesn't know, boss."

Delaney moved back and Jake's eyes widened suddenly. He stepped back against the table, clearly terrified.

"It's all right." But then Delaney saw where Jake Morgan was looking, and cursed. "I told you to stay in the car, Candy."

Candy Morgan ignored him, fixing Jake with a look of pure venom. "If you know anything, you tell him now, Jake."

Jake backed further against the table. "I don't know anything, Candy. Don't hurt me."

"Nobody's going to hurt you, Jake, I already told you that."

Candy stepped forward. "I wouldn't bank on it."

Delaney sighed. "You can wait in the car, or I can get the DC to take you back to the nick and from there back to Holloway. Your call, Candy."

Candy looked at Delaney for a moment. "You're part of this now, Inspector. You don't want to let me down." She gave Jake a last cold look and went back to the car.

Delaney bit back a sigh of relief and turned to Sally. "Take this place apart. There's got to be something here."

He strode over to the workbench and angrily opened the drawers, scattering their contents, his rage barely contained. He tipped the last drawer over the floor: pencils, screwdrivers, nails, screws, an oil can, a chisel. Nothing that said anything about where Morgan could have gone.

Sally took Jake by the arm and led him over to a couple of chairs that stood against the oil-stained brick wall.

"Sit down, Jake."

His eyes flicked nervously to the doorway.

"She's not going to hurt you. I promise."

"She burned Howard. She burned him with the hose."

"She did, but she isn't going to hurt you. She was ill, but she's better now. Do you understand that?"

Jake shook his head slowly. Nothing made sense to him at the moment.

Sally kept her voice soft. "When she burned Howard it was because she was sick. But she's better now. She's not going to hurt anyone. Not you, and certainly not

Jenny. She wants to help Jenny. You can understand that, can't you?"

Jake nodded. "Jenny's a good girl."

"She is, and we need to find her." Sally looked across at Delaney, who was angrily reading through bills and receipts, throwing them aside.

"I don't know where she is."

Sally sat beside Jake and patted him reassuringly on the leg. "I know you want to find her as much as we do. So think. Was there anywhere you used to like to visit together? You, Howard and Jenny?"

"We used to go to lots of places."

"Like where?"

"The countryside."

"Anywhere in particular?"

"To see the cows. Horses sometimes."

"Can you remember where that was, Jake?"

Jake nodded enthusiastically and smiled. "It was the fields."

"London Fields?"

Delaney looked across as Jake shrugged. "Just fields, with cows in them and horses."

Delaney raised an eyebrow at Sally and went back to looking through the paperwork. Sally smiled reassuringly at Jake again. "You can't remember any of the names?"

Jake shook his head. "Just countryside. Jenny would say let's go to the countryside and Howard would drive us all."

"To the fields with the cows and the horses?"

Jake nodded enthusiastically. "And the river."

"The river?"

"Yeah, we'd go all over on it. Long journeys."

"On the river?"

"Yeah, on the big river in his barge."

Delaney came over now. "He's got a barge?"

Jake smiled broadly. "He's got a Dutch barge."

Delaney swore under his breath and looked at Sally pointedly. "A Dutch barge is sea-going."

CHAPTER
TWENTY-ONE

The gentle swell of the Thames splashed lyrically, rocking the barge slightly from side to side. It was a soothing motion that at any other time, in the hot, still, thick air of the summer's evening, would have lulled Jenny into a gentle sleep. But she wasn't sleeping, she was huddled against the interior side of the boat, her legs wedged under the table that stood against one wall. Her eyes fixed on the still bright sunlight sparkling like a million broken stars on the water outside the window.

The barge seemed to rock deeper in the water and she heard the sound of heavy work boots walking across the wooden floor. She looked up at the scarred face of her father and seemed to shrink back a little into the cracked and faded leather of the bench she was sitting on.

Howard Morgan's face creased in a smile, but his worried darting eyes held no humour in them, and Jenny was not reassured. She was confused, and she was frightened.

"Where are we going?"

"I told you that when you were old enough I'd take you away, didn't I?"

Jenny nodded her head. "Yes."

"Well you're old enough now."

"Am I?"

"You're a big girl now. So I'm going to take you away like I promised."

He laid his hand over Jenny's small, fragile fingers and she tightened them into a curl, the hot, sweaty feel of her father's hand making her uncomfortable.

"What about Aunty Candy?"

Morgan drew his hand away, the anger flashing across his face like the turn of a fast tide. "Don't talk about her."

"Can't she come with us?"

"No."

"Why?"

Morgan slammed his meaty fist on the table. "Because I said so." As Jenny flinched, Morgan caught himself and smiled at his daughter. "I'm sorry, I shouldn't have shouted, sweetheart. I was angry. But not at you. At her."

"Why are you angry with her?"

"Because she took you away from us. Without asking. She took you away and you could have been hurt."

"But I wasn't hurt. She said she was going to protect me."

"Protect you against what?"

Jenny huddled up against the window again. "She just said she'd look after me."

"Well I'm here now. And Daddy looks after you the best, doesn't he?"

Jenny didn't reply for a moment, and then nodded as she saw the darkness gathering in the corners of her father's eyes.

"Good girl."

Delaney pulled a piece of paper loose from a pile of bulldog-clipped receipts and waved it at Sally Cartwright.

"What have you got?"

He pulled out his mobile and hit a speed-dial button as he flashed a small grin at her. "It's a bill. Mooring charges."

"Way to go, boss."

"Unless we've already missed him." Delaney turned his attention back to his phone. "Bonner. It's Delaney."

Downriver, where the large houses on the banks were home to the rich, the famous and the criminally wealthy, the tide swelled, sending eddies and currents that lifted silt from the river bed and gently tugged at the reeds and weeds that lined the banks. Reeds and weeds that held all kinds of wildlife. Fishes that had been sheltering from the hard, relentless beat of the summer sun came closer to the surface, drawn by the insects that crawled and danced and darted in the air. And below, his hair snaking loose in greasy tendrils and his eyes as milky as a dead cod's, the head of Billy Martin was tangled in the deep roots of the bulrushes and clinging weed that held him close. As the surging rise of the tidal water tried to suck him from their tight embrace, the weeds pulled him back as though his bloated body was a treasure that they were loath to lose, and the fish and the crawling things feasted on the rotting parts of his exposed flesh.

Delaney got out of his car, Candy and Sally beside him as he walked down the riverside path to where Bonner and a horde of uniformed police were gathered.

Bonner nodded to him. "Guv."

"What's happening?"

Bonner nodded at the barge, which was rising higher in the water as the tide poured water back from the North Sea and into the Thames estuary. "Still here. Another twenty minutes he'd have had the tide and been gone."

"We'd have got him on the water."

"Maybe. Just as well you found that mooring receipt."

Delaney waved a dismissive hand. "That's all down to DC Cartwright here. She managed to get Jake to speak where we failed."

Bonner flashed a smile at Sally. "The gentle touch. Is that what they call it?"

Sally wasn't amused. "The human touch, I believe, Sergeant."

Delaney looked across at the barge, his hand on his brow shielding his eyes from the low glare of the sun as it flashed off the silver water of the Thames. "Why haven't we moved on him?"

"Making sure he's not armed first. We didn't want to risk anything with the girl in there."

"So where are SO19?"

"On their way. And the coast guard and river patrol."

Delaney could see movement on the barge and took Bonner's binoculars from him.

"It's Morgan."

Through the lenses he could see Morgan clearly. Could see the tension written in his face like a clenched fist and saw what he was doing. He cursed under his breath and gave the binoculars back to Bonner.

"He's pouring petrol all over the boat."

"Shit."

Candy took Delaney's arm and swung him round. "You've got to let me go and get her."

Delaney shook his head. "That's not going to happen, Candy."

"You can't leave her in there."

"I don't intend to."

Bonner stepped in front of her. "What are we going to do, Jack?"

Delaney looked back at the boat, Morgan was still swinging the petrol can. "I guess someone has to go and talk to him."

Sally shook her head. "We should wait here, boss. Wait for SO19 and the hostage negotiating team."

"Haven't got time for that. I'm going over." Delaney kept his eyes fixed on Morgan as he moved about the boat.

"He killed his father, probably killed his mother and God knows who else. You should wait for armed response."

Delaney looked back at Sally. "And what about the girl if he torches the boat?"

190

"He's not going to do that, is he? Not with him on board too."

"From what we've heard, we know he's capable of pretty much anything."

Candy stood in front of Delaney. "If you don't go and get her, then I will."

Delaney moved her firmly out of the way. "You stay here. I'm going." He looked back at Sally. "When SO19 arrive, you tell them to take no shot unless I signal it." He looked back at the sergeant. "We clear on that, Eddie?"

Bonner nodded his head.

Sally stepped forward. "I'm coming with you."

"Absolutely no way."

"Think about it. Someone needs to be there for the girl."

"That's why I'm going."

"If you have to deal with Morgan, then someone has to get her safe. You can see that, can't you?"

Delaney considered for a moment. She was right. If Morgan lost it, then someone had to get the girl off.

Candy stepped up. "Then it should be me."

Delaney dismissed the idea. "Absolutely not. He's unbalanced as it is; seeing you might tip him over the edge." Delaney gestured at Sally. "Come on then. You concentrate on the girl and follow my lead on everything, okay?"

"Sir."

"I mean it, Constable. This is no time for heroics."

They walked slowly over to the path and moved towards the boat.

Inside the barge, Morgan shook the last drops of the gasoline from the container and looked through the window at Delaney and Sally approaching. "Stay away!"

"It's Inspector Delaney and Detective Constable Cartwright. We're coming in."

As they came down the steps into the cabin, Morgan took a lighter from his pocket and held it up in his left hand.

"I'll use it."

Jenny, huddled in the corner of bench and table, screamed as Delaney stepped quickly on to the small deck on the front of the boat and held his hands up.

"We're not armed, Howard. How about you put down the lighter?"

"You've seen what I've done with the petrol. You try and follow us, I'll torch it."

Delaney stepped forward, down a couple of steps into the cabin. He cast his eyes quickly around the room. A narrow living space with a galley kitchen and a wood-burning stove, the wraparound bench and table that Jenny was sitting at. A small TV on a built-in sideboard. A DVD player with some films. Delaney recognised one of the titles from somewhere but put the thought aside. He slid his eyes back to Morgan as Sally came slowly down the steps behind him. "This isn't what you want, Howard."

"You don't know what I want."

"We found her for you; you can trust us. You don't want Jenny to get hurt, do you?"

"That's why you have to let us go."

"And how's that going to work?"

"We've done nothing wrong."

"She's your daughter, Howard. Of course you've done nothing wrong."

Morgan nodded. "It was Candy. She took her. I'm keeping her away from her, so she can't hurt her. I'm her dad. She should be with me."

Sally smiled reassuringly at Jenny, who was still huddled terrified in the corner.

"You're scaring Jenny. Why don't you let her come to me? I'll take her somewhere safe."

Morgan shook his head and looked back at his daughter. "Jenny, stay where you are."

Sally took a step forward and held her hand out to Jenny. "Come on, Howard, let me take her out of here. The petrol is making her eyes sting."

As she took another step forward, Howard shouted at her, holding up the lighter and flicking the flint wheel a little with his left hand. "Stay where you are."

Delaney gripped Sally's arm with steel fingers, holding her in place.

"It's okay, Howard. Nobody's going anywhere. We just want to talk."

"Everyone wants to talk, but what good does it ever do?"

Delaney paused, not sure he had an answer. "Just put the lighter down. And let Jenny come to us."

Morgan was emphatic. "She stays with me."

"Nobody's saying we will be taking her away from you, Howard. We just need to sort everything out."

"You're lying."

Sally moved a step forward and Morgan raised the lighter again. She stopped. "You're her father. Of course she'll stay with you."

"Candy took her away. You're going to let her keep her, aren't you?"

"She shouldn't have taken her. That was wrong."

"Are you going to send her back to prison?"

"We all need to sit down and talk about things. We need to sort everything out."

"She told you, didn't she? Candy told you everything."

Delaney kept his eyes flat, neutral, but Sally couldn't meet his gaze and Morgan nodded, vindicated.

"That's why you're here."

"Just come off the boat, Howard."

"Dad, please . . ."

Morgan looked over at his terrified daughter. "Don't worry, sweetheart. This is all going to be for the best."

He held the lighter out again and flicked it a couple of times, the sparks darting out and licking the air.

Chief Inspector Campbell slammed her car door shut behind her and walked angrily over to where Bonner stood with his binoculars held to his eyes. Beside him a couple of SO19 officers were prostrate on the ground with their rifles trained on Morgan as he moved in and out of shot in the window.

"What the hell's he doing in there, Bonner?"

Bonner lowered the field glasses and smiled apologetically at his boss. "He went in to get the girl out."

194

"He didn't wait for armed back-up? He didn't wait for the trained hostage professionals?"

"He evaluated the situation and assessed that there wasn't time to wait, ma'am."

Campbell glared at him, her voice dripping with sarcasm. "He evaluated the situation, did he?"

"That's right, ma'am. That was his assessment."

Campbell took the binoculars from Bonner and trained them on the boat. "He should never have let the girl go in the first place."

"That was my assessment too, ma'am."

Campbell glared at him. "Shut it, Bonner."

"Morgan has poured petrol all over the boat. Threatening to torch it. That's why he went in. To protect the girl."

Campbell nodded at the SO19 snipers. "What's their position?"

"They're waiting for the word."

Campbell turned to a sniper. "You take a shot, is it going to set the petrol off?"

"Shouldn't do, ma'am."

"Delaney said he'd signal if it was looking like Morgan was going to do anything and it was safe to take him down."

Campbell looked at the prone officer who was watching her. "You don't do anything without my say-so. Those are my officers out there."

The rifleman nodded his head. "Ma'am."

Morgan flicked the lighter once again, the sparks more visible as the sun set lower.

Delaney held his voice calm. "Let's get off the boat and talk, Howard. You want something, we know that. And we want something too. And you know what? It's the same thing. We both want Jenny safe. We're singing from the same hymn sheet here. Can you see that?"

Morgan snaked his tongue between his lips and licked the corner of his mouth. He tried to swallow some saliva but he had to strain his throat muscles. His eyes stung with the salt of the sweat dripping into his eyes and the petrol vapour that was hanging like a fine mist of poison in the overheated air of the barge.

"Jenny stays with me."

Back on the bank, Bonner smiled as he watched Delaney hold his hand up in a wait gesture. "That's his signal, ma'am."

Campbell hesitated for a moment as Morgan moved backwards, giving the marksmen a clear shot at him. She swallowed and nodded to the waiting snipers.

"Take him down."

The marksmen trained their rifles, relaxed their breathing and caressed the steel curve of their triggers just as Delaney moved in front of Morgan again, blocking their view.

"Take the shot!" Bonner shouted.

"Shit!" Campbell glared at him. "What in the name of sweet fuck do you think you're playing at? Are you trying to get Delaney killed?"

Bonner shrugged unapologetically. "They had a chance, they could have taken Morgan out."

Campbell was about to say more, but the sight of a Sky News mobile camera van parking further up the road stopped her dead in her tracks.

"What moron fuck tipped those clowns off?"

But as the tall figure of Superintendent Walker walked hurriedly towards her, with Melanie Jones hard on his heels, she had her question answered.

"Do you think it's wise to have cameras here, sir?"

"They've been behind us on this from the beginning, Chief Inspector. Their help has been invaluable."

Campbell threw the reporter a pointed look. "What help? Delaney tracked the girl down both times."

Walker glared across at the barge. "What is he doing on there?"

"Morgan's poured petrol all over it. Delaney's playing the hero."

"That man is a liability." Walker looked at the armed officers. "Have they had a clear shot?"

Bonner nodded. "Almost."

Walker's scowl faded as the cameraman arrived and Melanie Jones moved forward to interview him.

"Come on, Howard. Put the lighter down."

Morgan had tears in his eyes. "I'm done talking. Get off of my boat."

"No one's going to hurt you."

Morgan pointed out of the window to where he could see Candy waiting by the uniformed police. "She hates me. She's going to make Jenny hate me."

"Is that why you were taking Jenny away?" Delaney fought to keep his voice level.

Morgan's shoulders slumped slightly. "I don't want Jenny hating me like she did."

Delaney stepped forward. "Let her go then. Let Sally take her off the boat. We can sort this out."

Sally moved to the side of Delaney and held her hand out again to Jenny, who took it but didn't move from the table, which she kept in front of her like a barrier.

Morgan looked at his daughter. "I always loved you, Jenny."

Sally crouched down and smiled reassuringly at the girl. "Come on. We're going to be just outside." Howard said nothing, but the arm holding the lighter relaxed as Sally led Jenny off the boat.

Delaney stepped forward to take the lighter, but Howard stiffened, holding it up again. Delaney breathed in, the petrol in the air tasting of bad memories. Tasting of an opportunity to put all those bad thoughts that tumbled constantly in his brain behind him once and for good.

Morgan's eyes darted back and forth again as he stepped back. "It's time for you to get off my boat."

"Come on, you don't have to do this."

"It's over, isn't it?"

"Is this how you want her to remember you? Setting yourself on fire? Don't you think she's been through enough?"

Morgan's hand trembled as he held the lighter up. "I'll do it."

Delaney stepped right into Howard's face. "Then fucking do it! Put us all out of our misery."

Morgan took a step back, surprised. Delaney snatched the lighter out of his hand and started flicking the wheel in his face.

"Is that what you want, is it?"

Morgan backed up against the table. "What are you doing?"

"Pest control. It's what I'm good at. Do the world a favour if I torched us both."

He flicked the wheel again and laughed as Morgan almost whimpered, "Don't do it."

Delaney gripped the lighter in his fist, squeezing it. Then stepped back and jerked his head toward the exit.

"Go on, get out of my sight."

Morgan stumbled to the door as Delaney looked at the lighter in his hand and threw it hard across the cabin.

A flurry of uniforms and noise. Blue and black uniforms, padded jackets. A lot of shouting way past a time when the urgency implied would have been any use. Superintendent Walker making sure he was prominent in the shot as Morgan was bundled off the boat and led away.

Inside the barge, for a moment or two Delaney looked down at the open petrol canister on the floor, his eyes slate dull. He glanced across at the bench that Jenny had been sitting on. A ragged teddy bear was tipped upside down on the corner of it.

"Boss?"

Delaney looked up at the window. "On my way, Sally." He walked over to pick up the teddy bear and followed her to the exit. Stopping at the fore cabin to pick up the DVD he'd seen earlier. *Sin Sisters*. He turned it over so he could see the cover. The two women on the front were dressed in miniskirted, latex nun's outfits, one with a riding crop in her hand and a shock of curly black hair and laughing eyes. Jackie Malone. And the woman with her, heavily made-up, with a wig to match Jackie's hair. Melody Masters, according to the credits.

He slipped the DVD into his pocket and stepped off the barge, walking out into the golden light of the setting sun and the furious gaze of Diane Campbell as she bore down towards him. Ignoring her, he watched Morgan as he was led by uniformed officers to a waiting police van.

"What the hell do you think you were doing in there, Delaney?"

"Excuse me a minute, ma'am." Campbell was left speechless as Delaney walked to where Jenny was standing with Candy and a couple of uniformed officers.

"Here you go, Jenny, I think he's yours."

Delaney handed the teddy bear back to Jenny, who took it and hugged it as if she was a much younger girl. Today, he figured, she did feel a lot younger. In the days to come, the years ahead, she would come to realise that what had happened could have made her so much older.

Delaney put his hand on Sally's shoulder. "You did well."

"Thanks, boss. It's a good result. Celebratory drink?"

Delaney looked over at Campbell as she shouted into her mobile phone, and hesitated. If he could face down a psychopathic mechanic with severe emotional difficulties and a homicidal history, he supposed he could face his boss. But as Campbell closed her mobile, Superintendent Walker approached her with his pet Sky News reporter close behind. Delaney turned to Sally.

"Come on then, before people start asking questions." And he led her behind a bank of uniforms and away.

CHAPTER
TWENTY-TWO

Kate Walker lay on her bed, the covers thrown back, fine beads of perspiration dotting her forehead. She moaned softly in her sleep and twisted her body for the hundredth time in half an hour. In her dream she was walking up a familiar staircase, broad oak steps with a large hall below her on the right. The staircase turned to the right and led up to a wide corridor. A procession of portraits marched uniformly along the wall, and at the end of the corridor a wide, panelled white door stood slightly ajar. Kate walked slowly towards it, her bare feet soundless on the thick pile of the rich green carpet. She put her hand on the door, opened it further, and walked into the room. A pool of blood reached out, almost kissing her bare toes. And at the top of the elliptical pool was the fanned hair of Jackie Malone, her eyes still wide and uncomprehending, her pale skin still horribly violated.

Kate awoke with a start. She remembered where she had seen a murder scene like it before, and realised why Jackie Malone's body had swapped places with the corpse in her dream. Her dreams were telling her something, and she felt a chill run through her veins as she realised what it was.

* * *

Delaney groaned as he swung his feet off the sofa. He figured one of these days maybe he'd wake up without a hangover. A quick couple of drinks with Sally Cartwright had turned into a few more, and when Sally left for a relatively early night, Delaney carried steadily on. He finished up at about four o'clock in the morning and was poured into the back of a taxi by a large Irishman called Liam, who bounced at a pub in Queen's Park called the Greyhound, famous for its regular late opening hours and just as regular fights.

Tipping some cereal into a bowl, Delaney opened the door of his fridge and winced as he stepped back. He didn't have to take the bottle out to realise the milk had gone sour. He snapped up his jacket from the sofa and the DVD he had taken from Morgan's boat fell out and clattered to the floor. He picked it up, glanced at the cover briefly then put it in a sideboard drawer. He closed the drawer and took a step away, but then turned back and opened it again. He took out a small packet of white powder, licked his finger and dipped it in, then ran the powdered finger round his gums. It would numb the feeling there but it would spark his brain up a little at least, and Delaney figured he'd need his senses about him today. He dipped his finger again, just enough to keep him sharp, and put the cocaine back in the drawer.

He switched his mobile phone on, and some few seconds later, as he was locking his front door, it rang. He answered it and immediately held it away from his ear, wincing as Campbell's voice barked out at him.

203

An hour and a half later, Delaney was drumming his fingers impatiently, looking at the bland face of Detective Inspector Richard Hadden and not particularly caring for what he saw. He'd been sitting in Hadden's stark and windowless office being interviewed by the man about Jenny and Howard Morgan for over half an hour now, and was sick of the sight of him. Hadden was five nine, with fair, thinning hair, trendy glasses and the kind of smug expression that made Delaney want to pick up his coffee mug and smash it straight into his face. Only trouble was, assaults against fellow officers were just the sort of thing Hadden investigated.

Instead Delaney fought down his urge for violence and summoned a weary smile. "Like I said, Richard, I acted as I did to save the life of a young girl."

"It could well be that you put that girl's life in danger. For goodness' sake, Inspector Delaney. I know you call yourself Cowboy, but this isn't the wild west. You can't go taking the law into your own hands."

"I don't call myself anything of the sort. I did what I did because I had to make a decision. And I made the right decision."

"The review will see about that. We have protocols for a reason, Detective Inspector."

Hadden wrote calmly in his notebook, ignoring Delaney for a moment or two, and then looked up at him with a cold smile.

"It's little more than a week since we had to interview you about other irregularities with police procedure, isn't it?"

"That was bullshit too, and you know it."

Hadden smiled again, and again Delaney wanted to give him a serious dental bill. Hadden looked down at his notes and shrugged. "A kilogram. That's a lot of nose candy still missing from evidence."

Delaney laughed out loud, despite himself. "Nose candy? What's up, Richard, they send you off to jargon school? You actually thinking of doing some proper police work? Getting the lingo right so you can rap with the gangstas?"

"Your attitude isn't helping your cause."

"What are you going to do? Charge me with saving the girl's life?"

Hadden closed his notebook and stared at Delaney for a long, condescending moment. "We'll let you know what we are going to charge you with when we decide."

"Whatever tickles your pickle, Richard."

Delaney stood up and walked out of Hadden's office as fast as he could, before he could say or do anything he might regret.

As Delaney walked back into his own office, he was surprised to see Kate Walker sitting at his desk, and a little annoyed.

"Can I help you with anything?"

Kate picked up on the shortness of his tone and stood up. "You could start by losing a bit of the attitude. I've come with some information I thought you might find useful."

Delaney nodded a little guiltily. "Sorry. Bit of a bad morning."

"I heard you were in with DI Hadden."

"That's right."

"I always thought the man was an insufferable prig myself."

Delaney smiled. "Close enough. What have you got for me?"

Kate pointed at the murder scene photographs that she had left on Jack's desk. "Jackie Malone. The way her body was mutilated. The positioning of her body."

"What about it?"

"I've seen it before, Jack."

"Where?"

Kate handed him a DVD. *The House of Knives*. "It's a classic sixties French film. A black-and-white art-house slash and gore. There is a woman mutilated and murdered in it in exactly the same way as Jackie Malone."

"You think it's a copycat killing?"

Kate looked at him. "No. As you know, Jackie Malone's injuries were post-mortem."

"So . . .?"

"So I think what you have here, Jack, is a seriously sick film buff."

Diane Campbell was at her window lighting up a cigarette when Delaney knocked and entered her office. She glared at him. "What the fuck happened out there yesterday, Jack?"

"Yeah, good morning to you too, boss."

"Save it, Delaney. I'm not in the mood."

"We got the girl back, didn't we?"

"You should have waited."

"If I'd waited he could have got away."

"You don't know that."

"You're right, I don't know that. In fact, he probably wouldn't, in which case he was quite prepared to kill his own daughter, set light to the boat and blow them both halfway across Essex."

"We have people trained in hostage negotiation for a reason, Jack."

"Yeah, because we're too damn scared just to take them down first chance we get. And don't tell me that what happened at Stockwell station has got nothing to do with that."

Campbell glared out of the window. Finding no answers in the car park below, she looked back at Delaney and sighed. "And what's happening with Jackie Malone?"

Delaney shrugged and gestured noncommittally. "We think we're looking for at least two of them. Nothing concrete as yet."

Campbell took a long last pull to finish her cigarette and flicked it out of the window. "Your connection with her? Anything you want to get off your chest?"

Delaney helped himself to a cigarette from Campbell's packet on her desk and joined her by the window. "Like what?"

"Come off it, Cowboy. She calls here looking for you. Repeatedly. Next thing she's lying in our deep freeze with more holes in her than a Swiss cheese on fondue night."

"I didn't see her."

"Why was she trying to get hold of you?"

Delaney blew a stream of smoke out of the window. "Seems like she was worried about something."

Campbell snorted drily. "Seems like she had good cause."

"That's what Dr Walker said."

"Kate Walker meets a lot of people who clearly had good cause to be worried."

"I know."

"So why did Jackie phone you? If it was a police matter, why not speak to Eddie, or anyone else on the shift?"

Delaney shrugged.

"There's nothing in your relationship with this woman I should know about?"

"If there was, I would be telling you."

She looked at him for a moment or two and then shrugged. "I've got a meeting. Why don't you walk me to my car?"

Delaney nodded and fell into step beside her as they walked out of her office and then headed downstairs toward the front office and the car park.

"What exactly was your relationship with her then?"

Delaney scowled. Not at the question, but at the memories it brought. "For Christ's sake, Diane, I've told you, there was no relationship."

"It's no big deal if you visited her. As long as we know. It can't have been easy for you."

"Excuse me, ma'am but that's . . . if you'll pardon the expression, a load of horse shit you're shovelling there."

"It's not me holding the spade. And it's not me that's got a strong smell of the country about him right now."

Delaney stopped and looked at her. Like Campbell, he had been a cop far too long not to pick up on the importance of things unspoken.

"What all this about, ma'am?"

"You've got your promotion board next week, Cowboy. And after the last debacle I just want to make sure no skeletons are going to come dancing out of the closet, rattling their chains." She smiled at him, the corners of her eyes softening. "Or should I say their whips and chains?"

"It's not funny, ma'am."

Campbell halted, pulled up by the plain criticism in his tone. "No, you're bloody right, it isn't."

Delaney shrugged apologetically. "I don't know why she called. I'm assuming she was scared, needed my help. I don't know why it was only me that she thought could help her."

"Never assume, Detective. It makes an ass out of you."

"I intend to find out the truth. You can depend on that, and you can depend on me."

She nodded again. "I had to ask. Someone took that cocaine out of evidence and the finger was pointed at you."

Delaney swung the door shut behind them as they headed into the car park and across to the chief inspector's car. "Hadden only takes his finger out of his arse to point it at me, but my record's clean."

"Like I said. I'm not the one holding a spade. Just don't make the mistake of thinking that you don't have enemies in the force, Jack."

"That was all a load of shite and you know it. Do I look to you like I use the stuff?"

Campbell looked at him closely. "We all deal with our demons."

"Yeah, well, it's strictly Bell's, book and candle with me."

"Whoever lifted a kilogram of grade A cocaine from our stores probably didn't do it to powder his own nose."

"Or hers."

"Or hers," the chief inspector agreed, and got into her car. Delaney watched as she gunned the engine and pulled swiftly away from the car park, darting into the traffic like a salmon heading back to its spawning ground.

Delaney walked back into the building. He nodded absent-mindedly to PC Dave Patterson, walking past him to the custody booking area and beyond that to the evidence holding store. He quickly tapped the entry code into the security pad and walked into a brightly lit, windowless room. A large counter stood in front of him, behind which were the shelves and wire-caged storage areas for evidence seized during arrests.

The officer on duty was a thirty-two-year-old brunette called Susan Halliday, who had Marilyn Monroe's body and an even brighter smile. Many was the time Delaney would have flirted with her but knew there was no point. Susan had been living with his boss for over four years now, the most open secret at the station. Delaney honestly didn't know why Diane Campbell was always so grumpy in the mornings.

Susan Halliday flashed her brilliant orthodonture at him. "Sorry, Jack, your usually drugs delivery hasn't arrived this week."

"That's not funny, Susan." Delaney's smile belied his answer.

"So what can we do you for, sir?"

"I just want to look at the evidence log for the Jackie Malone crime scene."

"Sure."

She went to the records area, pulled out the relevant file and extracted a couple of sheets of paper, which she handed to Delaney.

Delaney ran his eyes down the list of items taken from Jackie's flat. He read the list twice to make sure, but he was quite right. Among the list of DVDs was *Head Girl, Crime and Punishment, Spunk Junkies*. But *Sin Sisters*, which he remembered seeing on the night of Jackie Malone's murder, was very much conspicuous by its absence.

"Everything all right, sir?"

Delaney smiled. "Absolutely perfect."

But the expression on his face as he walked back into his office told a different story. Bonner hung up the phone as Delaney entered the room.

"What's up with you then, boss? You look like you've got a pain somewhere only a doctor should be looking at."

Delaney shook his thoughts away with a covering smile. "Any word on Billy Martin?"

"Absolute zip. But we're scouring every dive, brothel and bar from Wembley Park to Bethnal Green. He'll turn up sooner or later."

"He usually does."

"What are they charging Morgan with?"

Delaney shrugged. "Whatever it is, he isn't going to be out for a good long while."

"And his sister?"

Delaney shook his head. "Shouldn't think they'll charge her with anything." He picked his jacket up from the back of his chair. "Come on. You're with me. You can drive."

"What's on?"

"I've got a meet with one of London's genuine scumbags."

"A grass?"

"My bank manager."

Delaney used to joke that he liked both kinds of music, country and western. It was an old joke, but that didn't bother him. It was how he'd got his nickname, Cowboy, and the music playing in his car as he pulled to the side of the street would have made Johnny Cash smile in his grave. The latest in a long line of southern belles with a voice of pure sunshine. Some man was going to do her right by doing her wrong and that was just the way she liked it. Oh yeah, baby, that's the way she likes it. So much for women's liberation, thought Delaney, eat your heart out, Tammy Wynette. He flicked the music off and opened his car door, turning to Bonner. "I won't be long. If I'm not out in ten minutes, come in and shoot the bastard."

"You know, boss, sometimes I don't think you show the proper respect for the capitalist system we are sworn to protect and serve."

"Make that five minutes."

Chief Superintendent Walker sat back in the padded leather chair in his plush office, which was neat and spotless. The paintings on the wall were not prints and the brandy in the decanter sitting on his walnut cabinet was not from a supermarket at just over ten pounds a litre. He smiled as DC Sally Cartwright responded to his summons and entered the room. He looked at her appraisingly. She could be sitting behind the reception desk of a top London advertising agency, or modelling bikinis, or singing banal pop songs; instead she had come to work for the police force. His police force. Maybe she expected her healthy good looks to curry favour, and maybe they did. In the cut and thrust of police work on the factory floor, as it were, they might serve her very well. But Chief Superintendent Walker couldn't care less what she looked like. She was a police officer and that was that. One of his pieces to move about the board. He glared angrily at the file she held in her hand.

"Do you have a boyfriend, Detective Constable Cartwright?"

"Sir?" Her smile fading.

"Somebody on the force? Somebody to chat to on refs. Someone to sneak off with. Have a crafty fag, a quick kiss, a fumble in the corridor."

She shook her head, puzzled. "No, sir."

"What the bloody hell kept you with this then?"

He snatched the file from her hands. She blinked nervously. "Records, sir."

Walker waved a dismissive hand. "Go." Sally walked slowly back to the door. "And where the blue bloody hell is Delaney?"

She shrugged apologetically at him and closed the door behind her.

Walker drummed his manicured fingers on the polished mahogany of his desk, his eyes hardening as he read the report that the detective constable had just delivered.

Jasper Harrington was in his early thirties. As polished as the pine desk he sat behind. Which was to say, if you were to take a penknife and scratch beneath the surface, you wouldn't find a great deal of character in either. In truth Harrington looked a lot like Richard Hadden, and if Delaney hadn't disliked him before he met him, he certainly did now.

"Thirty thousand pounds really is quite a large sum of money to carry around on your person."

"I'll be all right. I have a police escort."

Harrington flicked a small condescending smile. "If you could tell me what you need the cash for? I'm sure the bank could arrange proceedings in a far safer manner for you and your capital."

214

Harrington had a large stack of bundled twenty-pound notes on the desk in front of him. Delaney gestured at the cash. "Is this the bank's money?"

"Technically not. But we still have a duty of responsibility."

Delaney held his hand out. "A duty which you have fulfilled. By getting the money out and returning it to me."

The manager still hesitated. "Things can be done far more safely electronically now."

"It's not a loan, is it?"

"No, sir."

Delaney stood up and opened a small overnight bag he had brought with him. The look in his eye made Jasper Harrington sit back a little too sharply for his normal studied poise.

"If it had been a loan you'd have every right to keep me here, filling in forms, asking endless questions," Delaney said as he started filling the bag with the stacks of notes.

"Naturally we need to take certain steps . . ."

"But this isn't your money. It's my money. And what I do with it is my business. Not your business, not the bank's business. My business. We clear on that now?"

Harrington nodded, swallowing nervously. His throat had suddenly gone very dry. As a bank manager he wasn't used to dealing with dangerous, violent men, but he could see that that was what he was dealing with right now.

Delaney walked out, pulling the door shut quietly behind him.

Harrington took a moment or two to recover his composure, and then picked up the phone, punching in some numbers quickly.

Delaney walked up to his car, where Bonner was snapping his fingers to the rhythmic rapping of a white English teenager singing about slapping his bitches around. Delaney leaned in through the window and turned it off.

"What have I told you about my radio?"

"Jeez, Cowboy, if I had to listen to one more song about a lonely trucker missing his sweetheart Mary-Jane-Jo-Bobbi I'd have ended up cutting my wrists."

"Touch it again and you won't need to bother."

"Had a couple of calls whilst you were sorting out your pension in there."

"Good for you."

"You want the good news or the bad news?"

"No such thing as good news, Bonner."

"We've found Billy Martin."

Delaney slid in to the passenger seat and threw the sergeant a knowing look. "You see."

"Out near Henley."

"Only he isn't going to tell us a thing? Right?"

"Right."

"Somebody beat us to him and made sure of it."

"What's that, Irish intuition?"

"Call it a stab in the dark." He reached over and pushed the preset button on his radio, and Kenny

Rogers' smooth voice flowed out like a twenty-year-old single malt.

"Are we going to Henley, then?"

"We're going to Wigmore Street first."

"What's there?"

"Nothing you need to know about." Delaney held the bag close to his chest as Bonner pulled out into the traffic.

CHAPTER
TWENTY-THREE

The same river that had earlier swallowed him into her cold depths in the dead of night had disgorged Billy, tiring perhaps of his company, as did all who had spent more than a little time with him in life. But in the full brightness of day, that river was a different thing. The air was busy with the sounds of tourists, of wildlife, of oarsmen stroking in their skiffs and sculls, of powered craft chugging softly through the water, of gentle lovers strolling and laughing far in the distance on the footpath. The banks seemed closer together by day, and the masonry of the bridge ahead was a soft grey, not a forbidding black. The sunlight sparkled on the surface of the water like the flash of revelation. The depths below were soothing, inviting. On a day such as this, when the relentless sun burned like an all-cleansing fire, the human spirit looked back to its past and would slip into the water to be reborn. Born again in the cool, ancient water as a beautiful creature of supple movement and flight.

But the thing that lay on the bank would never go swimming again, would never dart and shimmer in the cool water, and, truth to tell, had never been considered beautiful.

Delaney pushed roughly through a crowd of morbid onlookers and ducked under the yellow police tape, wincing as his neck muscles objected. He walked over to the group of officers processing the scene, followed by an amused Bonner.

"You're getting old, Cowboy."

"Every day." He was surprised to see Kate Walker in attendance. Henley was out in the sticks, and although her accent blended into the background as smoothly as a cucumber slice in a crust-trimmed sandwich, she was a town girl work-wise. Strictly city limits.

"Bit out of your jurisdiction isn't it, Dr Walker?"

"I was asked." Kate turned her attention back to the thing that had washed up on the shallow bank. The time in the water had not been kind to Billy Martin. His corpse was bloated with gas and his skin was loose and grey; a rough stroke would slough that skin straight off the body.

"Lucky for us he was carrying ID. His mother wouldn't recognise him."

Delaney watched, feeling neither pity nor loss, as Kate carefully tilted the head to one side. Billy Martin was the kind of person Delaney joined the police force to hurt. Not physically hurt, but in every other way he could. To stop him and to stop his kind. He was a pimp, a rapist, a trader in other people's misery, and Delaney wouldn't have thrown him a rope of piss to save him from drowning. What he did feel as he looked down on Billy Martin's aborted body was disappointment. His death was linked to his sister Jackie Malone's death, Delaney was sure of it, and now whatever secrets

Billy Martin had to tell were beyond his powers of persuasion to extract. Delaney dealt with the living; it was up to Kate Walker now to probe Martin's inner recesses and find, if any, what secrets the bloated corpse might conceal.

"What have you got?"

Kate looked back up at Delaney, squinting still in the bright sunlight. "He was tied up with coat-hanger wire. Hands and feet. Then dumped in the water."

"Alive?"

Kate nodded grimly. "For a while."

"They say drowning is one of the better ways to die."

"Not like this. He must have been terrified out of his wits."

"Billy Martin didn't have a lot of those."

"You knew him?"

"He's Jackie Malone's brother. Her maiden name was Martin."

"What happened to her husband?"

"He died of a heroin overdose eight months after they got married and six months after she fell pregnant."

"Not a lucky family."

"Never were. Can you make a guess at what time it happened?"

"Judging by the state of his skin and the time he was found, I would say he's been in the water a few days. Roughly about the time of the Malone murder. Can't be more specific, I'm afraid."

"Anything else you can tell me now?"

Kate nodded towards one of the forensic officers. "He had a quarter of an ounce of cocaine on him. Kept sweet in a waterproof plastic container."

"Convenient."

"Yeah."

Delaney took in the dark lustre of her hair, the brilliant flash of emerald from her eyes, the way she almost always had a hint of a smile dancing on her lips, then he caught himself and looked down again at Billy Martin's grossly disfigured face.

"Thanks, Kate." A dismissal. He walked over to speak to the Scene of Crime Officers, feeling her gaze on his back but not turning round.

Half a mile or so upriver from where the body of Billy Martin was found was an old ivy-covered brick pub called the Saracen's Head. Bonner, at the bar, scowled as Delaney fed the jukebox some more coins and punched buttons. It was an old-fashioned country pub. The kind that had a large fireplace and bowls of water and nibbles for dogs. A pub with history, with original oak beams and warm brick walls, and photos of the Victorian forebears of local people who still used the place. A half-a-yard-of-ale glass hung on the wall, and the stone flags on the floor in front of the bar were worn smooth and slightly concave by the countless pairs of feet that had walked across them over the passing centuries.

It had tradition and heritage, everything Bonner hated in a pub, Delaney surmised, judging by the look on his face as he joined him at the bar. Bonner took his change from a twenty-something barman who had the same enthusiasm for his work as a duck has for orange sauce, then handed Delaney his pint, his frown deepening as the sound of a Dixie Chick, regretting losing her virginity to someone named Earl, started playing in the background.

Delaney took a swallow of his ale. "Jesus, Eddie, what is this shit?"

"They call it Old Peculier for a reason, boss. It's supposed to taste like that. I thought you'd like it." He smiled, taking a pull on his own cold pint of lager.

Delaney put his glass back on the counter, wiping his lips as Kate Walker came in through the front door and walked over to them. She smiled tentatively at Delaney. "Hot out there."

"It is."

"Thought I'd join you for a drink, if it's not a problem?"

Bonner moved a bar stool across for her. "Of course it isn't."

Kate flashed a quick smile at the young barman, who had suddenly become more interested in his job. "Vodka and tonic, please."

The barman nodded enthusiastically and took down a glass. Kate looked across at Delaney and arched an eyebrow. "Anything for you, Inspector?"

Delaney gestured at his glass of ale. "I'll trade this for a whisky, please."

Kate looked over at Bonner. "Sergeant?"

"I'm fine with this, thanks."

The barman lifted a hefty whisky glass to the optic, but Kate stopped him before he could pour. "The good stuff, and make it a double."

He nodded and poured out a large shot of Glenmorangie and put the glass on the bar.

Kate gestured. "Scottish whisky all right with you?"

Delaney picked up the glass. "We live in troubled times, Dr Walker. So needs must when the Devil drives."

"It's Kate. Please."

Delaney swirled the whisky around the glass, the sun lighting it to a sparkling tawny gold. He held it up to Kate. "*Slainte.*"

"What does that mean exactly?"

Delaney considered for a moment. "That I'm probably living in the wrong country."

Kate clinked her glass against his and drained her vodka and tonic in one. "I have to go."

Delaney looked surprised. "You just got here."

"Just for a quick one, it's so damn hot out there. And besides, I'm driving. Got a date with Billy Martin waiting for me back in the office."

"Be careful. He's got a reputation," said Bonner.

Kate looked pointedly at Delaney. "Haven't they all?"

Delaney almost smiled. "Drive carefully." He watched her as she walked to the door. There was definitely an animal litheness in her movement, a sensuality that wasn't lost on him or on the young barman, who was watching her leave with open admiration. Delaney glared at him and he turned back quickly to polishing beer glasses. Delaney took another sip of his whisky and had to concede to himself that he liked it. A day for surprises all round.

Bonner leaned forward, interrupting his thoughts. "So, Billy Martin, what do you reckon, boss?"

Delaney shrugged. "He's not going to win any more beauty contests."

"He was a piece of work. No doubt about that. Seems he upset the wrong people this time."

"I want you to go back to Jackie Malone's flat. Canvass her neighbours again. See if he had been there on the day she was killed."

"You reckon she was murdered because of him?"

"Some people just get in the way, don't they? They're in the wrong place at the wrong time."

Delaney watched through the pub window as Kate climbed into her open-topped BMW. The music changed, the Cowboy Junkies singing "Blue Moon", and he was back in another place, another time.

Sinead turned the dial on the radio, twiddling it with mock annoyance.

"How many times have I told you not to fiddle with the radio?"

Delaney's wife laughed; it was a musical laugh, full of sunlight and joy. "Just because you like that rubbish doesn't mean the rest of the world should suffer."

"I should wash your mouth out with carbolic soap, young lady."

Delaney spun the wheel, turning in to the forecourt of the petrol station. The adverts finished and the

Cowboy Junkies started to play. "Blue Moon". One of Delaney's favourites. "Now you can't tell me that isn't proper music."

His wife laughed again. "I can't tell you anything, Jack. I've learned that much by now."

Delaney got out of the car, popped open the petrol tank and was reaching for the fuel nozzle when the plate-glass window of the shop exploded. Delaney instinctively raised his arm to protect his eyes from the storm of flying glass. His wife's scream carried over the sound of the shotgun blast and two men came out of the shop. Thick-set men dressed in black with balaclavas covering their heads, shotguns held at waist level, sweeping the forecourt in front of them.

They shouted at Delaney, their shotguns trained on him, but he couldn't hear them, and he watched frozen for a moment until his wife screamed at him and her words finally registered.

"For Christ's sake, Jack, get in the car."

And he did so, watching as a transit van drove across the forecourt with its back doors open. One of the men jumped in and the other ran to catch up. Delaney turned the key in the ignition and gunned the engine, not listening as his wife shouted at him, putting the car in gear and screeching after them, swerving to avoid an incoming car.

The second man jumped into the van, half falling back with the motion and landing with a bone-jarring crash on his knees, but a hand to the inside wall of the van steadied him and he brought his shotgun round to bear on the pursuing car. Sinead screamed again, and the sound ripped into Delaney's consciousness like a dousing of ice-cold water as he realised what he was doing. But it was too late. The shotgun blasted, and Delaney's windscreen exploded, the car spinning out of control as the screaming blended with the screeching of brakes and the crumpling of metal . . . and a curtain of blood and black descended over Delaney's eyes, over his life.

Delaney jolted awake from sleep, back in his flat, and it was night-time. Four years had passed, and there was not one single night since when he had not woken from the same nightmare. Only this time it was different. This time when he turned at the sound of his wife's musical laugh, it wasn't her eyes that he saw sparkling back at him, but Kate Walker's. Kate Walker's slender alabaster throat, her ebony hair, the blood red of her lips and the green brilliance of her eyes. Her lips parted and her hot, moist breath brushed over him like a velvet kiss.

He ran a hand across his forehead and it was wet with sweat, his sheets rumpled. He wasn't sure what it was he was feeling, but it was only partly guilt.

He reached over to the bottle that stood on his bedside cabinet, poured himself a measure of whiskey and swallowed fast. If it was a fever he had, then the medicine he was taking wouldn't provide a cure, but he took another swallow and hoped that the burn of the alcohol would do its job and keep the dreams from him at least. But it never had yet, and in truth he wasn't sure that he wanted them kept away any more.

CHAPTER
TWENTY-FOUR

Bonner had spent the morning speaking to Jackie Malone's neighbours, even though he knew it was a waste of his time. He had better things to be doing on a Saturday, and true to his prognosis he had nothing new to report. It was the land of the three wise monkeys. Nobody saw anything, nobody heard anything and nobody was saying nothing to nobody. Bonner had left the next-door neighbour on the right-hand side until last. The top flat. The same set-up.

He sat uncomfortably on the wooden kitchen chair, squirming a little, trying to get his buttocks comfortable as the hard ridge in the centre of the chair bit between them. He watched as Melissa poured him a cup of tea. Her real name was Karen Stuple but she felt the name Melissa sounded sexier. Bonner didn't think she looked like a Melissa, or a Karen come to that; to him she was more of an Ingrid or a Tonya. She was from Germanic stock and it showed, with long, powerful legs and a decidedly Teutonic chest. She was the kind of woman the poet Betjeman would have enjoyed watching play tennis or riding about town on her bicycle. Bonner looked at her legs, balanced on four-inch spiked heels and encased in black stockings and suspenders, then upwards from her creamy muscled thighs to her generous upper body, moulded by a lacy basque into something almost cartoonish. Jessica Rabbit meets Betty Boop. The loose green cardigan on top did little to detract from her sexiness, Bonner thought, nor the thick red lipstick or the sunshine-yellow hair. Bonner liked his women to look like women, and with Melissa there was very little doubt. If her hair colour came from a bottle and her chest from a plastic surgeon's shopping list, he didn't mind at all. It just showed she cared more about her appearance than other women, and that was a trait that Bonner thoroughly approved of.

Today, though, he was focusing on business, or trying to. He had his notebook open on his lap and his pen in his hand.

"Come on, love, she's dead. Not a pleasant death."

Melissa shivered. "I heard."

"Or Billy Martin's."

"What's happened to that prick, then?" She put two mugs of tea on the table and sat opposite him. Bonner watched distracted as she placed a cigarette between her ruby-red lips and fired it up, her lip muscles twitching and the cigarette doing a lazy circular dance as she drew deeply. Her chest swelled as she inhaled and Bonner had to flick his eyes away from her cleavage. The heat wave was showing no signs of abating and a small drop of sweat was running slowly down her right breast.

"I said what happened to him, then?"

Bonner blinked and looked up at her face. "He went for a bit of a swim. Didn't wear his lifebelt."

Melissa sucked in more smoke, her cheeks hollowing and her lips pouting. She let the smoke slip forth in a lazy stream, and Bonner almost sighed along with her.

"Good," she said finally, and Bonner nodded in agreement. Billy Martin's passing from the world was universally unmourned, but he still had a job to do, and the sooner he got business out of the way, the sooner he could attend to other matters. He nodded to the smoke-stained wall to his left.

"Jackie Malone. You telling me you didn't hear anything?"

"I already told your uniforms. Nothing at all."

Bonner gave her his policeman's look. "You told them nothing or you told them you heard nothing?"

"You've got my statement. I didn't hear a thing."

"She was murdered right next door, for goodness' sake."

"I wasn't listening. I'm a working girl, remember. I have to concentrate."

"So you didn't notice anything out of the ordinary? You didn't hear anything unusual?"

"She was a specialist, wasn't she, Eddie? It was all unusual there." She threw him a knowing look, half amused, half challenging. "Wasn't it?"

Bonner closed his notebook. He was only going through the motions anyway. The woman didn't know anything, that much was clear.

"What about her son? Where did Andy go, do you know that?"

Melissa looked at her watch and blew out another stream of smoke. "Who knows with that one? Thirteen years old going on thirty. He's probably with his other uncle, travelling. He was never here much, you already know that. You spoke to his uncle?"

"We're looking for him."

Melissa shrugged. "I wish I could help, love, but I didn't hear or see a thing." She ground out her cigarette in a small plate on the table and drained her mug of tea. "That the official business over with, is it?"

"For now."

"Right." She stood up and took off her cardigan. Her voice suddenly uncompromisingly authoritarian. "Get next door then and get on your knees."

She reached behind her to pick up an improbable-looking object with straps and buckles from the kitchen table. Bonner nodded, the dry tip of his tongue nervously licking the corner of his lips.

Sometimes he really loved his job.

Later that afternoon, Delaney ground his cigarette stub with a quick flick of his shoe and watched as a police van pulled to a stop in the car park outside White City police station. The back doors swung open and a couple of uniformed officers climbed down, leading a middle-aged man between them. In his forties, he was dressed in filthy black jeans, with beads, bangles and long greasy hair. Half hippy, half Hell's Angel, more metal in his face than God or nature ever intended. Jackie Malone's elder brother. He scowled as he saw

Delaney lounging against the wall and spat on the ground.

"Might have known."

Delaney walked over to the officers. "I'll have a quick word with him, thanks, guys."

"All yours."

"There was no sign of the boy?"

One of the uniformed men shook his head. "We asked around too. Nobody has seen him for a long time."

"Okay."

The officers walked away, rubbing their hands as if to clean off the taint of Russell Martin.

"What do you want, Delaney?"

Delaney pushed the man against the wall and wasn't gentle about it.

"Suppose you tell me where the boy is, for a start?"

Martin struggled angrily. "And suppose I tell you to go stick your head in a pig?"

Delaney kneed him quickly in the groin; he doubled over in pain but Delaney hauled him up by his throat and leaned in close.

"You fuck with me, Russell, and I'll make your eyeballs bleed. Do you know what I am saying to you?"

Russell Martin looked away and Delaney slapped him as hard as he could, open-palmed against the side of his head.

"Do you know what I am saying to you?"

Martin grunted and rubbed his head. "I've got rights."

"You've got the right to remain silent. But you exercise that right and I'll spoil you for your girlfriend. You fuck with me, you piece of pikey shite, and I'll spoil you for any woman."

"What do you want from me?"

"I want to know where Andy is."

"I don't know where he is. I haven't seen him for weeks."

Delaney slapped him again on the side of the head. "I'm telling you, don't fuck around with me."

Martin was nearly in tears. "I don't know where he is. I swear."

"I don't care what you swear; you lie to me and you'll live to regret it."

"I've been on the road for four months and he wasn't with me the last couple. He came back to his mum, that's all I know."

"You spoken to her lately. Or your brother?"

Martin shook his head, "I heard what happened to them, but it's got nothing to do with me."

"Who has it got to do with, then?"

He shrugged. "I don't know. We weren't exactly close."

Delaney curled his lip, genuinely disgusted. "You're a real piece of shite, you know that."

Martin shook his head angrily. "I know what I am and I know what they were. This has got nothing to do with me."

Delaney leaned in angrily again. "It's got everything to do with your nephew right now."

Martin flinched back and shook his head. "I wouldn't do anything to hurt the boy."

"That's right. You're a regular Mary Poppins, aren't you?"

"I don't know where he is, Delaney. It's the truth."

Delaney looked at him for a long moment. "You wouldn't know the truth if it fucked you in the arse." He gave him a rough shove towards the road. "Stay where I can find you."

Russell staggered and caught his balance. "Yeah, right."

"I mean it. Don't make me come looking for you."

Martin hurried away out of the car park entrance without looking back. Delaney palmed a cigarette into his mouth and lit it, a dark look in his eyes as he drew the soothing smoke in and watched Jackie Malone's brother scurry away. He took a couple more drags and then walked across the car park, heading towards the road.

Pacing about on the deep-pile carpet of his office on the second floor, Chief Superintendent Walker was talking on his mobile phone, and he was far from happy.

"I don't care what your problems are. I told you I'm dealing with it." He walked over to the window and looked out, anger sparking in his eyes like an electrical storm as he saw the person they were discussing heading out of the car park.

"I told you I'd take care of it, so just let me do my job!" He snapped the phone shut.

Kate threaded through the crowd of off-duty police already packing the Pig and Whistle at five o'clock, and made her way to the bar. Delaney was sitting on a stool in the corner, nursing a pint of Guinness, watching Sally Cartwright beat Bob Wilkinson at darts but not really paying any attention. His thoughts were elsewhere. Kate took a penny out of her pocket and slid it along the bar counter in front of Delaney. He picked it up and looked at it.

"If they were that easy to get rid of, I'd gladly give them to you."

Kate nodded at his glass. "That doesn't solve anything."

"It does if you drink it."

Kate laughed and Delaney decided he liked the sound. He'd decided that a long time back, of course, but he was beginning to admit it to himself.

Kate smiled at him. "When you're right, you're right. Same again?"

"My turn." Delaney gestured at the barmaid. "Large vodka and tonic, please."

"I've still got a bit of work to do. I can't be drunk."

"You work with dead people. What can it hurt if you slip with your scalpel?"

Kate looked across at him. "You are joking?"

"I am."

Kate hesitated. "It's just paperwork."

Delaney looked at her thoughtfully. "So twice in as many days. You following me?"

"I just dropped some files off and I saw you heading here." She shrugged. "I've had a hell of a day, and what do they say about misery loving company?"

Delaney laughed unexpectedly. "You like to say it as it is, don't you?"

"Not a lot of call for subtlety in my job."

"I suppose not."

Delaney looked at her again as he took another sip of his drink. "On Monday night, at Jackie Malone's flat . . ."

"Yes?"

"I was rude to you. I'm sorry."

"There's no need to apologise."

"I was in a bad mood. I'd spent the day at Northfields cemetery. It was our wedding anniversary."

"I heard about your wife. I'm sorry."

It was Delaney's turn to shake his head. "I just wanted you to know."

The barmaid handed Delaney the vodka and he held it out to Kate. "So, is work over for the day?"

Kate looked at the drink and then levelled her sparkling eyes at him as she took the glass. "Does this mean we're friends now, Jack?"

"I don't have friends. People don't like me."

"People change."

"Like hell they do."

Again the laugh from Kate, and Delaney suddenly realised he had to be careful.

Kate looked at him, her smile smoothing into a serious line as she bit her lower lip. "I haven't spoken to my uncle on a personal basis since I was nine years old."

Delaney looked at her wide-open eyes and could feel the blood pumping in his heart. Maybe it was adrenalin kicking in, fight or flight. He came to a decision. He clinked his glass against hers.

"I think I'd like to be your friend, Kate."

Her smile was a thousand watts now.

CHAPTER
TWENTY-FIVE

Delaney found that he was enjoying Kate Walker's company. The first time since the death of his wife that he had enjoyed a woman's company so much. Kate glanced at her watch and Delaney felt guilty at the disappointment he felt.

"Running out on me again?"

"Time's up, I'm afraid."

"Oh?"

"Got to give a speech at my old university. Then dinner with a friend."

"A male friend?"

Kate looked at him curiously. "Lady friend. A doctor. She's trying to persuade me to go and work for her."

"Are you considering it?"

Kate shrugged. "I kind of like my work."

"Queen of the Dead?"

"Something like that. Not quite as glamorous."

Delaney looked at her, puzzled. "As who?"

"It was a literary reference."

Delaney smiled. "I read *The Beano* as a kid."

Kate laughed. "Your dumb-cop act doesn't fool me you know."

"You think I've got hidden depths?"

"I reckon you're a regular walking city of Atlantis."

Delaney laughed again. "You sure you're not a psychiatrist?"

Kate shook her head and looked at him appraisingly. "I like working with my hands too much."

"And you're good at your job."

Kate leaned in, her voice a little husky. "So I've been told."

Delaney looked at her and felt himself becoming lost in her eyes. Imagining what would happen if he just leaned across and kissed her. Wondering if her lips tasted as good as they looked, as good as they sounded. Then he caught himself and sat back, looking at his watch.

"You best get along to your dinner."

Kate reacted to the shift in his tone. "I could cancel it. You look like you could do with some company."

"No, you get along, Kate. I'll be okay."

Kate stood up, leaning over him, and for a moment he knew she was about to kiss him on the cheek, just a farewell kiss, but Delaney realised it would be more than that. He could feel it and his cheek burned; he wanted it, he wanted more than that, but he hated himself for it. Kate took a breath, straightened up and painted on a smile as Delaney raised his glass and took a defensive drink.

"I'll see you later, Jack."

Delaney nodded. "Yeah."

"Thanks for the drink."

He watched as she walked out of the pub. Wanting to call her back but keeping his silence. He thought there was an almost imperceptibly more exaggerated swish to her hips as she walked away, and if there was, he realised that it was all for his benefit, and suddenly he felt even more confused. The blood was pumping in his ears again and he had to loosen his tie as he swallowed another measure of his drink. He drained the glass and shook the thoughts away; he already had enough in his life to feel guilty about. He gestured at the barman, and soon his glass, at least, was full.

The pub got even busier with the relief coming off shift, and Jack Delaney joined in with the usual meaningless banter as he sank a couple of pints, but in truth it washed over him, his mind elsewhere. After half an hour or so he made his farewells and left.

Back at his flat, he closed the door behind him, checking his post on the mat, picking up a number of bills, junk mail and a small padded envelope with his name and address on it, written in crude block letters. He tossed the mail on a small table and walked through to his lounge. The evening sun was streaming through the windows, still hot, still bright. He pulled the heavy curtains shut. Taking off his jacket and starting to sweat as the room became even more like a sauna. He opened the padded envelope and pulled out a DVD. He loosened his tie, walked over to the DVD player and took out the DVD that was in it, *Sin Sisters*, replacing it with the new, unlabelled disc. He poured himself a large glass of whiskey and pushed play.

White noise and static hissed on the screen for a moment or two and then cleared. Delaney sat back in his chair to watch.

On screen was a static shot, filmed with a good-quality camera. A Victorian front room. Thick curtains drawn over lace nets on the windows, a small gap throwing a golden shaft of diffuse sunlight into the room. A piano with old photos in silver frames on top of it; the floor plain dark wood but polished so it shone, with a single faded rug. Dark furniture in the background, a display case on thin sculpted legs, a sideboard with broad gothic doors. A jardinière stand with a white ceramic pot on it, but no flowers.

And music playing. "Pie Jesu". Delaney's eyes watched motionless, the flickering light of the television dancing and reflecting in his pupils as he took another dispassionate swallow of whiskey.

A young girl walked into shot. She was around nine years old and you could see she was nervous. She walked slowly towards the camera wearing a simple white dress with ribbons in her long dark hair. She stopped and knelt down like a supplicant, opening her mouth into an oval.

A dark-suited figure moved in front of her.

Saturday morning. The twenty-eighth day in a row without rain in London, and the capital was looking set to break heat records for the month.

A television studio is a world without a ceiling, but that didn't make it any cooler. It is a place of wires and cables and chaos; and like any other universe it has its own laws, its own morality, its own little gods.

In the director's room a number of monitors showed a group of primary school children of about nine or ten years of age. They were singing "All Things Bright and Beautiful". Alex Moffett, in his late thirties and prematurely balding, took off his designer glasses and paused the tape.

"Okay, Caroline, that's fine. Cue up the bishop for me."

Caroline, a perky media school graduate in her twenties, with short bleached hair teased into spikes, combat boots, a tartan skirt and a T-shirt with "The Dog's Bollocks" hand-written across her front, shuffled a box of tapes and shrugged apologetically. She flicked through the box again and shook her head.

"The bishop's back in the office. The runner should have brought it up by now."

Moffett glared at her.

"What is it I always say?"

Caroline looked at her boss's angry face. A little amused, a little scared if truth be known, although Moffett wasn't a scary-looking man.

"Never work with bloody amateurs."

"Never work with bloody amateurs, that's exactly bloody right. Christ, I need a drink."

Caroline looked a little taken aback as Moffett stood up and slipped into his jacket.

"Alex, we record in one hour!"

"I have been producing this show for five bloody years, sweetheart. I know what our sodding schedule is."

"Of course."

Caroline smiled, placating, and turned back to her monitor. Moffett muttered under his breath and headed for reception. He didn't even acknowledge the nod from the security guard who sat behind the desk, just pushed the big green button to the side of the doors and headed out to the car park.

He scowled dismissively at a huddle of studio employees who stood at the kerb of the road that ran parallel to the studios, blowing smoke and gossiping. If gossip was currency in the TV industry, then everyone was a millionaire. If you weren't sticking a knife in someone else's back, then you had no business being there. Moffett headed past them further down the road and pulled out his mobile phone, punching in a number with frustrated urgency.

"It's Alexander. What's happening?"

He listened, teasing a hanging nail on the corner of this thumb between his teeth, then shook his head, unhappy.

"I don't like it." He sighed, his temper rising like a needle on a thermostat. "Sod your bloody golf game. I'm shooting Jesus' bloody sunbeams in forty-five sodding minutes! I tell you, I'm beginning to get very nervous here, so do something about it or I will."

He listened for a moment or two longer and his shoulders sagged.

"I'll see you later."

He clicked his phone off but didn't head back to the studio. He stood a while longer, worrying at his hangnail. Finally he tore it loose, gasping with pain as it ripped into the quick and a bright spot of blood appeared. He sucked it, tasting the iron and copper, and grimaced. He didn't like omens.

Delaney was also uncomfortable that Saturday morning. Five days since the anniversary of his wife's death, and he was at his sister-in-law's again, perched on the edge of her sofa like a distressed seagull on a wall. He fitted a finger under his collar and pulled it out to cool his neck. He would have loosened his tie but he knew that if he did, busy female hands would seize it and tighten it even more uncomfortably. The truth was that Delaney had never been a suit-and-tie man.

He looked across as the lounge door flew open in an explosion of anarchic energy. Siobhan, dressed for her First Holy Communion, came bursting into the room like a human cannonball, the happiness and innocence shining from her eyes like a beacon.

"What do you think of the dress?"

Wendy followed her in. "Siobhan. Be careful. Watch your hair."

"You look a picture, darling. Daddy's sweetheart."

Siobhan clambered into his arms and he hugged her.

"Everything all right, Jack?"

Delaney found a smile and nodded at Wendy. She held her hand out to Siobhan. "Come on then. We'd best be getting on. Can't be late for the big day, can we?"

"They'll make a convert of you yet, Wendy."

Wendy shook her head. "I may be a hypocrite, Jack. But not that big a one."

Delaney stood up and took his daughter's other hand.

"Come on, darling. Let's get your membership card to the biggest club in the world."

The Church of St Joseph was old. Dating back to the Norman Conquest, it had history in its very bones. High vaulted arches crossing above the nave. Stained glass filling every window. Dark wooden pews worn smooth over the years by countless people sitting and praying. Around the church were the fourteen pictures of the Stations of the Cross. Behind the altar a tall crucifix. The agonies of Christ captured in brutal realism. Blood trickling from the crown of thorns, a gash in His side where a Roman soldier had been ordered to put Him to early death so as not to spoil the Sabbath rituals. His hands and feet stained with dried blood as it pooled around the hard iron of the nails that had been hammered through His tender flesh and bone.

Delaney sat in one of the forward pews. He ran a finger under the collar of his shirt again and tried to get comfortable on the hard wooden bench. He stretched his legs out and crossed them. Wendy sat beside him and dug him in the ribs. He nodded apologetically and sat up straighter.

Forgive me, Father, for I have sinned. He didn't say the words aloud but they echoed in his head as if he had shouted them to ring in the rafters of the ancient church.

Forgive me, Father, for I have sinned.

At the back of the church, in an upstairs gallery, Mrs Henderson, a kind-faced, mild-mannered lady of fifty-two, sat at the organ and positioned her feet on the pedals. She turned the sheet music, placed her hands on the keyboard and began to play. Sweet music filled

244

the air. The music of celebration and worship. The music of ritual, thought Delaney, as the sound carried him back to his own childhood. To another church in another country and another time.

Jack could feel the blood pumping in his veins as he knelt in front of the altar, waiting for Father O'Connell to return. He shifted uncomfortably, the cold stone painful on his sore bare knees.

Jack Delaney was an altar boy, the youngest of a group of five or six boys from the village who came to church every Saturday morning to practise. The other boys had been sent home half an hour or so ago and Jack had been ordered to wait on his knees and think about his sins. Jack did think about his sins. He thought about them a lot. Especially the one thing he had done and could never take back, no matter how hard he prayed to go back in time and undo it. That was why he hardened his heart to what was going to come. Whatever it was, he deserved it.

Jack could hear movement in the vestry and clenched his hand into a fist to stop it from trembling. He had sinned and now he had to face the consequences.

Father O'Connell was a man capable of great anger. You only had to listen to his old-fashioned sermons on a Sunday morning to know that. He was very clear on what he despised, and what he thought of sin and sinners and what should become of them. And Jack was a sinner right enough. His father swore that he was born to sin as a duck was born to water. And his father should know.

He looked up as a shadow fell on the polished floor in front of him and he heard the soft swish of a black cassock. Father O'Connell was not particularly tall, but to a kneeling ten-year-old his five foot ten gave him Olympian proportions, while his rough white beard and sore red eyes lent him the look of an Old Testament prophet of doom. Jack shivered despite himself. He was usually afraid of no one, would front up to much bigger kids in the school playground if they messed with him, but Father O'Connell had a reputation. He liked to hurt boys. He kept a strap in his vestry and none of the parents in the area objected if he used it to keep their unruly children in line. And there were rumours.

"Jack. What are we to do with you?" The priest's booming voice echoed around the stone walls of the church, rich with disappointment.

"I didn't mean to do it, Father."

"You didn't mean to drink the bottle of communion wine?"

"No, Father."

"Was it the Devil that made you do it then?"

"I'm thinking it must be, Father. For sure as you're standing there I have no inkling of why I'd do such a thing."

"No inkling?"

"None whatsoever. As God is my witness."

"But God is your witness, isn't he, Jack?"

"Yes, Father."

"So it was the Devil in you that had the inkling, is that what you are thinking?"

246

"Now you come to mention it, Father, that must be the right of the matter. For I have no inclination in myself whatsoever to be drinking wine. It tastes disgusting."

"And yet you drank a whole bottle of it."

"And was heartily sick."

"Then maybe you have learned a valuable lesson, Jack."

"I certainly have learned my lesson, Father," he said hopefully.

"It was the Devil in you. You're sure of it now?"

"Certain sure, Father."

"It is a bad business when you let the Devil into your body, boy."

"He must have snuck up on me, Father. I'll be vigilant from now on. I promise it to you."

"But if the Devil is in you, boy, we have to get him out, don't we?"

"Do we?"

"The Devil is like a cancer, boy. Like a sickness. We must purge him, son. It is our Christian duty."

"Purge?"

Father O'Connell laid a heavy hand on Jack's head, and Jack flinched.

"Our Christian duty, son. Come with me to the vestry."

And as Jack looked up into the middle-aged man's eyes, he saw not anger but some kind of feral hunger, and he trembled even more as he was led to the vestry door.

★ ★ ★

The hymn came to a close and Delaney wiped the back of his hand across his forehead, damp now with sweat. Wendy handed him a tissue, which he took gratefully as the twin doors to the church opened and a procession of young children, boys and girls, came in. The girls in white dresses, the boys wearing red ties. They walked slowly up the aisle in a line to the altar. Delaney smiled at Siobhan as she passed, but Siobhan kept her eyes ahead, looking at the cruciform figure of Christ hanging behind the altar. Wendy put a hand on Delaney's knee and he squeezed it, holding on just a little too tight.

Wendy smiled reassuringly at him. "She looks a million dollars, Jack. A million dollars."

Siobhan came to the altar and knelt at the little rail. The priest made the sign of the cross in front of her with his hand, and Siobhan shut her eyes and opened her mouth, putting out her tongue so he could place the communion wafer on it.

Kate looked around the empty CID office. She paused at Delaney's desk. It was neat and ordered. Files stacked tidily, pens in a pot, loose papers collected, everything aligned. The desk of a man who liked to keep control of things, Kate surmised. Not least his emotions. A photograph stood centrally on the desk. Silver-framed. A smiling woman holding a young baby. Delaney's wife and daughter, Kate guessed. She picked up the photograph; his wife was very beautiful. Kate

248

couldn't begin to imagine what he must have gone through when she died.

She put the report she had brought him on top of his files, suddenly feeling guilty, and started as Bob Wilkinson came across, a thinly veiled anger in his eyes.

"Come to gloat, have you?"

"What are you talking about?"

"Come off it, Dr Walker. We all know you're no friend of Jack Delaney."

Kate shook her head, puzzled. "You've lost me."

"What are you doing here, then?"

"I promised Jack a copy of the autopsy report on Billy Martin."

Bob Wilkinson was a little taken aback. "Right."

"And for your information, whatever differences Jack and I had in the past are just that. In the past."

"I'll take your word for it."

Bob Wilkinson went to move away, but Kate gripped his arm firmly. She lowered her voice to a whisper. "What are you talking about, though? What's going on?"

"There's rumours flying around. That's all."

"What kind of rumours?"

"About Jack."

"What about him?"

Bob leaned in and lowered his voice too. "They're saying he was involved in Jackie Malone's murder."

Kate shook her head, shocked. "That's ridiculous!"

"You and I know that," said Bob Wilkinson, letting the implication hang in the air.

"You've got to do something."

He shrugged. "I'm just a foot soldier, what can I do?"

Kate looked across the office, her face hardening as Chief Superintendent Walker came out of DCI Campbell's office, forcefully pulling the door shut behind him. He strode angrily down the corridor, not even glancing at his niece.

Wilkinson looked pointedly at Kate. "If something bad is coming down on Jack Delaney, and if you are his friend like you say," he looked across at the superintendent's retreating figure, "then he's going to need friends with connections in high places."

"I'm not sure I have any influence there."

"Maybe it's time to find out."

Kate considered for a moment, looked down at the photo on Delaney's desk and hurried after her uncle. Time to swallow her pride and ask for help.

Outside the church, Delaney leaned against the cool stone of the old flint wall and caught his breath, telling himself it was just the heat. But the feverish pump of blood in his heart told a different story. He took a couple of deep breaths and forced himself to relax. He started as the mobile phone in his pocket rang and had to take a moment or two to answer it. "Jack Delaney?"

The voice on the other end of the phone was breathy and low. A woman. "Did you get the film?"

"Who is this?"

"It doesn't matter who I am. Did you get the film I sent?"

"I got the film." Sweat was breaking out on Delaney's forehead once more.

"Did you enjoy it?"

"Who is this?"

"You can call me a friend."

Delaney barked a short dry laugh. "*My* friend?"

"I don't know you."

"Whose friend, then?"

"Jackie Malone's friend."

Delaney sighed, running his hand across the top of his forehead again.

"What do you want?"

There was a small chuckle on the other end of the line. A chuckle that had as much warmth in it as a penguin's foot. "That's the twenty-four-dollar question?"

"You want money?"

"No. I don't want money."

"What do you want then?"

Delaney could hear the woman on the other end covering the phone and hissing to someone: "Give me a minute." He heard a man's voice replying to her but couldn't make out the words.

Delaney's patience was wearing thin. "What do you want?" He spoke curtly into the phone.

"I want justice for Jackie. I want retribution."

"Why don't you come in and talk about it?"

Another harsh laugh. "I don't think so, Jack. People involved in this business seem to get hurt, don't they? Jackie. Her dropkick brother Billy."

"What do you know about Billy Martin?"

"I know they both ended up getting terminally hurt. And I never was like Jackie. I don't play the rough games. And this is a sick business."

Delaney frowned. "What business?"

"Blackmail."

Delaney sighed again. "I see."

"Billy Martin thought he had stumbled on a little goldmine, but Jackie didn't want anything to do with it. She gave me the tape to look after. Anything happened to her, she said to send it to you."

Delaney nodded. "Where's the boy?"

"I don't know anything about a boy."

"Who am I talking to?"

"Anyway, that's it. I don't want anything more to do with it. She said you'd know what to do with the DVD. She said you'd take care of those responsible. She didn't trust the police but she trusted you to make sure they got what was coming to them."

Delaney could hear the man in the background shouting at her, urgent, angry. He thought he could make out the name Carol, or Karen.

"I've got to go."

"Just tell me where —" But the line had gone dead. Delaney closed his phone angrily and looked over to the church doors, where children flanked by happy parents were spilling noisily out. Delaney watched them for a moment or two and then ran to his car.

Wendy came out with Siobhan. Shielding her eyes against the sun and squinting as she looked around for Delaney.

"Jack?"

252

But Delaney had gone.

In his car he lit up a cigarette and took a few deep drags, then picked up his mobile phone and tapped a number in. "Sally, it's Delaney. I want you to get Jackie Malone's file out. Trace all her known associates and go back as far as you can. I'm looking for a Carol or a Karen. Probably on the game. And do the same with Stella Trant's file too. And I want it yesterday."

"Yes, boss, but . . ."

"Just do it, Sally. There's something I need to take care of."

He closed the phone and it rang immediately. He looked at the number. Campbell. He switched the phone off and took a few more hits on his cigarette as he turned the key in the ignition, his eyes dark pools of anger.

CHAPTER
TWENTY-SIX

Alexander Moffett's tongue poked thickly from his mouth. His eyes bulged painfully, small blood vessels in them breaking as he twisted. The veins and muscles of his neck were thick with effort, like cords or snakes writhing under his skin. He grunted with desperation. With madness. His head rocked back and the skin on his neck burned and tore. Struggling just made the noose tighter, however, and his breathing stopped completely with a last horrible gurgle. His legs strained downward but his toes couldn't find the floor. His eyes bulged even more and red tears leaked from the corners of his eyes, his tongue so swollen now as to fill his mouth, blocking it even if he could draw air. He jerked once, maybe twice more, and was still. The eyes rolled back, and the body swayed silently on the rope in a gentle circle like a drunken, grotesque ballerina.

Behind him on a large flat-screen television, Billy Martin was screaming soundlessly as Kevin Norrell picked him up and threw him, hands and feet tied with coat-hanger wire, into the cold night water of the Thames.

A hand reached down, ejected the DVD and turned off the television. His face was reflected in the wide, staring pupils of Alexander Moffett, but as the man left the room, his image went with him.

Parked a few doors up from Moffett's house in Paddington, Delaney crushed a cigarette into his already full ashtray and automatically put another in his mouth. Flaring a match, he watched blue-suited forensic investigators hurry into the house, past flashing lights, and uniforms stretching out yellow and black tape to cordon off the area from curious passers-by. Nothing to see here. Not any more, thought Delaney.

Inside, Chief Inspector Diane Campbell nodded sourly at the uniformed constable who stood to the side of the door opening into Moffett's study. She walked into the room swearing quietly under her breath. It was an opulent room. A man's study from another era. Book-lined walls. A deep-pile carpet underfoot. A large globe of the world from a time when most of it was coloured pink. A sideboard with decanter and crystal glasses. A large mahogany desk with a green leather inset. A humidor stocked with the finest cigars from Cuba. The only modern things were the flat-screen TV and the telephone. It was a man's room. A dead man's room.

Moffett's body had been lowered, the rope cut down from the three-hundred-year old beams that spanned the ceiling. Bonner stood to one side as a police photographer finished taking shots of the deceased. Moffett's face was stained purple with the blood pooling in the loose skin. His eyes were dull and his tongue protruded like an obscene gesture. Campbell brushed a hand angrily in the air as a fly buzzed past, and turned to Bonner.

"Where is Dr Walker?"

"On her way, ma'am."

She sighed and looked at her watch, then glared back at Bonner. "And more to the bloody point, where's Jack sodding Delaney?"

Bonner shrugged as Campbell's mobile phone went. She snapped it open. "Campbell?"

She listened, her lips tightening with anger. "Bring it in. All of it." She snapped the phone shut and glared angrily at Delaney as he walked into the room. "Your phone switched off, was it?"

Delaney shook his head. "Must have been out of range. I called in; Dave Patterson gave me the shout."

"Obviously. Or you wouldn't be here, would you?"

Delaney picked up on her tone. "What's that supposed to mean?"

Campbell nodded to the body on the floor. "Alexander Moffett. What do you know about him?"

"Just what I was told by Slimline." Delaney shrugged again. "Television producer. God slot. Sunday morning, singing children, all that. Now dead."

"He certainly is that."

Delaney looked at Moffett's grotesque corpse. "Was it suicide?"

Campbell looked at him for a long moment. "Did you know him personally, Jack?"

"I don't think I went to the right school."

"Just answer the bloody question."

Delaney's eyes flattened. "What going on, Diane?"

"You've never met or had dealings with Alexander Moffett?"

"You have a point to make, why don't you just make it?"

Campbell held up a piece of paper. "His suicide note."

"And?"

"And in it, Detective Inspector Delaney . . . in it he tells us why he committed suicide. It says that you were blackmailing him."

Delaney gritted his teeth angrily. "I never met the man."

"Not only that, but you were selling him cocaine and turning a blind eye to the party games he played with young children. The private films he made."

Delaney nodded, the penny dropping. "Ah."

"For money, Delaney. Lots of money."

"And you believe this?"

"Why would he lie?"

Delaney shrugged. "And why would he kill himself now?"

"Because he has a young child of his own, Jack. Coming up to her ninth birthday. She lives with her mum, but he has access. And he was scared of what he might do."

"He told you this?"

Campbell held up the sheet of paper. "All in the letter."

"Convenient that it's typewritten."

"He couldn't live with himself any more so he thought he'd make amends."

"It's all bullshit, Diane."

Campbell glared at him. "Don't call me that."

"How am I supposed to fit into all this?"

"Jackie Malone. It all comes back to her."

Delaney looked over at Bonner, but Bonner's face was impassive, unreadable. He looked back at Campbell. "Go on?"

"Alexander Moffett didn't just make shows for Sunday morning television."

"I'm listening."

"He made all sorts of films. Pornography. Like *Sin Sisters*, for example, starring your old friend Jackie Malone."

"What's that got to do with me?"

Campbell carried on, ignoring him. "The thing is, he made other kinds of films too. Films for a specialised market. Kiddie porn and other very nasty stuff." She held up a DVD case. "Jackie Malone dying."

Delaney went very quiet and Campbell gave him a hard, flat look. His phone suddenly rang, shattering the silence. Delaney answered it before Campbell could object.

"Delaney?" He could hear Kate's worried voice on the other end of the phone and kept his face neutral as she spoke.

"It's Kate. Someone's setting you up for the murder of Jackie Malone."

"It's in hand. Don't say anything to anybody, okay? I'm dealing with it."

He clicked the phone off.

"Who was that, Jack?"

258

"If it is any of your business, it was my sister-in-law. Some of your people have been questioning her."

"Standard procedure. You know how it works."

"Anybody upsets my daughter and they'll have me to deal with."

"Let's get back to the kiddie porn, shall we, Jack."

"It's got nothing to do with me."

"We found copies in your flat."

"You've been to my flat?"

Campbell's look was pure granite. "Yes, we've been to your flat."

"You had no right."

"We had every right. We had a warrant and we found the cocaine."

Delaney shook his head angrily. "Jesus Christ, Diane, half a dab."

"I told you not to call me that. And damn near a kilo is a little more than a dab. I told you to talk to me, didn't I? About Jackie Malone, about your relationship with her." She shook the suicide note at him and pointed at Moffett. "And now this sick dead fuck is saying you killed her."

Delaney sighed, resigned. He could see the way this was going, but couldn't see a way out of it, for now. "This is a set-up, Diane. I didn't take that cocaine, it's a plant. I've got nothing to do with those films or with Moffett. I've never even heard of him. And I sure as shite had nothing to do with Jackie's murder. You know that!"

Campbell shrugged angrily. "You've left me with no choice, you stupid prick."

"Just do it then."

"Detective Inspector Jack Delaney, I am arresting you on suspicion of murder. You do not have to say anything, but it may harm your defence if you do not mention, when questioned, something which you later rely on in court. Anything you do say may be given in evidence." She turned to Bonner. "Cuff him and take him in."

Bonner shrugged apologetically and held out the cuffs. Delaney turned round and held out his wrists, looking back at Campbell. "Is this going to affect my promotion?"

"Just take him away, Sergeant."

Bonner led Delaney out of the room as Campbell glanced down at the dead body of Alexander Moffett and shook her head. She looked at the shell-shocked uniforms who were gathered about the room.

"And for fuck's sake, someone give me a cigarette."

Outside, Delaney walked ahead of Bonner and a uniformed officer to a waiting car. As Bonner opened the door for him to get in, Kate drove into the driveway and jumped out of her car.

"What the hell's going on, Jack?"

"Unpaid parking fines."

Kate rounded on Bonner. "Eddie. Come on. What's going on here?"

Bonner shook his head. "It doesn't concern you, Dr Walker."

Delaney looked at her impassively. "He's quite right, there's a dead man in there. Stick with him."

Kate turned back to Bonner. "Where's Campbell?"

"She's inside. Not in a good mood."

"It's not going to improve any."

She turned sharply on her heel and walked into the house. Bonner put his hand on Delaney's head, bending him into the car. Delaney sat in the back and Bonner turned to the uniform. "I can take it from here, thanks, Jimmy." The policeman nodded and headed back towards the house. Bonner walked around and got in the front seat, firing up the engine. He tilted the rear-view mirror so he could see Delaney's face.

"What's going on, Jack?"

"You tell me."

"That's not the way it works. You know that."

Delaney held up his hands. "Not really. Not used to sitting in this position."

"I had to put the cuffs on."

"Sure you did."

"She wasn't a happy bunny, Cowboy. No point both of us pissing her off."

Delaney nodded his head and looked out the window. "You reckon this good weather will hold?"

"We'll make an Englishman of you yet."

"Not in this lifetime."

Bonner laughed drily. "As for good weather, you said there was a shit storm coming and you were right. And it's all coming your way, Cowboy." He shook his head and readjusted the mirror.

Kate walked into the study, her heart hammering in her chest. She fought hard to stay calm. Delaney needed her to stay focused, she reckoned. And strangely, the knowledge made her heart beat a little faster.

Campbell gave her a curt acknowledgement as she entered and gestured at Moffett's body. "I need to know if it was suicide or if he was helped."

Kate knelt down by the body of Alexander Moffett, opening her police surgeon's bag and letting the familiar routine steady her nerves. She felt as if every eye in the room was trained on her. She looked at the ligature marks around the dead man's neck. Rope burns that, had he survived, would have marked him for the rest of his life. But he hadn't survived. The man's death was clearly tied up with Jackie Malone, but she didn't know how. She looked up at Diane Campbell.

"What exactly do you think happened here?"

"We don't know, Dr Walker. He was found by his housekeeper."

"A suicide note?"

"A typed one, left on his computer."

"What did he say in it?"

"Said he couldn't live with himself. Couldn't live with the guilt."

Kate looked back down at the swollen face, twisted in agony. "He chose a particularly unpleasant way to go."

Campbell nodded. "I have a hypothetical for you."

"Go on."

"Somebody orders a man — at gunpoint say, or some other threat — to stand on a low stool. The rope has been fixed, the noose tied. He tells the man to put the rope around his own neck. He has a gun on him, so who knows, he probably would do it. Then the stool is kicked away and the man is strangled."

"What's the question?"

"Is there any way of telling that? Any way of telling it was murder and not suicide."

Kate shook her head. "Under those circumstances, probably not. If there was a struggle, we could get some indicators — skin under his fingernails, that kind of thing. Otherwise it's very hard to prove."

"What about fingerprints off the rope?"

Kate shook her head again. "No chance. We'll test for fibres, but the surface is too rough for prints."

Kate tilted the man's head and looked at the bruising around his neck.

"I can tell you one thing."

"What?"

"This wasn't a quick death. He would have taken a while to die. He'd have to really hate himself to do it."

"Unless he had help."

Kate looked down at Moffett again.

"Yeah. Unless he had help."

In the back of Bonner's car, Delaney looked down at the cuffs on his hands and flexed his wrists. There was no chance of sliding them off, the sergeant had made sure of that. He shifted sideways on the seat and looked at Bonner in the rear-view mirror.

"You getting a buzz out of taking me in, Eddie?"

"Someone had to do it, boss. That's what the taxpayers pay their taxes for." He shrugged. "Nothing personal."

"From this angle, it feels kind of personal."

"What is it we always say? If you've done nothing wrong, you've got nothing to be scared of."

"We know the system better than that, though, don't we?"

Bonner nodded with a sly smile. "I'd be lying if I said we didn't."

"It's a frame. I don't know why. But someone has put me in it. Think about it."

Bonner shook his head again. "Not my job, Cowboy. I'm just a policeman, and only a sergeant at that. I don't get paid to think."

Delaney grunted. "Cheers, mate."

"I'm not your friend, Delaney. I never was. I work with you. End of story." He met Delaney's eyes in the mirror. "That is, I used to work with you."

Bonner turned his attention back to the traffic and Delaney slumped against the side of the car. He hoped Kate Walker would be careful who she spoke to. One of his colleagues had set him up. They had killed more than once, and to Delaney it was perfectly clear that they would happily kill again.

Siobhan screamed. High-pitched and terrified. She yelled again and Wendy laughed as she pushed the swing higher. "Don't stop!" Siobhan loved to go as high as she could. She loved it and was terrified by it at the same time. She remembered last year when her dad had taken her to an amusement park. She couldn't get enough of some of the rides. Ones that went high in the air and crashed to the ground. Ones that whirled like gigantic whisks, spinning and wheeling and turning and dipping. She'd laughed, screamed herself hoarse on that day. Her dad had paid for her to go on the rides time and time again, but wouldn't go on them himself, even though she and Wendy had teased him mercilessly. He claimed he had an inner ear problem which meant he couldn't go on spinning rides. Siobhan laughed as she remembered it.

Across the park, a tall man in a dark raincoat sat on a bench and watched as her aunt swung the little girl higher and higher. The man took a long, thin cigar from a case and lit it, the flame from his silver lighter flaring his pupils to pinpricks and flashing the blue of his eyes. He watched Siobhan as she swung higher, her excited, terrified screams loud in the hot evening air. And he smiled.

Delaney looked out of the side window at the traffic speeding past. People hurrying home to their Saturday tea. Hundreds of different lives locked in the bubbles of their own cars. Their own worlds. He thought of the tens of thousands of faces he must have seen through the lens of a car windscreen over the years. Commuters returning home. Sales executives knocking off early. Office workers keen to make happy hour at their local. Nurses, teachers, civil servants, account clerks and shop assistants, bank managers and chemists. People who could work nine to five and switch off with the clock. People who could go home to normal families and normal lives. Something that Delaney couldn't do. He sometimes wondered what his life would have been like if he had become an accountant or a solicitor instead of a policeman. His wife would probably still be alive, he knew that. They'd be living in a nice house in a suburb somewhere outside of London, sitting on the green belt with the country on his doorstep. A wife at home with him and their children, kicking a football in the garden and getting told off for spoiling the vegetable patch. But Delaney wasn't a solicitor, and his wife wasn't alive and complaining about broken tomato plants. She was dead. Delaney looked away from the window and a cold calm came over him.

Bonner swung the wheel, turning the car off the main street into a suburban cut-through, and as he did so, Delaney leaned forward, held his hands out and quickly looped them over Bonner's head, pulling the chain of the cuffs tightly into his neck.

Bonner swerved and fought to keep control of the car. His voice a painful rasp. "Jesus, Jack. What are you doing? You want to get us killed? Jack?"

But Delaney didn't answer. He flexed the powerful muscles in his forearms and pulled harder. Bonner started choking, unable to speak. He held his hands to his throat, trying to prise Delaney's fingers loose, and as his legs jerked uncontrollably, his foot stamped down on the accelerator and the car swerved off the road,

266

mounted the pavement and smashed headlong into a lamppost. Bonner flew forward, Delaney dragged behind as the airbag exploded in the sergeant's face and the gurgling stopped.

CHAPTER
TWENTY-SEVEN

Delaney unhooked his cuffed hands from Bonner's neck and whispered in his ear, "Nothing personal."

He awkwardly manoeuvred his hands into Bonner's jacket pocket and pulled out the key for the cuffs. He had just slipped them off his wrists when the wrecked front passenger door was wrenched open and a large, muscular man in a tracksuit leaned in.

"Are you guys all right?"

Delaney nodded, catching his breath. "I think so, but if you've got a mobile, could you call an ambulance?"

Delaney opened the back door and climbed out.

The large man gave him a puzzled look as he fumbled in his pocket for his phone. "Jesus. What happened here? You drove straight into that lamppost."

Delaney held out his warrant card. "It was an accident, the steering went."

The man nodded towards Bonner. "Is he okay?"

"He'll be fine. The airbag knocked him out."

"You're both lucky to be alive."

"Tell me about it."

The jogger pulled out his mobile phone and punched in the call. "Ambulance, please. There's been an accident."

He described what had happened and their location, but when he turned back to speak to Delaney, he was gone.

Bonner groaned and opened his eyes, and looked around him. As his memory came painfully back, he blinked up at the large man, who finished his call and smiled down at him reassuringly.

"You're going to be all right. I've called an ambulance."

"The guy who was with me?"

The man shrugged. "He was here a moment ago. He's probably gone to get help."

Bonner groaned again and shifted in his seat, releasing the seatbelt and wincing at the pain that ran from his shoulder to his waist and exploded in his head with each movement.

"You'd probably best try not to move. Wait for the ambulance."

Bonner slumped back, resigned, surveying the wreckage and damning Delaney to all kinds of Irish hell.

Bill Hoskins sat back in his battered wing-backed armchair, which was almost as old as he was. He stirred some sugar into his tea, the spoon clinking as it hit the sides of his enamel mug. He picked up a remote control and turned the volume up on the television set. The news was on and the public were being warned that a serving detective in the Metropolitan Police had violently resisted arrest and was on the run. The reporter went on to report that Jack Delaney was wanted for questioning in a series of murders including that of Jackie Malone, a prostitute who was found slain and mutilated in her flat last Monday.

The picture of Jack Delaney flashed on the screen and Bill shook his head. Something about the murder and the time and the date didn't seem right. He put down his mug of tea, then levered himself out of his chair, his old knees creaking almost as loudly as the wooden floor as he walked across to the door.

Sergeant Bonner came back into interview room one, pulled out a chair and sat down awkwardly, wincing with pain. His face looked like he'd just gone nine rounds with Mike Tyson and his ribs hurt like hell. He put a file on the long wooden table and then leaned back, looking into the eyes of the man sitting opposite him. Bill Hoskins was in his late sixties and had a crumpled, colourless face that matched the creases in his shirt and his faded grey jacket. He scowled at Bonner.

"I thought you were getting me a cup of tea."

"They ran out."

Hoskins sniffed, unimpressed. "Right."

"Let's go over it again."

"Do we have to?"

Bonner glared at him and Hoskins nodded, resigned.

"You were there in your capacity as caretaker all day long. You could swear to that?"

"I don't have to swear. I told you, didn't I? I don't lie."

"We never get any liars in here, Mr Hoskins. Funny thing, that. A police station and we get all sorts in. Rapists, burglars, murderers, arsonists, racists . . . No liars, though."

"I am none of those things, and I was there all day."

Bonner glanced down at a sheet of paper in his hand. "Ten o'clock in the morning to seven o'clock at night."

"That's what I said. And —"

Bonner held up a hand to stop him. "Yeah, yeah, I know. I want you to look at a photograph for me now."

"All right."

Bonner slid a photo across the table.

Hoskins picked it up and nodded. "That's him. Regular visitor he was. Sometimes he was carrying flowers, sometimes a bottle, you know what I mean?"

"I can imagine. And you're prepared to swear in court you saw him on the day in question?"

"He came in just before twelve o'clock."

"What time did he leave?"

"About six o'clock that same evening."

"You're sure about that. That's a very long time for this kind of visit."

"Not for him it wasn't. He was a regular."

"I want you to think very carefully. You could definitely swear to it in court?"

"I'd swear to it on my life."

Bonner's eyes glinted as he nodded pointedly. "So he didn't leave any time between twelve and three o'clock?"

"I told you. He came in and he didn't leave. I was there all day."

Bonner closed the file. "Thank you, Mr Hoskins. You've been very helpful."

"I can go now?"

Bonner nodded. "We'll be in touch."

"And about bleeding time." He stood up awkwardly and walked to the door.

Bonner leaned across the table and picked up the photo, studying it with a troubled expression in his eyes. But the eyes that looked back at him from the photo weren't troubled at all. The eyes of Jack Delaney almost seemed to be smiling.

Kate Walker sat at the bar of the Holly Bush in Hampstead, sipping on a Bloody Mary and letting the noisy chat of the other customers wash over her. She swirled the drink in her hand. The Holly Bush had their own secret recipe for Bloody Marys and always put a splash of red wine in to finish it off, lending sinister authenticity to the drink. She took another sip and steadied her breathing, trying to order the wild thoughts that were dancing in her brain. It made no sense to her. The preliminary examination of Moffett had been fairly straightforward. As she had told Diane Campbell, there was no way of telling whether it was a genuine suicide. There had certainly been no indications of a struggle or resistance, and she couldn't see the autopsy throwing up any contradictory information. That was straightforward. What wasn't straightforward was how Jack Delaney fitted into it all. Although Campbell had told Kate very little, she had spoken to the other officers there and was shocked at what she heard. They were accusing him not only of murder, but also of blackmail, stealing evidence, selling drugs and profiting from paedophile pornography. There was very little in this world that was certain, she knew that, but she was certain that Delaney was innocent of the charges. She absolutely knew it. What she didn't know was what to do about it. She understood it wasn't safe to talk to his colleagues from what he said on the phone. So who was she supposed to talk about it to? Maybe it was time to swallow her pride and talk to her uncle, as Bob Wilkinson had hinted she should. He would know what to do. There must be protocols. She finished her drink and stood up. She'd speak to him tomorrow.

Wendy sat on the sofa, her knees together, her arms wrapped protectively around herself. The television played the theme tune for *Casualty* and Wendy snatched the remote control up to switch it off. She'd had enough misery for one day. It had been some time since the police had left and she still felt a bag of nerves. She worried a fingernail between her teeth and sighed. Siobhan hadn't understood why the policemen had been there; she hadn't understood why her daddy wasn't with them, where he had gone after her First Holy Communion, and Wendy didn't have the words to explain. She couldn't believe Jack had been arrested for murder. She couldn't believe he was on the run.

The phone rang and Wendy jumped. She took a moment or two to settle her breathing and answered it.

"Hello."

"It's Jack."

"Jack, for God's sake, where are you?"

"It doesn't matter."

"Of course it matters. I've had a house full of detectives questioning me, questioning Siobhan."

"Is she all right?"

"She's upstairs sleeping."

"I want to talk to her."

"And what are you going to say to her?"

She could hear his frustration on the other end of the line. "For Christ's sake . . . I don't know, Wendy."

"Exactly. So let her sleep."

"Everything is going to be okay. Tell her that."

"How?"

"I don't know how. But tell her it will."

"Should you be talking on your phone? Can't they trace it?"

"It's a personal mobile, they don't know anything about it."

Wendy nodded, taking a deep breath. "Did you do it?"

"You think me capable of murder?"

Wendy sighed again, blinking the tears out of her eyes. "Yes, Jack, I do."

It was light outside as the sun sank slowly in the west, and although it had been far hotter during the heart of the day, the heat still hung heavy in the air. Inside Kate's hallway, however, it was cool and dark. The doors leading to the kitchen and the dining room and the lounge were all closed, and the stained-glass window on the front door was darkly coloured. The floor was laid with original Victorian tiles, a geometric mosaic in red, green and cream. A spilling of light through the stained glass spattered ruby colours on the hall floor like a splash of old blood. But in the corners and the depths it was dark.

Kate walked up to the front door, jangling her keys through to the right one, and slipped it into the keyhole. With a practised flick of her wrist she turned the key in the lock and opened the door. She was about to step inside when she felt a cold trickle run up her spine. She turned back to the road behind her and checked the approach to the house. She had had a feeling she was being watched ever since she left the pub, and even though the road was deserted she couldn't shake the feeling off. She was a medical doctor not a clinical psychologist, but given the circumstances, she knew that a certain amount of paranoia was justified.

She shivered slightly and turned back, bending over to pick up the mail that was scattered on the doormat. She straightened up and closed the door, distracted as she flicked through the envelopes, then a movement caught her eye and she looked up, her heart hammering in her chest as she saw a large man step out from behind the coat stand. Her knees buckled and she screamed in genuine terror.

CHAPTER
TWENTY-EIGHT

"For God's sake, Jack, what are you doing here?"

"Waiting for you."

"You nearly gave me a bloody heart attack."

"Sorry."

Kate blinked at him, astonished. "Is that it? Sorry!"

"I didn't mean to scare you, but I had to make sure you were alone."

"What the hell are you doing here anyway? How did you get in?"

"You keep your back door key hidden under a pot in your garden. Not wise."

"You were arrested. Shouldn't you be in jail?"

"I didn't like the idea."

Kate shook her head. "You better come in, make yourself at home." The words seemed ridiculous given the circumstances.

She led him down the hallway, opening the door at the end to the kitchen. Delaney followed her in and looked around. "Nice."

A stone-flagged floor, high ceiling and a conservatory that had been added to make a dining area. The late evening sunlight spilled in through French doors leading to a well-designed and very well-maintained garden. Kate picked up a large kettle from the hotplate of her Aga and filled it with water at her original butler's sink.

Delaney called out to her, "Have you not got something a little stronger?"

Kate put the kettle down and opened a cupboard, taking out a bottle of single-malt whisky. "No Irish, I'm afraid."

"That's okay. Maybe I'm starting to appreciate what the mainland has to offer."

Kate picked up two glasses and carried them across to the farmhouse table that Delaney was sitting at. She poured out a couple of hefty measures and clunked her glass quickly against his. "*Slainte*."

"Yeah." Delaney took a quick swallow and smiled gratefully at Kate.

"What did you do, Jack?"

"I escaped."

"How?"

"I throttled Eddie Bonner. Made him crash the car."

Kate took a swallow of her whisky, winced a little, and then took another.

"Do you think that was a good idea, all things considered?"

"I had to do something. I didn't murder Jackie Malone."

Kate looked at him for a beat. "Did you sleep with her?"

Delaney looked back at her, surprised by the question, then shook his head. "No. I didn't sleep with her."

"Just good friends?"

"Not even that. I just looked out for her now and again. I could talk to her."

Kate nodded sympathetically. "She's certainly landed you in a whole world of trouble."

Delaney shook his head again. "Not Jackie. Whoever killed her has put me in the frame for it, and that is something they are going to live to regret."

"I know you didn't kill her, Jack."

Delaney finished his whisky and Kate picked up the bottle to pour him another.

"And what makes you so sure?"

"You told me you'd spent the day at your wife's grave."

"I did."

"Did anyone see you?"

Delaney shrugged. "Not that I'm aware of."

"Other mourners? Someone who runs the place?"

"I don't know, Kate. I wasn't really in a state to notice much."

"So you have no alibi?"

"No."

"And no clue as to who really murdered Jackie Malone or Billy Martin, or Alexander Moffett?"

"None at all."

Kate took a sip of her drink and looked at him sympathetically. "Then you really are in the shit, Jack."

Delaney finished his second glass. "Neck high."

Chief Inspector Diane Campbell leaned forward to look at the film that was playing in miniature on her

278

laptop computer. A Victorian front room. Thick curtains drawn over lace nets, a small gap throwing a golden shaft of diffuse sunlight into the room. A piano with old photos in silver frames on top of it, the floor plain dark wood but polished so it shone, with a single faded rug. Dark furniture in the background, a display case on thin sculpted legs, a sideboard with broad gothic doors. A jardinière stand with a white ceramic pot on it, but no flowers.

And music playing. "Pie Jesu". Campbell licked her dry lips as a young girl walked into shot. She was around nine years old and you could see she was nervous. She walked slowly towards the camera wearing a simple white dress with ribbons in her long dark hair. She stopped and knelt down like a supplicant, opening her mouth into an oval. A dark-suited figure moved in front of her and then gestured off camera. A young boy, only just in his teens if that, walked into shot. A pretty boy, with long dark curly hair, dark eyes and red lips.

The girl and the boy looked at each other as the man held his arms out like a Louisiana missionary and spoke with a dead man's voice.

"It's time to make some beautiful music, children." The voice of Alexander Moffett.

There was a knock on the door and Campbell's heart leapt in her chest. She quickly closed her laptop and called out, "Come in."

Bonner came through the door. Campbell looked at him angrily. "Do you have any good news for me, Sergeant Bonner?"

"I don't, ma'am."

Campbell's temper rose as she shouted back at him. "Then find him, for Christ's sake. Bring him in, Eddie. I don't care how and I don't care in what condition. We clear on that?"

"Ma'am."

Campbell fixed him with a long, cold look. "I'm not going down on this alone, Sergeant. If I go, you go with me. This is your fuck-up, you sort it. You hear me?"

"Loud and clear."

"Get the fuck out of my office then."

Bonner left, pulling the door hard behind him. Campbell looked at her laptop and folded her hand into a tight fist.

Kate poured a splash more whisky into Delaney's glass and a last measure into her own. She looked at Delaney, her voice slurring a little now, a smile tugging the corners of her lips and mischief definitely dancing in her eyes.

"What made you think you could trust me? Coming here?"

Delaney smiled, the strain showing in his tired eyes, but enjoying her company.

"Woman's intuition."

Kate laughed, a musical laugh. "Oh yeah. Yours?"

"Yours."

"Pretty sure of yourself."

"And they're not going to look for me here, are they?"

"Why not?"

Delaney leaned forward. "Because everyone knows we can't stand the sight of each other."

"People change."

"Like hell they do."

And the smile was in his eyes too. He leaned forward and Kate tilted her chin upwards, her lips warm and parted. And they kissed.

Delaney lost himself in the warmth, the taste of whisky on her, the openness in her wide, beautiful eyes. Eyes he could drown in. Then he caught himself and pulled back.

"Sorry."

Kate shook her head. "You've got nothing to be sorry about." She held his head and pulled him back in to her, her teeth nipping his lower lip, hungry now. Passionate.

They stood up, Delaney shrugging out of his jacket and wrapping his strong arms around her pliant body. Holding her, needing her. Kate stood back, catching her breath, her ivory face flushed with desire. She held her hand out and Delaney took it, and she led him from the kitchen, to the stairs towards her bedroom. And Delaney almost made it.

"No. This isn't right, Kate."

"Jack . . ."

But Delaney put a hand to her lips so that she couldn't speak.

"Don't, Kate. This isn't the right time."

"It feels like it to me."

He shook his head. "With everything that's going on. I've already involved you in too much already."

Kate looked at him for a moment. "I haven't done anything that I haven't wanted to do."

Delaney nodded, conflicted. "I'm sorry."

Kate looked away, embarrassed suddenly. "There's a big sofa you can sleep on."

She led him through to the lounge and Delaney sat gratefully on a wide red leather sofa.

"What are you going to do, Jack?"

"I don't know. Someone's very scared. I have to find out why."

"It all comes back to Jackie Malone?"

Delaney nodded. "Yeah, I think it does."

"Somebody murdered her. And whoever it was, someone on the force is protecting him. Setting you up for the fall."

"Looks that way."

"I hope you find the bastards."

Delaney's eyes hardened. "Oh, I'll find them, Kate." He was lost in his own thoughts for a moment and then smiled apologetically at her. "I'll be out of your hair in the morning."

Kate looked at him and then nodded, finally, with a small smile of her own and left.

Delaney lay back on the sofa, his mind dancing with thoughts he wasn't sure he wanted to be having. This wasn't a time to be getting emotionally involved with someone. And he knew that that was exactly what it was. It wasn't about sex. If it was, he'd already have been in Kate's bed. He'd lied to her earlier about Jackie Malone. They were more than just friends; he had slept with her. Not often, but every now and again, when enough Guinness and whiskey had chased the guilty thoughts of his wife out of his turbulent and troubled brain, he had visited her and they had slept together. And she had written about it in her diary. But they were just friends, there was no emotional context at all apart from that. They could talk, they could relate to each other and they could have sex without it meaning a damn thing. Until the next morning, of course, when Delaney would wake with more than a hangover. He'd wake with the guilt returning tenfold. Guilt that made his stomach cramp and his throat gag drily. That made him hate himself all over again.

Kate coughed quietly, and Delaney snapped out of his reverie. She had returned with a duvet under her arm and a new bottle of whisky in her hand. She put the whisky on a small table and handed Delaney the duvet.

"Are you sure this is what you want?"

Delaney nodded, not meeting her eye. "Thanks."

Kate paused, then smiled and ran her fingers gently through his hair. "If you need anything, you know where I am."

She walked back to the door and Delaney called after her. "Kate."

She turned back, surprised. "Yes."

"Thanks."

"Sure."

And she left.

The nurse was a small, dark-haired woman in her early twenties with delicate, almost Oriental features. Her hands were small too, delicate again, but precise. She moved a pillow under the woman's head. The woman's eyes were closed, her breathing operated by an artificial respirator. The mechanical pumps making an obscene sound. Her body was invaded by tubes and wires, and the beat of the heart monitor sent out a contrapuntal and discordant rhythm to the respirator. She was living in form only.

Delaney stood at the bottom of the bed as the nurse finished adjusting the pillow so that the woman's dark hair fanned out neatly on it. There was no twitch beneath her eyelids, no smile tugging at the corner of her lips, and there never would be again. She was dead. All it needed was for Delaney to let them turn the machine off.

The consultant was sympathetic. "If there was any hope at all, I would advise against it, of course, but the brain stem has suffered too much damage. To all intents and purposes she is already dead."

Delaney looked at him for a long moment, scared to ask the question but needing to know the answer. "And the baby?"

The consultant shook his head sadly. "I'm sorry."

Delaney's head nodded downward as he gave permission. He couldn't hold back the tears any longer. As the obscenity of the pump ceased and the heart monitor line became still, his world went dark.

The small nurse passed him with a sympathetic look, and he wanted to reach out and hold her. To beg her to do the same for him. To pull his plug, because he couldn't bear it. He couldn't live with his wife's death, and what was more, he didn't want to. But he didn't do anything. He was powerless. Impotent. Wasted. All he could do was stand there and sob.

Delaney lay curled, almost foetus-like, on the sofa, his head twitching as in his dreams he looked down once again on the face of his wife. He could almost hear her heart slowing and stopping, the blood lying still in her veins, her breath sighing to a close, and tears fell from his eyes all over again.

Kate sat gently beside him and put her arms around him, cradling him like a child. Delaney awoke, the memories clinging to him like a physical presence, a thick cobweb of pain. Kate murmured reassurance and Delaney held her as though a hurricane might blow him away if he didn't. Kate looked into his eyes and touched a finger to his lips.

"Come to bed." She took his hand and stood up, and Jack didn't even hesitate as he let her lead him from the room.

CHAPTER
TWENTY-NINE

Kate stood under the shower. The pressure was turned to maximum but she didn't have the water as hot as she normally did. In fact there was a lot about her this morning that wasn't normal. For one thing, she was smiling quietly to herself, and for another, as she soaped her body with a sponge it was more of a caress than a scrub. She hummed as she poured shampoo into her hand and worked it through her thick tresses of hair.

She rinsed the soap clear and sang too. It was the first time she had sung in the shower for a long time. She bit her lower lip a little guiltily as flashes of memory came back.

"Tell me, Jack. Talk to me." Low, breathless, husky.

"Dig your nails in. I want to taste blood."

"Pleasure and pain, Detective Inspector. Very Catholic."

Delaney laughed, looking into her eyes, at the mischief sparking within them. "I want to remember the moment."

And Kate dug her nails into his buttocks, pulling him deeper into her. "Oh, you'll remember. I'll make sure of that."

And she set about keeping her promise.

The water pooled at Kate's feet as she leaned into the jet and caught her breath. Just remembering the night before made her hot and bothered again. Hot and bothered in the nicest possible way, and Kate shook her head at herself. Delaney was on the run. He was a wanted man. Wanted for murder. This was certainly not the time to be getting involved, or the man to be getting involved with.

She wrapped her robe around her as she walked into the kitchen and put the large enamel kettle on the range to boil; then, smiling playfully, she slipped the robe off again and walked into her bedroom.

"Time to go to work, Jack."

But Delaney already had.

Kate sighed; she should have known better.

DC Sally Cartwright was having a bad Sunday morning. Jack Delaney doing a runner meant no one was getting a day off any time soon. She sat at her desk in the CID room with her head reeling. She couldn't believe that Delaney had been arrested and was now somewhere on the loose. Maybe she hadn't been on the force long enough to develop what Bob Wilkinson called his infallible gut instinct for slags, but she knew one thing for sure, and that was that Jack Delaney was no slag. She drank her coffee thoughtfully as Bob, perched on the edge of her desk, leaned in.

"I'd watch your back if I were you, Sally."

"Why?"

"Because people reckon you were close to him."

Sally shook her head, shocked. "What are you saying?"

"Just rumours. He has got a reputation, you know."

"For Christ's sake, Bob, he's old enough to be my dad."

Wilkinson laughed. "From what I've heard, most of the women on the relief would've been banging him like a drum."

"Well he wasn't banging me, and this isn't funny, Bob."

Wilkinson nodded seriously. "I know."

"What are we going to do?"

Wilkinson shrugged. "Who was it said there's something rotten in the state of Denmark?"

"Hans Christian Andersen?"

"Whoever it was. Something in this whole set-up stinks." Wilkinson looked across as Bonner walked in at the end of the room, his face a picture of bruised pride and even more bruised flesh. "And that slag's not so squeaky either."

"You don't trust him?"

"Put it this way, love, you turn your back on him, you'd best be wearing iron knickers, you know what I'm saying?"

"I thought he was quite close to the inspector."

"Trust me. The only thing that slag is close to is his own right hand." He looked at Sally pointedly. "He'd fuck his own grandmother and her postman if he thought there was something in it for him."

Bob stood up and finished his coffee. "I'd better get back. Like I said, just watch your back."

Sally turned back to her paperwork but couldn't concentrate. She went across to open the window; the heat in the office was unbearable. She leant a little into the cool breeze as it blew through the open window, running her hand around her neck, wiping a damp palm on her skirt.

"Hot, isn't it?"

Sally turned back, startled and flustered, to see Bonner standing right next to her.

"Yeah."

He leaned in and spoke quietly. "You heard anything from Jack?"

Sally shook her head.

"The damn fool. What's he playing at?"

Sally looked at the bruising spoiling Bonner's normal good looks. "I'm guessing you're not too happy with him?"

Bonner ran a hand over his face. "I don't blame him for this."

"You don't?"

Bonner shrugged. "Maybe a little. But I would have let him go if he'd asked. He didn't need to kill us both to do it."

"You'd have let him go?"

Bonner nodded, his face a picture of sincerity. "Murder. It's not Jack's style, for Christ's sake. He's been fitted up."

"It's what a lot of us think."

"We're going to have to stick together, Sally. He needs our help."

Sally shook her head. "What can we do?"

Bonner stood up straighter as Diane Campbell walked into the room, her face thunderous. He lowered his voice. "I'll let you know. But if he gets in touch, tell him I want to see him."

"Bonner. My office, now," Campbell barked at him.

Sally watched as Bonner walked across to Campbell's office. As he closed the door she pulled out her mobile phone and looked at a text message. She stood for a moment or two in indecision, then, making her mind up, snatched her jacket off the back of her chair and hurried out of the office.

Kate was sitting at her desk, trying to work but unable to concentrate, when her mobile rang. She snatched it up and frowned angrily at the withheld number, then answered it. "Kate Walker?"

"Kate, it's Delaney."

"Jack, where the hell did you go?"

"Sorry."

"Sorry? For Christ's sake, do you know how I felt?"

"I didn't want you to get involved."

"And you thought fucking me was the best way to achieve that, did you?"

"It wasn't like that."

"Then what was it like? I had to check my bedside cabinet to see you hadn't left a couple of twenty-pound notes behind."

"Kate . . ."

"My name's not Jackie Malone, you know."

"I didn't want you getting hurt."

Kate snorted angrily. "Good job!"

"It's your career. You can't afford to be associated with me. Not right now. I just wanted to do the right thing."

"Then don't patronise me, Jack. I want to help." There was long pause and Kate could hear Delaney breathing, thinking.

"Okay."

"Okay? Is that it?"

"Yeah, Okay."

Kate smiled. Damn the man.

Half an hour later, Kate was looking out of a wooden-framed window on to a picture of English tranquillity. Lush green grass, sedate willows lining ordered and well-tended gravel paths. Somewhere a fountain tinkled and Kate could imagine the cool water in the air, giving gentle relief from the relentless sun. In the centre of the park was a small lake with a semicircle of trees behind it, and splashing on the water was a family of moorhens. It was a beautiful spot to spend eternity, she thought.

She turned back to the caretaker who looked after the cemetery. "It's a lovely place, Mr Hoskins."

The caretaker nodded. "I try and keep it nice."

"You do it very well."

"People don't get the respect they deserve in life, do they?"

Kate shook her head in agreement. "Not often. Not in this world."

"So when they die and come here, I like to think they all get respect. At least they do from me."

"And Jack Delaney's grateful for it?"

"He always brings fresh flowers. Always leaves a little something in the donations box. He doesn't think anyone sees, but I do. I see everything."

"I can imagine."

"I don't spend it on myself. Now and again I buy flowers for them as don't get any visitors."

"That's good of you."

He grimaced. "Yeah, well, no one's going to be putting any flowers on my grave, miss."

Kate gave him a small smile. "You're absolutely certain of the date?"

"Positive. I never forget a date. It goes with the job really. Spend all my day looking at them."

Kate nodded gratefully. If Delaney was here grieving for his dead wife all day long, then he couldn't have been in Ladbroke Grove murdering a prostitute. "I might need you to make a statement later."

"I've already done that."

Kate looked back at him, surprised. "I'm sorry?"

"At the nick. One of your sergeants, he's got my written statement."

"Which one?"

"Can't remember his name, arrogant little cockerel."

Kate nodded again gratefully, pretty sure who he was referring to.

Outside in her car, Kate hesitated for a moment, flipping her mobile phone round in her hand. She watched as a young couple came and placed a bunch of flowers by a small memorial marker, then made a decision. She thumbed the number in quickly and set her jaw firmly as the call was answered.

"Superintendent Walker, please."

There are all kinds of secret places in London. Buildings hidden away in the labyrinths of old cul-de-sacs and dead ends that lie moments away from the main thoroughfares. The Church of Saint Mary is one such place. A small gothic church, with its own walled garden, set back at the top end of a cul-de-sac just a stone's throw from the middle of Oxford Street, but, as the morning services had finished, it was as quiet now as a building can be in London.

The sun still beat down, as relentless as it had been all summer. Dazzling the pavements with light and melting the tarmac of the roads, so that the tarry smell hung in the air like a modern-day smog. But inside the church it was cool. As cool as a mountain stream and a menthol cigarette. As cool as a Martini served dirty in a New York cocktail bar. But still Delaney sweated, and it wasn't the fact that he was wearing his leather jacket that moistened his neck and sent small beads of perspiration running from his broad forehead to drip into his eyes and along his nose. It was the church itself. He tasted the sweet saltiness of his own sweat and dragged his coat sleeve across his brow. Ever since he was a child, churches had unsettled him. He had a rational mind, but he nonetheless felt a tangible presence whenever he was in a church. He didn't think it was God. In Delaney's opinion, God was just as likely to be in a hotel bedroom, or a supermarket, or a bowling alley as in a church. Given the amount of horror perpetrated on a daily basis in His name, it was perhaps more likely that He *wouldn't* be in a church, or a mosque, or a synagogue.

Delaney looked around the small, beautifully constructed church with its sweeping stone pillars and exquisite carvings, its Renaissance paintings and heart-breaking realistic statuary, and felt the weight not of the presence of God, but of his own ever-present guilt.

He closed his eyes in silent thought for a moment or two, lost in unbearable memories. So lost that he didn't notice the figure slide quickly into the pew next to him and press something into the side of his ribs.

Startled, he opened his eyes to see Sally sitting beside him. He looked down as she pulled back the mobile phone with which she had just prodded him.

"You trying to give me a heart attack?"

"I thought you were asleep."

Delaney looked at her, and then laughed. His voice echoing around the small church like a rude intrusion. "Christ, Sally. I think you just put ten years on my life."

Sally looked around, shocked. "Don't, sir."

"Don't what?"

"Blaspheme."

"Blasphemy is the least of my problems."

"Still, sir. You know. In a church."

"Don't tell me you're a Catholic too?"

"Church of Scotland, sir."

Delaney looked at her, surprised. "I didn't know you were Scottish."

"On my dad's side. I grew up in north-west London. Went to church there. St John's. Run by an ex-padre, reminds me a lot of you."

"How?"

"He could be an irreligious bastard at times too, sir. And he liked a drop of whisky."

Delaney laughed again, gently this time. "Well, I do thank God for you, Sally, that's all I say."

Sally looked at him, suddenly serious. "What are you going to do?"

"What I do best."

"What's that?"

"Fuck things up regally."

Sally took his hand. "That's rubbish, sir. You're the best detective on the squad."

"And who says that?"

"You do."

Delaney smiled.

"And so do I."

Delaney looked at her. "How long have you been a detective constable?"

"Maybe it's just a week. But it's long enough to know the truth when I see it."

Delaney patted her hand gratefully. "So what have you got for me?"

"My dismissal, probably." She reached into the inside pocket of her jacket and pulled out a sheet of paper.

"My best guess is that the woman who called you about the DVD was Karen Richardson. A prostitute who used to work with Jackie Malone. They were busted together in a massage parlour out in Cricklewood some years back."

"You got an address?"

"I'm working on it."

"I need to know where she is, Sally. It's really important."

Sally sighed, frustrated. "I'm doing the best I can, but it's very hard with everyone watching me. I'm just a constable. They catch me . . ."

"I know. You're putting your career on the line for me, and I'm grateful."

Sally shook her head. "I'm just doing what I signed up to do. You're not the bad guy, boss."

"I'm glad someone believes me."

"You've still got a lot of friends on the force."

Delaney took the piece of paper. "Nobody else knows about her?"

Sally shook her head. "But Bonner —"

Delaney interrupted her sharply. "You didn't tell him this?"

"No."

Delaney nodded, relieved. "Good."

"But he wants to help."

"What did he say to you?"

"Just that, that he wants to help."

"You told him you were meeting me?"

"No, but I guess he worked out you might get in touch with one of us."

Delaney took her shoulders, looking into her eyes so she could see how serious he was. "This stays between you and me for now. Okay?"

"Of course, sir."

"And don't call me sir. If I get back on to the force after this little lot, I'll be lucky to be a uniformed constable."

"He said that if you got in touch, he wants to see you." She paused. "I don't think you should do it. I don't think he can be trusted."

"Oh, I think he can be trusted all right." Delaney smiled, but it had all the warmth of a dead man's hand. He took out his phone and hit Bonner's number on speed dial.

CHAPTER
THIRTY

Bill Hoskins walked over to the gas ring he kept in his maintenance hut, flicked a match to light the gas and put the kettle on. Some minutes later, he was settled in his armchair with a mug of tea, some Rich Tea biscuits and a book. He was reading *The Moonstone* by Wilkie Collins. It was a long book, longer than most he read, but he loved a good mystery and he liked to take a page or two on his tea breaks.

A short while later, his tea finished, the book lay flapping open in his lap. In the summer heat he had gently nodded off to sleep. He was awakened by the sound of the door opening.

"Hello?"

He squinted into the bright sunlight spilling into the room and he could tell that it wasn't the attractive young lady who had come to see him earlier in the day, as he'd hoped, but someone entirely different. He sighed, irritated. "What do you want?"

As the shot rang out, he had his answer. He opened his mouth to protest, but the words died with his breath on his lips. He slumped back in his chair, the book falling to the floor. Bill Hoskins never would get to find out who had stolen the Moonstone. He'd taken his last page.

Kate sat nervously in her car, parked on a double yellow line. She looked at her watch and drummed her fingers on the steering wheel. Further down the street she could see a traffic officer slowly walking along the line of illegally parked cars. Where was Delaney? And what the hell was she doing anyway? She was a forensic pathologist, for goodness' sake, not Tonto to Jack Delaney's Lone Ranger. What was she doing running around London trying to find a murderer?

The traffic officer looked across pointedly at Kate and she swore under her breath and turned the engine over, pulling back into the traffic just as Delaney came out of the church carrying a small overnight bag. She stopped, ignoring the angry honks from behind, and leaned over to open the door for him. The traffic officer watched as Delaney opened the boot of the car and put his bag inside. He closed the boot and walked slowly forward. The officer's gaze was lingering a little too long for Kate's comfort.

"For God's sake get in, Jack. That copper's looking at you."

Jack got into the car, pulling the door closed behind him. "He's just Traffic."

"He might well be, but your face has been all over the place."

Kate floored the accelerator and headed into Oxford Street. "Where to?"

"Angel."

"What's there?"

"Eddie Bonner. I just spoke to him."

Kate looked across, concerned. "Do you think that's particularly wise after what I just told you about the caretaker's statement?"

Delaney shrugged. "I guess we'll find out."

Head north from King's Cross towards Holloway, up a long, busy hill lined with scruffy warehouses and aluminium-roofed offices, and after about half a mile or so you get to Angel tube station. Turn right and you are in Islington proper, if proper is the word. Delaney could remember when the area was in two halves. On one side of the divide lived the poor and on the other the rich, like a line had been drawn across the road. That had all changed now, since the late eighties and early nineties, from the Angel tube station all the way down the main road past the King's Head and beyond was the world of the chic and the sleek. Designer pubs crammed in with trendy restaurants and bistros. Chain bars that catered to the nouveaux hoorays, like the Slug and Lettuce, All Bar One and the Pitcher and Piano, had replaced the old Islington that Delaney remembered. Not that he didn't still have a drink in the King's Head when he got a chance, where you were as likely to share a pint with an Irish fiddle player as with a long-haired drug dealer with dreams of rock stardom that had long since crashed and burned. There was something about the untouched nature of the place that Delaney took to, and if it was an affectation that they still rang up the sales on an old-fashioned till with the amounts demanded in l.s.d. — the currency, not the drug — then it was a small price to pay for a little defiance amidst the ravages of progress.

Much as he might have wanted to, Delaney didn't tell Kate to turn right as they reached the top of the hill. She turned left past the Angel tube station and then right, off the main thoroughfare into a series of back streets that led to a bleak industrial wasteland in a matter of a few short minutes. They drove in silence until Delaney cursed colourfully as the car bucked and bounced over the uneven and broken road surface. He turned to Kate. "Sorry."

"I think we've got more to worry about than a little swearing, don't you?"

Delaney shrugged in rueful agreement and Kate laughed, a nervous laugh, a little too loud, betraying the tension coiled like an ache in her stomach.

Delaney put his hand on her knee. "It's going to be all right, Kate."

A twist or two further along the battered road led them to a series of old Victorian warehouses, long abandoned and shambled together in mutual disrepair. Kate drove slowly up to the ramshackle, slope-shouldered building that Delaney had pointed to and stopped the car.

"Be careful, Jack."

He leaned across and kissed her. "If I'm not back in ten minutes, call the police."

"Not funny."

Delaney opened his car door, and Kate put her hand on his arm. "Maybe I should come with you."

301

"I want you to stay here."

"It's a set-up. Bonner could have cleared you and he hasn't."

"You told me. Just keep an eye on the building. Anybody comes in after me, you phone, all right? That's all you have to do."

Delaney got out of the car and walked around to the boot. He popped the lid open and unzipped his overnight bag, moving some clothing aside to reveal a cloth-wrapped object hidden at the bottom. He picked it up, unwrapped it and hefted it in his hand. An unregistered gun he had had for about four years now. He checked it was loaded, even though he knew full well it was, and laid it across his left thigh as he shut the boot and walked across to the warehouse door. He stopped at the entrance, looked around the corner and then walked in.

It was dark inside and it took a moment or two for his eyes to adjust. As his vision slowly returned, he could see the place was a very old building in complete disrepair. It was partly demolished, and a series of half-destroyed rooms led mazelike to a big open area. Crumbling walls, garishly streaked with different-coloured paint, spread out erratically into the distance. Upper levels visible through collapsed floors. It was like the ruins of a modernist castle. On one wall a futuristic soldier with a bare chest and improbable muscles and armed with a hand-held rocket launcher had been painted above a garish slogan written in large blood-red letters: "PAINTBALL 3000 — SURVIVAL HURTS". The different-coloured paints splattered on the walls now made sense to Delaney. The post-apocalyptic effect had clearly been designed with the local yuppie market in mind. War games for young professionals letting off steam by pretending to blow ten degrees of shit out of each other. Delaney smiled at the irony. A few miles down the road, the disaffected, drug-dealing youth were doing it for real.

Delaney made his way slowly through the series of rooms. Placing his feet carefully so as not to dislodge the randomly scattered piles of old brick and masonry. It was clear that there were plenty of places for the paintballers to lay an ambush, and Delaney felt the small hairs on the back of his neck rise as he moved from one area to the next.

He put his back against a wall and called out.

"Bonner!" His voice echoed around the cavernous spaces.

"I'm over here."

As Delaney edged cautiously around the wall, the sound of a brick falling came from behind him. He dropped into a crouch and scowled when he saw that it was Kate. He held up a hand to get her to stay where she was and put a finger to his lips. Kate nodded, but walked slowly up to him and whispered in his ear.

"I couldn't just wait in the car."

Delaney glared at her and whispered angrily, "Well wait here. I mean it."

Bonner called out. "What are you doing, Jack?"

"I'm making sure there isn't a scope with my head in its sights."

"I'm on my own here. I came to help, for Christ's sake. There's things you need to know."

Delaney made a stay gesture to Kate and raised his gun. Kate shook her head, disapproving, but didn't say anything. Delaney moved slowly away from her and looked around the corner of the wall, then walked up to the open area where Bonner stood with his jacket off and a gun held in his right hand.

"I came alone, Cowboy."

Delaney looked around, the gun sweeping in his hand.

"There's only me. You can put that away."

"I should just take your word for that, should I?"

"I'm here, aren't I?"

"What's it all about, Eddie?"

"Like I said. Things that you don't know, Jack. Things that happened."

"You going to tell me?"

"That's why I'm here."

Delaney nodded him for him to continue. "I'm listening."

Bonner stepped closer. "It's just a question of being in the wrong place at the wrong time. They needed a fall guy and everybody knew you were banging Jackie Malone. Didn't take a genius to put your name in the frame."

"Who is it, Eddie?"

"They told me that Jackie's death was an accident. You know she choked to death."

"Go on."

"But they'd have killed her anyway. I didn't know everything that was involved. I didn't know about the kids, Jack, I swear that. And I know it wasn't you that took the cocaine from evidence."

"You?"

Bonner shrugged with a guilty smile. "I was caught at it a long time ago. Deals were made. People took their cut. You know how these things work."

"Not in my world, Eddie."

"So I had to do what I was told. Things are getting way out of hand, though . . ."

"Who is it, Eddie? Who told you to cover up the caretaker's statement?"

"You've got loose lips in your camp, Jack. You should know who to trust."

"What are you talking about?"

"I'm talking about Kate Walker. She's a regular little canary."

Delaney shook his head, taken aback. "That's ridiculous." He fought the urge to look back at Kate.

"I'll tell you everything, but I need to know you'll cover me. I'm out of my league here, Jack, but we can help each other."

Delaney could hear the desperation in his voice. "Put the gun down then and let's talk."

Bonner held his gun steady. "I need insurance first."

A shot rang out like the crack of a bone, bouncing around the half-demolished walls, and echoing into silence. A spurt of blood fountained. Delaney gasped soundlessly with the sudden shock of it, his knees bent and he dropped towards Bonner.

The second shot rang out as Delaney cradled Bonner in his arms, pulling him back behind the wall. The bullet smashed into Bonner's outstretched leg and he spasmed soundlessly.

Kate took Delaney's arm and pulled him around the corner as a third bullet gouged concrete from the floor. Delaney propped Bonner against the paint-splattered wall. His face was as pale as porcelain, and he held a hand to the hole in his head, letting the blood trickle through his fingers like warm soup.

Delaney leaned in. "Jackie Malone. Who killed her, Eddie?"

Bonner swallowed drily. "Kevin Norrell." He looked at his fingers, at the viscous liquid staining them, and back up at Delaney, the confusion painful in his eyes. "Is it real?"

Then he slumped forward, his mouth gaping, his eyes open but seeing nothing in this world. Kate knelt beside him, propping his head and feeling for a pulse.

A brick fell from the upper level, crashing to the floor below, and Delaney whipped his head round. A door slammed upstairs. Delaney stood up, his eyes cold with fury. Kate grabbed his arm but he shook it off.

"Wait here."

Delaney sprinted across the open space to a wrought-iron staircase on the other side. He held the gun forward and ran up the stairs into a large empty room. Some sunlight slanted in through the filthy windows that lined one of the walls. The floor was rotten, rain-spoiled planking ripped half up, and in places whole gaps where the floor below could clearly be seen. To the left a door hung half on its hinges, leading to a darkened corridor beyond. Ahead was another closed door. Coming to a decision, Delaney ran across the room and charged the door open. He flew into the next room, skittering on the bare wooden floor. It was empty except for an open door that swung on to an outside staircase. Delaney could hear the sound of a car being driven away at speed, but by the time he reached the doorway it was gone.

He walked back down the stairs to where Kate was waiting by Bonner's inert body.

Kate watched him, shaken, as he put the gun in his jacket pocket. "Have you got a licence for that?"

Delaney ignored the question. "What did he mean about you selling me out?"

Kate shrugged. "I spoke to Bob Wilkinson, Jack. But I can't believe he would set you up."

Delaney looked down at Bonner. "Nor can I. And Eddie Bonner would lie as easily as breathe."

He watched impassively as Kate checked Bonner's pulse once more. "He's not going to do either again."

"There's no chance?"

Kate shook her head. "Do you think he set you up? Was the shot meant for you?"

"Not the first one. No, I think he was telling the truth, he got seriously out of his depth. They followed him, planned to take both of us out."

"Who's Kevin Norrell?"

"Pond scum out of west London, hired muscle mainly."

"And he's behind all this?"

Delaney shook his head. "He hasn't got the brains. He's just an animal for rent."

Kate stood up and dusted her trousers. In the distance, the faint wail of a police siren could be heard.

"We can't stay here."

"Come on." Delaney took her hand and led her quickly towards the exit.

"Where are we going?"

"West."

CHAPTER
THIRTY-ONE

Emerald Cabs was a seedy outfit based in Northwood Hills, a run-down, one-horse town west of London, out on the Metropolitan line. Stuck between Pinner and Northwood proper, it was a shabby, halfway kind of place with no real identity, something 'twixt and 'tween. It used to be a kind of breakwater, to the tide of London but the growing spread of housing development had pushed brick, steel and pollution further and further out, breaking though Northwood Hills to wash the flotsam and jetsam of modern London into Northwood and the green belt that lay beyond.

The office of Emerald Cabs was functional but scruffy. As much a front as a legitimate business. They did have a small fleet of cars, nothing luxurious, and a handful of disgruntled drivers who drove them. But Norrell didn't rely on the cab firm's turnover to keep him in pig product and beer, he earned his keep mainly through debt-collecting and hurting people. They say if you are good at something it's usually because you like doing it, and Kevin Norrell certainly liked hurting people.

He sat in front of a battered pine desk at the far end of the office, his grotesquely enlarged legs stretched out on a chair in front of him. He was dressed in baggy shorts and a cut-off T-shirt that revealed massive biceps and forearms. His face was red, flushed with the heat and marked with a permanent rash of angry acne. He had a large Wimpy hamburger in one hand and a thick milkshake in the other. Two similar-size burgers waited in a brown bag on the desk. He took a bite and smiled. Norrell was a man of simple tastes, and stuffing a half-pound cheeseburger into his face was pretty much at the top of his list of most pleasurable experiences. A bag of golf clubs stood in the corner, but it was a long time since he had played the game; walking long distances was not an option with his build. He took another bite of his burger, nearly finishing it, and sat back grunting with pleasure in his chair.

Delaney watched him through the filthy glass outside the taxi office and turned to Kate. "Wait outside this time."

Kate nodded, seeing no point in arguing.

Norrell looked up as Delaney walked into the office. "Help you?"

Delaney could see his face altering as recognition slowly dawned on him. He put down his burger, wiping the cheesy mayonnaise from his face, and lifted his massive legs off the chair opposite him, sitting upright.

"What are you doing here?"

"What do you think I'm doing here, Kevin?"

"Fuck knows."

"You want to think about it a little? I know you haven't got a lot to work with there."

310

"No. I want you to get the fuck out of my office. You got no business here, Delaney."

"That's Detective Inspector Delaney to you."

"And it's suck my cock to you."

Delaney smiled. "You and I need to have a little talk."

"I've got nothing to say to you."

"Nothing to say about Jackie Malone?"

Norrell's eyes flicked nervously sideways.

"Or Billy Martin."

Norrell stood up, his shoulders dropping, his face shifting into animal meanness.

"I don't know what you're talking about. Now get the fuck out of my office."

"Or what?"

"I heard Jackie Malone was hurt real bad. Be a shame if that was to happen to you or your pretty lady friend outside."

Delaney looked across at the window to see Kate watching them both.

"Nice bit of cunt like that. Be a shame to see it all sliced up."

Delaney stepped forward, picking the telephone off the desk in one smooth movement and smashed it with full force into Norrell's face. Norrell cried out in pain as his front teeth broke and blood poured into his mouth. He shook his head, astonished, and reared above Delaney, who punched him as hard as he could in the stomach. It was like punching a bag of concrete that had been left out in the rain and then in the sun for a week. He might as well have hit him with a limp balloon. Norrell didn't even react, just slapped Delaney on the side of his head with his open palm. A red light exploded in Delaney's brain as he staggered back, his legs suddenly weakened. Norrell followed him in a lumbering waddle, his thighs so large he couldn't walk without them rubbing together. Delaney shook his head clear and jabbed out with a punch to Norrell's bloody chin, snapping the large man's head back but not rocking him off his axis. Norrell swung a meaty fist at Delaney's face and Delaney ducked under it, punching out again at Norrell's chin. Norrell just grunted and spat more blood on the floor.

"You're starting to piss me off now."

"You were taking shots at us an hour ago, you dumb prick. What am I supposed to do, bake you a cake?"

Norrell looked at him. "I haven't been anywhere near you. I've been here all day."

Delaney kicked at Norrell's knee, knocking him off balance, and Norrell gasped with pain as Delaney punched him as hard as he could in the temple. It should have put him on the floor. It didn't. He stood up and staggered forward, enveloping Delaney in a bear hug. Delaney snapped a couple of punches at Norrell's head but he couldn't get any force behind them and Norrell started to squeeze. Delaney felt as if he had been caught in some kind of industrial vice. He struggled as he felt his ribs constricting and the air being forced from his body. His punches became feebler as he felt his consciousness draining. He grunted, drawing in some oxygen, and summoning his last ounces of energy, slammed his knee up into

Norrell's groin. Norrell grunted a little, but didn't relinquish his boa constrictor grip. Just my luck, thought Delaney, as a blackness started to descend and he felt himself passing out. Norrell's balls must have shrivelled to nothing after years of steroid abuse; probably didn't feel a thing.

Suddenly Norrell let out a cry and stepped back, his arms opening, dropping Delaney gasping to his knees. Norrell looked even more puzzled than usual as Kate swung the golf club again, a three wood, gripping it low on the shaft like a baseball bat and smashing it with a sickening crack into his temple, dropping him to the floor like a bull elephant hit with a stun gun. The floor shuddered and Delaney, still gasping for breath, looked up at Kate.

"Where did you learn to play golf?"

Kate knelt down and put her fingers to Norrell's neck. "He's still alive."

"Not going to be able to answer a lot of questions, though, is he?"

"Was that what you were doing, interrogating him?"

"Yeah."

"Interesting technique."

"I could have got him to talk."

Kate smiled tolerantly. "You'd rather I'd let you finish the fight?"

Delaney winced again as he got to his feet. "I guess not. Thanks."

Kate put the club back into the golf bag propped against the wall. "What are we going to do with him?"

"Put him in the car."

"What with? A fork-lift truck?"

Delaney looked at the prostrate figure. "Good point." He walked across and searched through Norrell's jacket thrown over the back of a chair. Nothing. He looked in the desk's single drawer, taking out a stubby revolver, smelling the barrell before placing it on the desk, then searched through the papers in the drawers.

Kate knelt down to check Norrell's pulse again. "He might be badly hurt, Jack."

"Be a bonus."

"I'm serious. He needs to get to a hospital."

Delaney slammed the drawers shut. "And I need to know who he's working for." He wasn't sure what it was he was hoping to find, but whatever it was, he hadn't found it. He wasn't surprised, just annoyed.

Kate looked at Norrell, a trail of drool pooling on his lower lip. "How do you know him?"

"I busted him on a drugs-dealing charge a short while back."

"And?"

"Cocaine, good quality. We took him down with about a key of the stuff."

"So why isn't he safely locked up?"

"Because the evidence went missing. That's what Bonner was talking about. He took it. The CPS wouldn't proceed and rhinoceros boy here walked free."

Delaney's mobile rang and he looked at the caller's number before answering it.

"What have you got?" He listened intently to the reply. "You've found her?" He looked across at Kate

and smiled. "You're a star, Sally. I owe you big time."
He shut his phone up and checked that the telephone
he had smashed into Norrell's teeth was still working. It
was. Score one for petroleum by-products. He handed
it to Kate. "Call an ambulance."

"Then what?"

"Then we're out of here."

"Out where?"

"To see a tom."

"Tom who?"

Delaney smiled as Kate dialled 999. "A tom is a
brass, Kate. A prostitute."

"Any particular reason?"

"Because she just might know what the hell's going
on."

The traffic not so much crawled as stumbled and
wheezed round Cambridge Circus. Like sick, broken
and arthritic creatures, automotive elephants following
a trail of pitch and tar to a secret graveyard. The
temperature was now over thirty-eight degrees,
breaking all records for the time of year. The tarmac on
the road was melting and the vehicles' tyres stuck
slightly to it as they inched nose to tail from
Shaftesbury Avenue down to Covent Garden.

Delaney led Kate past the theatre that stood on the
circus, past one of the pubs that Jeffrey Bernard
frequently got unwell in and up to a doorway next to
another small minicab office. There were a couple of
tacky coloured signs offering a variety of exotic
services. What was it about cab offices and prostitutes?

Delaney wondered. A fat tourist stopped to watch as Kate looked at the notices, a bead of sweat rolling down his forehead as he gazed at her like a starving man might look at a joint of beef.

"What's Greek?" she asked Delaney.

Delaney glared at the fat man, who was reddening even more in the face, his mouth hanging open as he watched Kate. Delaney took Kate's arm and steered her through the doorway. "Let's just say it's not a lunch option."

The hall was narrow and stifling; the heat trapped inside radiated off the walls like an oven. There were no carpets on the floor, although the two-toned wood showed where carpet had once been, and it looked like the wallpaper hadn't been changed since the mid-seventies. A half-eaten McDonald's meal was thrown in one corner, and the air was rich with the scent of cheap perfume and even cheaper air freshener.

Kate picked her way delicately as she followed Delaney up the narrow staircase to the second floor. Delaney pushed the button next to a colourful yellow card that had the name Aisleyne written on it, with the legend "Blonde and Busty" below.

Muffled footsteps were heard behind the door, and then a voice.

"I'm busy. Come back in twenty minutes."

The footsteps receded again and Delaney leaned on the buzzer, letting it ring. The footsteps came back, as did the voice, angrier this time.

"I said I was busy."

The door opened to reveal a woman in her early thirties, surgically enhanced to prove one part of her advertising slogan, with a straw-coloured wig on her head to prove the other.

"Hello, Karen."

Karen sighed, recognising Delaney. "Fuck."

She tried to close the door, but Delaney slammed his foot in the gap, shouldered the door open and pushed her back inside with the palm of his hand. Kate followed them in and shut the door behind her.

Delaney glared at Karen. "We can do this the easy way, but one way or the other you are going to talk to me."

Karen sighed. "All right, Delaney. You win. Not here; come through to the kitchen."

They turned down the corridor, passing a bedroom door on the right, and into a kitchen area where a small television was showing some daytime reality show. A door led off it. The room was sparsely decorated with faded, torn wallpaper and some small, functional units; a hot plate for a kettle, a fridge for some cans of beer. Not a kitchen for a chef, but perfect for a forty-pound-a-blow-job tart, thought Delaney.

A long-haired man in his forties with two days' worth of stubble and a Motorhead T-shirt sat at the table rolling a joint. His face had the kind of pale sickliness found in grubs that live under rocks; it was wrinkled and spotted with blackheads. He looked up, outraged, as Delaney turned off the television.

"The fuck you think you're doing? I'm watching that."

Delaney glared at him. "Take a break."

"You what?"

Karen nodded towards the door. "Do what he says, Daniel."

"I'm not having some Irish prick tell me what to do."

"It's me that's telling you. Go on, give us ten minutes."

The man stood up and glared belligerently at Delaney. "You got ten minutes." Delaney held his stare until Daniel turned away and headed out of the kitchen. "He give you any grief over this and you tell me. Okay, Karen?"

"He won't do anything."

"Either way."

Karen turned back to Delaney as the man left. "What are you doing here, Inspector?"

"You know why I'm here."

"No I don't." She looked over at Kate as if seeing her for the first time. "And who's the bint?"

"Be nice, Karen."

Karen was about to respond when a small man in spectacles, wearing a short-sleeved shirt and a neatly knotted tie, came into the kitchen.

"What's going on?"

Karen nodded at him angrily. "Get back in the room, I'll be through shortly."

The small man shook his head angrily. "That's not good enough. I've paid my money."

Delaney stepped towards him. "Why don't you take a hint and leave?"

The man shook his head. "I paid my money. I want my service."

Delaney pulled out his warrant card. "Maybe you'd like to be serviced down at White City."

The man bristled, his red eyes tightening behind the steel frame of his spectacles.

"You can't do that. The nature of my business transaction with Aisleyne here is perfectly legal and you know it. I'm going to take your name and report you." He looked across at Kate and smiled. "Unless of course this other one is available."

Delaney would have moved towards him but Karen stepped forward, reaching into her pocket, and stuffed some notes into his hand.

"Come back later, Reginald. Give me half an hour."

"I can't come back later. I've got work to do."

"Do you want me to tell Marjorie?"

The small man paled and seemed to deflate somehow.

"There's no need to be nasty."

Karen smiled. "I'll make it up to you."

"How?"

"I'll do the egg custard, no surcharge."

The small man nodded, pleased, and made his way out into the corridor.

Delaney gestured towards Kate as the front door shut. "This is Kate Walker. She's a colleague."

Karen shrugged. "So why are you here?"

"Don't be stupid. You know what we're here for."

"She don't look the type."

"Don't fuck me around, Karen. I can make your life a whole lot more miserable than that loser pimp of yours."

"He's not my pimp."

Kate uncrossed her arms. "You phoned him, Karen. You obviously want to help."

Karen shook her head.

"I don't want to get involved, Delaney. People are getting hurt all around you. I don't want to end up like Jackie Malone or her lowlife brother."

"That's not going to happen."

Karen shook her head, conflicted.

Delaney leaned in. "It's your choice. You tell me everything you know and I put a stop to this. If you don't, you could be next on their list."

"They don't know about me."

"I found out about you. You willing to take a chance they won't?" He reached into his pocket and pulled out a six-by-four photo of Jackie Malone's mutilated body. "You want to end up like this."

"For Christ's sake, Delaney, you've made your point. Put that away."

"Start talking then."

Karen sighed and picked up the cigarette papers from the table and a small bag of grass. "Jackie's boy, Andy."

"Go on?"

"It's all to do with him." Karen started rolling a joint. "He was supposed to be with his uncle. Only he wasn't. They had a falling-out. He came back to London."

"But he didn't go back to his mum?"

"No. You know what Andy's like."

"Yeah, he's thirteen years old."

"Anyway, he had mates. A whole bunch of them living in a squat up Finchley Road. All ages."

"And?"

"And he used to work the begging game. On the streets, down on the tubes. Billy used to organise it. Homeless sign, skinny dog, borrowed baby. You know the kind of thing."

"I know the kind of thing. So Andy used to beg in the streets?"

"But one day he got picked up by a social centre."

Kate looked over at her. "What social centre?"

Karen shrugged. "Looked after stray kids. Not your usual wagman, though."

"Wagman?" Kate asked.

Delaney waved Karen on.

"So Andy got taken to a home. Residential. Out in the country, though."

"Where in the country?"

"Somewhere near Marlow."

"Henley?"

Karen shrugged again, then lit up the joint and took a long drag on it. She held it out to Delaney, who shook his head, and then to Kate, who smiled politely.

"No thank you."

"So what was this place called?"

Karen shrugged at Delaney. "I don't know. Just a big house, somewhere between Marlow and, like you say, Henley. But the thing is. It was a set-up. A group of them, all with short eyes. They made films there."

"Short eyes?"

Karen nodded to Kate. "They liked children. Paedophiles. Nonces."

"And what happened to Andy?"

"He got away, didn't he? He's smart, that kid. Not a proper runaway like the rest of them. Christ, he's lived his whole life on the move."

"I know he's a smart kid, Karen. Are you telling me he did something stupid?"

"Yeah, he did. His uncle Billy found him and made him tell him all about it."

"And Billy thought he'd earn out of it?"

"Yeah. Blackmail. The cocksucker. But the point is, Andy knew who one of the men was. The one who did the filming. Alexander Moffett. His mum and I were in a porn film he made."

Delaney nodded, picturing her in a black wig and industrial levels of make-up. "Melody Masters. *Sin Sisters*. Right?"

Karen nodded. "That's right. She'd taken Andy to the set once, kept him in the car, and he saw Alex Moffett. So he knew where he was based."

She took another nervous drag on her joint. "Jackie didn't want anything to do with it, though, Jack. And neither do I. These people . . ."

"Where is he, Karen?"

"Who?"

"Andy. Where is he?"

"He doesn't want anything to do with you." She glanced over at Kate. "With any of you."

"You saw what they did to his mother."

Karen nodded, scared. "You reckon you can help him?"

"Yes, Karen. I can."

Karen looked over her shoulder at the closed door by the cooker, opposite the one they had walked in through. She took another long drag on her joint, her eyes glazing slightly but not so much as to mask the fear that lurked in them.

Delaney walked over to the door and opened it. Behind it was a bathroom, and standing in it was a boy with dark curly hair. Delaney immediately recognised him, just as he had when he had seen the film he had been sent. The dark-haired boy abusing a much younger girl. Jackie's son. Andy Malone.

Andy glared at Delaney as he walked into the kitchen, his head held high. "I ain't coming in with you."

"What's going on, Andy?"

"Why don't you ask your boss?"

"Who?"

Andy looked at him for a moment. "Don't tell me you don't know. That pervert Moffett's partner. One of yours, Delaney. Captain Scarface. Why don't you ask him?"

Delaney nodded, his face suddenly darkening like a front of bad weather. He looked across to Kate, who, despite the humid, sweltering heat in the squalid kitchen, had lost all the colour in her own face, and Delaney remembered what Bonner had said about someone on his team having loose lips.

CHAPTER
THIRTY-TWO

Delaney pulled his seatbelt around himself, jerking angrily as it stuck in its mechanism, and looked across at Kate.

"What did you tell Walker, Kate?"

"Just that I'd spoken to the caretaker. That he could give you an alibi for the . . ." she looked back at Andy as he glared at her from the back seat of the car, "for the day of the incident."

Andy squirmed uncomfortably and leaned forward between her and Delaney, his dirty face scrunched into a frown.

"Where you taking me?"

Delaney looked back at him. "We've got a visit to make first, and then we'll take you somewhere you'll be safe for a while. Now sit back and put your seatbelt on."

The boy snorted. "Fuck off." He sat back on the seat. "What are you going to do, arrest me?"

Kate smiled soothingly in the rear-view mirror. "It's going to be all right, Andy."

Andy snorted again. "Get real, Lady fucking Diana. You don't know the guy."

Kate looked out the window, wishing it were true.

Delaney finally gave up on his seatbelt, turned the key and gunned the engine.

The traffic was bumper to bumper once they hit the main road. It was peak rush hour; cars were overheating and being abandoned, clogging up the roads and slowing movement down to an infuriating crawl. Delaney slammed his hand angrily on the horn, joining in with a pointless chorus of honking that had absolutely no effect. He knew that the cemetery was open in the evenings for people to visit outside of work hours, but it closed at seven and there was only twenty minutes to go.

The sound of a siren joined in with the horns as an ambulance approached, heading the other way. Delaney looked out of the window, watching it pass, and then mentally slapped himself on the forehead.

"You're a doctor. You got one of those green lights, Kate?"

"Yeah, I have." She reached over to her glove box and took out her flashing green light. She opened her window and put it on the roof, and then flicked the siren on.

Delaney pulled out of the traffic, moving over to the right, and smiled approvingly as the cars ahead moved left to let them pass.

They arrived at the cemetery five minutes before locking-up time, but there was no sign of Bill Hoskins near the gates or in the parkland. They hurried down the path to the caretaker's hut, calling out his name as they approached. But there was no answer, and no sign of him. As Delaney reached the hut, he could see the door was open.

He turned back to Kate, who had a tight grip on Andy's arm. "Keep hold of him." Then he put his hand under his jacket, curling his fingers round the grip of his pistol, and walked into the hut.

There was nobody there. The armchair was empty. A book was lying face down on the floor. He looked around the hut, his professional eye sweeping round and taking it in. It was sparse but cosy. A battered upholstered wing chair. A small desk. A gas ring with an old aluminium kettle on it. A bookshelf with a number of well-read paperbacks. All mysteries, by the looks of them. Andy came into the hut, followed by Kate.

"What a dump. What are we doing here?"

"Shut it." Delaney opened the desk drawer. Inside were a number of work-related letters from the council, an address book and a home electricity bill. Delaney put the other items back in the drawer and kept the bill. It had Hoskins' address on it.

He turned round to see Kate looking closely at the armchair.

"What have you got?"

"A stain, Jack. It's small and it could be gravy or coffee . . ."

"But?"

"But I think it's blood."

Back in the car, Delaney handed the electricity bill to Kate and told her to look Bill Hoskins' road up in the A to Z. Kate flicked through the pages until she found the right one.

"It's about five minutes from here."

"Good." Delaney fired the engine up.

"What are you going to do if . . ."

"If he's still alive?"

"Yeah."

"I'm going to get him and laughing boy here somewhere safe, and then I'm going to go in."

He crunched into first gear and spun away, the gravel kicking up from his back tyres like shotgun pellets.

About fifty yards behind them, a grey Volvo pulled out of its parking space, a lot more smoothly, and headed in the same direction.

Bill Hoskins lived in a mid-terrace house built somewhere in the late Victorian era. A lot of the houses in the row were showing signs of disrepair, shabby paintwork, overgrown gardens. But Bill's was neat and orderly. His small front garden as manicured as the cemetery where he worked. Kate watched as Delaney took his finger off the bell button that he had just pushed for the fifth time, and knew with a cold certainty that Bill was never coming home. Delaney shouldered the door open and ran inside, but Kate knew there was no one waiting for him. There was going to be no one to miss Bill Hoskins. He had spent his life looking after the dead, and now his own body had been dumped somewhere, she knew it. Dumped with no ceremony, no respect. Suddenly Kate wasn't scared any more. She was angry. People were going to pay, her uncle most of all.

Wendy was a little flustered as she ushered Delaney, Kate and the boy into her kitchen. "It's a shame you missed Siobhan. She's at a friend's for her tea, but she shouldn't be too long." She lifted the lid on her large range cooker and put a kettle identical to Kate Walker's on the hob. Her hand was shaking a little so that the kettle rattled heavily.

Kate watched her. "I keep meaning to switch mine off. It's been so hot, and I could quite happily survive on salads."

Wendy looked over at her and smiled. "I know, it's been unbearable. Seems crazy to keep them on just for cups of tea." Seemed pretty crazy talking about the weather and range cookers to a strange woman in her kitchen, who had arrived with her fugitive brother-in-law and a filthy-looking child in tow too. She shook the thought away as she set out some cups and saucers and smiled reassuringly at the wild-haired youth standing next to her. The boy didn't smile back. Judging by the look in his slightly feral eyes, he probably hadn't smiled in a long, long time.

"Would you like a tea, Andy?"

"You got any lager?"

"Behave yourself," said Delaney sharply.

"Or what?"

Delaney gave him a flat look. Andy stared back at him for a moment or two and then looked away.

"Whatever."

Wendy smiled again, feeling the corners of her mouth as she forced the muscles to work.

"I've got a Coke."

Andy nodded sullenly. Wendy got a can of Coke from the fridge and handed it to Andy, who took it and sat at the kitchen table.

Delaney took his sister-in-law by the arm and led her into the hallway.

"Thanks for this, Wendy."

Wendy nodded. "It's okay."

"We'll be back for him in a couple of hours."

"What's it all about, Jack?"

"I want you to look after something for me." He pulled a letter from the inside pocket of his jacket and handed it to her.

Wendy looked at it, scanning the words quickly. "What's this? Thirty thousand pounds?"

"It's with my solicitors. It's part of a deposit for a flat. I listened to what you said the other day, and you were right. I need to have somewhere that Siobhan can stay."

"You could have kept it in the bank. You don't need cash."

"It's off the record. Keeps the amount under the next level of stamp duty."

"Isn't that illegal?"

Delaney looked at her without answering.

She nodded. "Right."

"Just keep it safe, should anything happen."

"Don't say that, Jack."

Delaney kissed her on the cheek. "It's going to be all right, Wendy."

Kate started the car and looked across at Delaney. "You sure we're doing the right thing?"

"We need to go to his house, Kate. We need proof. Something that will stand up in court. The word of that kid isn't enough. He's a thirteen-year-old child but he's already a career criminal, and a jury will see that. We need something tangible to tie your uncle in. We need hard evidence."

Kate pulled out into the road, flipping the visor down. Even at eight o'clock the sun was bright and dazzling as it dropped lower in the sky.

As their car turned left at the end of the road, out of sight, the man in the Volvo that had followed them from the cemetery earlier took off his sunglasses. The scar on his cheek throbbed a little in the heat, the white flesh becoming more and more prominent as his face grew more and more tanned. It was like scar tissue from a burn, and Superintendent Walker ran a finger subconsciously along it, stroking almost tenderly as he looked across at Wendy's house and smiled.

Kate leant on her horn as a slow-moving Range Rover blocked her path ahead. "Bloody Chelsea tractors. They should have been banned by now."

"I'd have thought they were just your thing."

"You'd have thought wrong."

"Not for the first time."

"And you a detective, too. You should know you don't judge a book by its cover."

Delaney turned amused eyes on her. "No. You've got to get between the sheets."

Kate laughed, and then her smile faded. "We're just going to break into his house?"

"Unless you've got any better ideas?"

"We should go in. Put it in the proper hands."

"I go anywhere near a police station and I'll be in a cell faster than you know it. And by the time anyone listens to you, if they ever do, your uncle will have covered all his tracks. You can be sure of that. There's no one left to testify against him except the boy."

"And Kevin Norrell."

"If he makes it."

Kate looked out of the window guiltily. It would be ironic if she had killed the one man who could have put her uncle away for good.

"Why you, Jack?"

"Why me what?"

"Why you? Why send you the tape? Why was Jackie Malone looking for you? Why are you in the middle of all this?"

"A couple of years ago, little Andy was involved in drug-dealing. Ten years old and working as a delivery man. Deals on wheels. Not uncommon nowadays."

"What kind of world are we living in?"

Delaney shrugged. "London."

Kate shifted gear, crunching the gearbox angrily.

"I was involved in his arrest. He was a kid, so there wasn't much we could do to him. They hadn't yet brought the age of criminal responsibility down to ten, but given his mother's record, he would have been taken into custody."

"What did you do?"

"I did a deal. He gave me the name of a major player and I covered up his involvement. He wasn't charged."

"I see."

"But even though he was a kid, he still put some major names in the frame. I promised Jackie I'd look out for him. She put him on the road with her older brother, a traveller, for a few years. Figured if they couldn't find him they couldn't hurt him."

Kate looked at him for a moment as they paused at a red traffic light.

"She was your friend?"

Delaney nodded angrily. "Yeah. She was my friend."

"And then Andy came back to London?"

"Yeah."

"Is it safe to leave him with Wendy and Siobhan?"

"She'll take care of him."

Kate looked at him pointedly. "I wasn't talking about Andy being safe."

Delaney shook his head. "He may be all kinds of stupid, Kate. But he's not that stupid." He pulled out his pack of cigarettes and took one out. The last one. He looked over at Kate and held it up. "Do you mind?"

"Did your wife like you smoking?"

Delaney was taken aback. If anybody else had asked that question, he would have snapped back at them that it was none of their goddam business. He didn't talk to anybody about his wife, apart from his daughter and his sister-in-law. Strangely, though, he didn't feel like making a smart defensive remark. He felt like talking to her about it. And he wasn't sure what that meant at all, apart from the fact that Kate reminded him of Sinead. Not just the looks, although the long dark hair was hers, and the intelligence in the eyes. It was more the comfort he felt with Kate now; he could be himself, and what was more surprising to him was that he did want to be himself again.

He smiled. "She asked me to give up shortly after we became engaged."

"And did you?"

"She never saw me smoke a cigarette after."

Kate laughed and said again, "And did you?"

"No. I never did." He looked thoughtfully out of the window. "Right up until the day she died."

Kate flicked a sympathetic glance sideways at him.

"I don't mind."

Delaney nodded and opened the passenger window. As it slid electronically down, the heat burst in. Delaney flicked the unlit cigarette out of the window and pushed the button to close it.

"Do you mind Siobhan staying with your sister-in-law?"

"It was the best thing for her at the time."

"And now?"

"Maybe it still is. I've been looking to buy a place of my own again."

"You're renting?"

"I sold the house. Pretty much everything in it. At the time it seemed like a good thing to do."

"You don't feel that way now?"

"You can't just sell your memories."

Kate nodded, lost in her own thoughts. "Maybe you shouldn't try."

Delaney nodded. "It was Siobhan's house too."

Kate suddenly looked back at the road. "Shit!" She flicked her indicator and pulled the car to a squealing stop at the side of the road.

"What are you doing?"

"Why weren't there any police, Jack?"

"What do you mean?"

"At Wendy's. There should have been police. Looking for you. Watching the house. We didn't see any."

"We wouldn't."

"They would have left someone somewhere, wouldn't they? Keeping surveillance."

Delaney nodded darkly. "Unless they'd been called off."

He pulled out his mobile phone. "Turn it round, Kate."

But Kate was already way ahead of him as Delaney made the call.

Wendy's eyes were wide with terror. She tried to cry out, but the best she could manage was a low whimper. She twisted her neck painfully, her face scraping on the polished oak of her hallway floor, the familiar smell of Mr Sheen clogging her nostrils. She coughed, choking as the gag in her mouth tightened, and tried to breathe deeply through her nose, willing herself not to panic, trying to calm the voice that screamed in her head. Walker looked down at her dispassionately and nodded to the boy with the thin rope in his hands.

"Tie it tighter, Andy."

Andy tightened the rope that held the gag in place and pulled Wendy's mouth into a rictus grin. Like Billy Martin and Jackie Malone, Wendy's hands and feet had been tied with coat-hanger wire, wound round and twisted hard so that it bit cruelly into her tender flesh.

Walker patted Andy fondly on the head and smiled like a teacher watching a favourite pupil apply a lesson well learned. Andy tied off the knot on the rope, careless of any discomfort he was causing Wendy.

Walker looked around angrily as the shrill ringing of the phone echoed loudly in the hallway. He looked down at the large Sabatier chef's knife he held in his hand. Twelve inches of broad steel with a solid wooden handle.

"Time to put her away, Andy."

The smile on Andy's face sent a chill through Wendy as her eyes, stark with fear, watched the steel blade rise. Roger had bought a set of them for her birthday one year. Something she had never forgiven him for. There were lots of things to forgive him for, she realised, lots of things over the years: too many golf trips with the boys, too many late business meetings, too many thoughtless comments, too many times she just wasn't noticed, or appreciated, or loved enough. Too many times she didn't feel special in his eyes. She never made her husband's eyes light up the way Delaney's did when he saw her sister, she knew that, but she loved her

335

husband in her way, and in the terror of her situation she realised that even if she wanted to forgive him all those things, there wasn't any time left.

The phone rang again. Echoing off the quarry-stoned floor of the kitchen like an alarm.

Walker slashed down with the knife. Cold. Clinical.

Delaney clicked the red button on his mobile and selected another number.

"Sally, it's Delaney. Is Walker in the building?"

"He left a while ago."

"You know where he was going?"

"He left a message for you, sir, if you phoned in."

"What message?"

"He said that before you do anything rash, you should think of your daughter. I guess he's concerned about you."

"Guess again. I think he's going to hurt Siobhan, Sally. Walker's been involved in this all along. He killed Eddie Bonner, or had him killed."

"What do you want me to do?"

"I'm going to my sister-in-law's house. You know where it is?"

"You want me to get a team down there?"

"No," he said sharply. "I don't want anything rattling him. Don't do anything till I tell you to, okay?"

"Of course, sir."

"I thought I told you not to call me sir." Delaney snapped the phone shut and looked at Kate. "Drive faster."

336

Kate floored the accelerator and charged up the bus lane, bumping cars aside, regardless of the damage to her paintwork and the outrage of the other drivers. Delaney gazed ahead, his eyes fixed, staring into a future he would not countenance.

The young girl waved goodbye to her friend, who returned the wave through the rear window of the departing car. As she stood watching and waiting for the car to disappear from view, she pulled her New York Yankees baseball cap lower on her head and sang "Clementine" quietly to herself. The cap was a present from her dad and the song was one of his favourites. He was always singing it, at least, so she presumed it was one of his favourites. And if the kids at school thought she was odd because she didn't wear a designer hat or sing the latest teeny pop idol song, she didn't care. All she cared about was making her dad happy again. Happy like he used to be when she was much younger. The memories of those times were blurred now, but she could remember his warm laughter as he hugged her mother. She could remember the smiles and the music, and now and again she saw flashes of it in his eyes when he laughed at one of her jokes or clapped when she sang him one of his favourite songs. She just wished she could put those moments on pause, like on the DVD player, and keep him happy like that for always.

The car turned the corner out of view and the young girl continued singing as she walked up the gravel path to her house, her head down, watching her feet as they scuffed through the raked stones.

The lock rattled, and Siobhan looked up, surprised to see the door open and a man standing in the hallway, smiling down at her, a wild-haired boy beside him.

"Hello?"

"Hello, Siobhan."

"You're very pretty," said the dark-haired youth, his smile revealing crooked teeth, a slash of ugly imperfection in the face of a gypsy choirboy.

Kate gunned the engine, spinning round the roundabout, cutting off someone on the inside and nearly losing control, but she was good, she righted her steering, accelerating again as she willed the traffic to part in front of her.

"Why do they do it, Jack?"

"Who?"

"People like my uncle."

"Human nature."

"It's evil. It's not human."

Delaney's eyes glittered darkly. "We're all capable of evil."

Kate glanced at him and shook her head. "You don't believe that."

"People like your uncle get hold of children like Andy and do what they do to them because people like us let them."

Kate looked angrily across at him. "Don't say that!"

"Children are left on the street like garbage and we complain when the wrong people sweep them up. We trust people in authority and we turn a blind eye when

338

that trust is abused in the worst kind of way. Teachers, policemen, social workers, priests . . ."

He trailed off. Kate flicked a glance across at him. "You sound like you're talking from experience."

Delaney didn't answer for a moment. "I live with it every day, Kate. It's my job. Cleaning up the vermin that comes crawling out of the gutters when we treat people like garbage. Vermin like Billy Martin and your uncle."

Siobhan stood in the doorway, reluctant to enter. Walker smiled at her, stroking the pad of his thumb along the scar on his cheek. "It's all right, Siobhan, my name's Superintendent Walker, I'm your daddy's boss." He pulled out his ID. "This is my warrant card. You've probably seen your daddy's, haven't you, just like this?"

Siobhan nodded and looked at the card, then back at Walker.

"Is he in trouble, then?"

Walker laughed, a big fruity laugh. "No, he's not in any trouble. Why don't you come in? This is Andy. He's a special friend of your dad's too."

Siobhan smiled, reassured. "Hello, Andy."

"Hello."

Siobhan walked into the hallway, slinging her satchel over a coat hook, and looked round, a little puzzled. "Where's Aunty Wendy?"

Andy grinned. "She's gone to the shops to get some lemonade."

Walker smiled again. "She won't be too long. Why don't you show me your room whilst we wait? I bet you've got some lovely toys."

Siobhan shrugged. "They're all right."

In the cupboard under the stairs, Wendy whimpered, tried to cry out, telling Siobhan to run, but the gag in her mouth and the rope holding it in place meant she could do no more than make a small mewing sound. She kicked her legs in frustration, but it just dug the wire deeper into her flesh and pulled the rope tighter around her neck. There was no air in the cupboard and the heat was unbearable. She struggled to get some oxygen into her lungs and failed. Her eyes widened for a moment as she heard the footsteps on the staircase above her head, and then they lost focus and closed. Soon she didn't feel the pain in her side where the knife had punched and penetrated her tender flesh; she didn't feel the cruel constriction of her tortured throat. She didn't feel anything at all.

Kate pulled the car to a screeching halt outside Wendy's house. Delaney threw his door open and jumped out, followed by Kate, who shouted after him, "Don't even think about telling me to wait out here."

Delaney nodded and headed for the door, taking a key out of his pocket as he ran.

Upstairs in Siobhan's bedroom, Walker smiled as he heard the key turn in the lock. He looked at Andy and put a finger to his lips. "Sit on the bed, Andy." Andy sat next to Siobhan, and Walker smiled at the young girl.

"Shush. That's your dad now. Let's give him a nice surprise, shall we?"

Siobhan nodded and whispered, "Daddy loves surprises."

"He's going to love this one."

Downstairs, Delaney picked up the slashed telephone cord and looked at the blood-stained Sabatier blade on the counter beside it. His daughter's scream rang out from upstairs and it felt like someone had plunged the knife into his heart. He snatched it and ran for the stairs; Kate caught his arm and whispered hoarsely, "Be careful."

Delaney shook her hand off and took the steps two at a time. Bursting into his daughter's room, he pulled up short as he saw that Walker had Siobhan held in front of him with a knife at her throat.

"Come on in, Detective Inspector."

Delaney kept his face neutral. He looked down at his daughter and spoke softly. "It's all right, pumpkin. Everything's going to be okay."

"Put the knife down, Inspector."

Delaney hesitated for a beat and then let the carving knife fall to the floor.

"Pick it up, Andy."

Andy stood up from the bed and picked up the knife.

Delaney watched him as he moved back. "You in on this, then, Andy?"

Andy shrugged. "Not to start with."

Walker nodded, his voice warm, amused. "He disappeared for a little while, but I think he's rather glad I found him again. Andy enjoyed the filming work I gave him, didn't you, son?"

"Yeah."

Delaney noticed the flat look in the young boy's eyes, and felt a chill in his soul.

"He used to help find the young stars for our films. He came and went as he pleased. Isn't that right?"

Andy nodded, and Delaney looked at him. "So what changed?"

Andy shrugged. "Uncle Billy found me. Saw I was holding some serious folding and wanted to know where I was getting it from." He smiled humourlessly. "He beat it out of me."

"The thing was, Andy knew Moffett from when his mum was making *Sin Sisters*," said Walker. "Billy went to Moffett and put the squeeze on him. Moffett hired Norrell to take care of the problem," he shrugged, "and the rest you know."

Delaney looked at the young boy. "So what now, Andy? Your mother loved you, you know. She'd have done anything to protect you."

"Which is why I had Moffett dealt with, as soon as I knew what was happening."

"So Jackie Malone's death was nothing to do with you?"

"Of course not. And Andy is a bright lad. He's learned from experience. Something it seems you're incapable of doing."

Delaney turned the full glare of his hatred back on Walker. "You think you can just walk away from all this? What do you think you're going to achieve here?"

Walker smiled thinly. "Closure, Jack. Isn't that what we are all seeking in the end?"

"Closure?"

"Because you're taking the fall, as our American cousins would say. I had information that you were keeping young Andy here against his will, and I acted on it. Isn't that right, Andy?"

Andy looked at Delaney, deadpan. "I told my mother about you and my uncle abusing me. That's why you killed them both."

"And that's why you killed Sergeant Bonner when he put two and two together. Your DNA is going to be all over him. You couldn't have been more helpful if you'd tried."

"Put the knife down, Walker, and I'll see you get help. You're a sick man."

"Because I showed affection and love? Because I cared for those kids when nobody else did?"

"Love," Delaney almost spat.

Walker was not fazed at all. "Yes, love, Delaney. Something those runaway kids never knew. Why do you think they do run away? Living on the streets like animals. We helped them. The home Moffett and our associates set up for them was the first real place they had ever felt secure."

Delaney looked over at Andy. "Is that right, Andy?"

Andy shrugged. "They were a lot better to me than my uncles ever were."

"You see, Inspector."

Delaney glared back at him. "Enough talk. Just let my daughter go now."

"All in good time."

Walker nodded at Andy. "Keep an eye on her."

Andy held the blood-stained Sabatier knife up as Walker put his own knife down on Siobhan's lilac-coloured chest of drawers. The lethal blade obscenely incongruous amongst the toy ponies and the Barbie dolls. He reached into his jacket pocket and pulled out a pistol.

"It's an unregistered gun. The one used to kill your good friend Bonner. We struggled, you died. Everything is cleared up."

Delaney looked at his daughter, his heart breaking as he saw the terror in her young eyes. "And Siobhan?"

"She'll be cared for. She won't die, I can promise you that."

"And my sister-in-law?"

"Already dealt with. You always were a violent man, Delaney. It's a matter of record."

Delaney felt the rage build inside him, felt the impotence. "Everything is disposable to you, isn't it? Nothing has a value."

"That's where you're wrong. You see, I understand what is valuable and what is not. But look at you, Delaney. You value nothing. How can you value others if you don't value yourself? You say you love your daughter, and yet you leave her to the sister of your dead wife to bring up. What kind of love is it that throws children away?"

Siobhan whimpered as Walker adjusted his grip. "Daddy?"

344

Delaney forced a reassuring smile. "It's all right, sweetheart, everything is going to be okay."

"Closure, Delaney. It's time for closure."

"Why me?"

Walker laughed. "Because nobody cares about you, Jack. Least of all yourself."

Delaney looked into Walker's eyes; they were cold, intelligent and quite insane. He was sure of that. He ran through his options. If he reached into his jacket for his gun, Walker would shoot him before he had time to clear it. He calculated the distance between him and Walker. Did he have time to reach the superintendent before he pulled the trigger?

Walker read his mind and smiled. "Don't even think about it."

"Give it up, Walker. This makes no sense. I've spoken to people. They know what's going on. There is no way you can just walk away from all this."

Walker laughed again. "You've spoken to no one, Jack. No one of any importance. You have no credibility. You haven't had for years. I've got a squad car round the corner. A forensic team. My people. Trust me, this will all be taken care of and it will all be down to you, Cowboy. Everything and everyone. Closure."

Walker's eyes hardened as Delaney heard footsteps behind him and Kate stepped into the room, Kevin Norrell's gun held in both hands and pointing at her uncle's head. "Drop the gun now or I swear I'll kill you."

Walker ignored her, keeping his attention focused on Delaney. "Goodness me, Cowboy. Is this your new mount?"

Kate pushed her hands forward, her aim unwavering.

Walker brushed the back of his hand across his cheek. "She used to be as pretty as your daughter once upon a time, Jack. Gave me this little scar late one night, so I could never forget how pretty."

"If you don't think I'll do it, you're wrong. Drop the gun and step away from the little girl."

Walker shook his head. "You could pull the trigger, I'd still have time to kill her." He looked back at Delaney. "Here's the deal. You tell Kate to put down her gun or I will kill your daughter. Do you believe me?"

Jack looked into his eyes and did.

"Tell Kate to put the gun down, Jack. Or I will do it."

Delaney looked over at Kate. Her long hair falling over her forehead in a curly tumble, her eyes bright with pure, glittering hatred as she stared at her uncle and said, "I'm not going to put the gun down."

The scream seemed to hang in the air like a parachute, the sound ripping into Delaney's consciousness like a dousing of ice-cold water as he realised what he was doing. But it was too late. The shotgun blasted, fire and destruction hurtling from both barrels towards their car. The windscreen shattering, the front nearside tyre ripping apart, the car spinning out of control. The screaming blended with the screech of brakes and the crumpling of metal as the car smashed into a barrier.

346

Delaney was out of the car, oblivious to the people rushing towards them. Oblivious to the shouts and the screams, as though he was cocooned in an impenetrable fog. He had his wife in his arms and he could barely see for the tears in his eyes as he laid her on the forecourt floor. Her curly hair fanning around her head like a nimbus. The blood pooled a little behind her head as he took his jacket off to make a pillow. And he said a prayer, for the first time in twenty-five years, pleading with God not to let her die. He knew it was all his fault. He could have stopped being a policeman for one minute but he didn't, and now his wife was dying on a cold petrol station floor. As the petrol station manager called an ambulance, Delaney held on to his wife's hand as if he could transfuse his own life into her, and he begged God to make it so.

"Come on, Jack."

Jack looked up as Father O'Connell held the door to the vestry open and nodded, resigned. The man's wind-scraped face and rough white beard made him look more than ever like a visitation from a tortured place. Jack shivered again despite himself as he walked into the room.

Father O'Connell shut the door behind him and pointed to a pair of armchairs that sat alongside a tall bookcase. "Sit down there."

Jack sat in one of the armchairs and Father O'Connell in the other, picking up a Bible from the table in front of him.

"Do you know what the Bible is, Jack?"

"I do, Father."

"Then you're a wiser man than most. And do you know what a priest is, boy?"

"It's a holy man, Father."

Father O'Connell laughed. "Indeed he should be." He patted the book in his hand. "You see, the Bible is a collection of stories. Hundreds of stories that teach us all how to live. Each and every one of them for a different crossroads, a different hurdle in life. A different decision to make. Do you understand, boy?"

Jack nodded, not sure that he could keep the lie from his voice if he answered out loud.

"And part of a priest's job, if you like, is to prescribe a particular story to a person when he needs it. Like a doctor prescribing medicine. Do you see?"

Jack nodded again.

"So the stories in the Bible are like spiritual prescriptions to cure spiritual ills. A dose of medicine that cures the black spots on your soul."

He leaned forward, fixing Jack with his wild bloodshot eyes. "So tell me truly, Jack. Do you believe in the Devil?"

"I do, Father."

"I see the lie in your eyes, boy. But my job is to make you realise that he exists. He lives, breathes and walks amongst us." He leaned in closer so that Jack could smell the musty wine on his breath, see the yellow tobacco stains on his crooked teeth, the passion dancing in his eyes like a jig, like a reel.

"My job is to make you believe in the Devil, boy."

"Time's up, Jack."

Delaney blinked. He looked at Siobhan, her eyes pleading, her voice muted by terror, then across at Kate, her hands steady, her eyes cold as an executioner's.

"Put the gun down, Kate."

Kate hesitated for a moment.

Walker stared across at Delaney. "See that look in your daughter's eyes, Jack? She's terrified. Jackie Malone had that look. Just before she died."

Delaney turned back to Kate. "Please . . ."

Kate still didn't take her eyes from her uncle, fury sparking from them as her hand trembled a little, then she slowly lowered the gun to the floor and stood up again.

"You see, she can be a good girl when she wants to be." Walker smiled at Delaney, then turned back to his niece, still smiling as his finger tightened on his gun's trigger, and shot her twice in the chest.

Kate flew backwards, gasping with shock as she crashed to the floor.

Walker's smile broadened and then died as he suddenly cried out in surprised pain, and looked down to see Andy twisting the cook's knife in his side. Siobhan screamed and broke free of Walker's grasp as he staggered back, grabbing hold of the knife handle and watching the blood flow over his fingers. He turned to Andy, who watched him emotionlessly. "Why?"

Andy bared his crooked teeth. "You told me you weren't there when my mum was killed. You lied to me."

Walker slowly lifted the gun again, but before he could point it, Delaney reached for his own gun and fired, shattering Walker's right elbow. Walker fell back against the wall, grunting with pain like a wounded animal as his gun fell harmlessly to the floor.

Delaney looked back at Kate, who lay motionless on the floor, her arms outspread and her hair fanned out in a monstrous echo of his dead wife. A monstrous echo of his own fault, his own culpability. People who got close to Jack Delaney got hurt. Wasn't that what Karen Richardson had said? He swallowed hard and turned his pistol back to Walker, who was on his knees now, gasping with agony. He levelled his gaze into Walker's pleading eyes.

"Don't do it, Delaney. Please don't do it."

Delaney brought the gun up and pointed it at Walker's face.

"Jack?"

Jack looked up at Father O'Connell. "Was your mind wandering, boy?"

"No, Father."

Father Connell walked back from the cabinet he had just crossed to and held up what was in his hands. "Do you know what this is, boy?"

"Yes, Father."

"This is the communion wine, is it not?"

"So it is, Father."

Father O'Connell nodded. "So it is. And would it be a sin, do you think, to be drinking it?"

Jack nodded, his face flushed as he realised that Father O'Connell was getting down to the serious business now, and squirmed a little in his chair.

"Yes, Father, I suppose it would be."

Father O'Connell looked at Jack for a while, making Jack squirm even more under the relentless gaze. Then he raised the bottle to his lips and took a long swallow.

"Does that make me a sinner then, Jack?"

Jack was confused; he didn't know what to say. Father O'Connell put the bottle of wine on the table and sat opposite him again.

"Are you familiar with the story in the Bible of the wedding at Cana?"

Jack considered for a moment; he was sure he ought to be, it did sound kind of familiar, but he didn't want to be caught in a lie.

"I'm not sure, Father."

"The one about Jesus at a wedding feast, when they run out of wine and Jesus turns the water into wine. Do you remember that one?"

Jack smiled. "Yes, Father. Dad's always saying it would be a handy trick to have, especially round Christmas."

"So you mind the facts? Jesus took a pitcher of water and turned it into wine for the guests and himself to drink."

"Yes, Father."

Father O'Connell leaned in again, all good humour leaking from his face. "So was Jesus a sinner too?"

Jack was thoroughly confused now; he shook his head, not trusting himself to say anything, but he had to try.

"But that wasn't the communion wine."

Father O'Connell pointed to the bottle on the table. "That's just a bottle of wine; it hasn't been consecrated. It was a sin for you to drink it, because you stole that drink. But in the main scheme of things it's not such a big sin, is it?"

Jack shook his head, confused. "No, Father."

"So what's the importance of the wine, do you think, Jack."

"I don't know."

"The point of it is that we all have choices to make, Jack."

"Choices?"

"Between good and evil."

"Do you mean like between the Devil and Jesus, Father?"

"It comes back to the wine, you see. When this wine has been consecrated, it becomes the blood of Christ, and you know what that means?"

"Yes, Father." It had not been so long since his First Holy Communion, after all.

"I don't suppose you do. But I'll tell you. What it means is eternal life, boy. Jesus is the best wine saved till last. By embracing him in the holy communion, he becomes part of you and you become part of him."

"Yes, Father."

"It is your choice to make. Throughout life, you are going to have all kinds of choices. Because just like you can choose to be part of Jesus, you can choose the other too. Because when I said that the Devil walks and breathes and lives amongst us, I meant that the Devil is human. He's not a mythical beast with horns and a red tail who lives in the pit of hell."

"He isn't?"

"No, son. He lives in Ballydehob or Luton. In New York or Bombay or Islamabad. He's us. He's you or me, if you let him be. Do you understand?"

"I think so, Father."

"So you have a choice to make now. You can go on stealing wine and getting into fights and trouble and bit by bit letting the Devil into you. Or you can choose not to." The old man leaned in and looked him in the eye. "Because in the end, choices are the only thing we've got. They make us."

Delaney swallowed hard and looked at the man who knelt before him. He looked into his pleading eyes, heard the sore gasp of his laboured breathing and remembered his wife as her support machine was switched off, her mechanical breathing as laboured as that of the man in front of him. He remembered his own unbearable pain as the heart monitor line went flat; he thought of the fear in his daughter's eyes; he remembered the cut and mutilated body of his friend Jackie Malone; and finally he thought about the shots fired into Kate Walker's body. He pictured the closing of her eyes, and her body stilling as it lay on the floor, discarded by the man in front of him as carelessly as someone dropping litter in the street, and he stepped forward, centering the gun on the man's forehead, pressing the cold metal into his sweating skin. And he made his choice.

"Please." Tears formed in Walker's eyes.

Delaney lowered the gun.

Walker sobbed as his body crumpled with relief. "Thank you."

Delaney shook his head coldly. "Don't thank me. Where you're going, when they found out who and what you are, you'll wish I had killed you."

Walker collapsed back against the wall and Delaney turned to Andy. "Thanks."

Andy looked blankly at Walker. "He lied." He turned and smiled at Siobhan, and another cold chill ran through Delaney's heart. "And I like your daughter."

Delaney picked up his sobbing child and held her in his arms, unable to stop the tears that stung his eyes and ran down his cheeks as he looked at the still body of Kate Walker.

CHAPTER
THIRTY-THREE

There was a slight chill in the air, and the young nurse shivered a little as Delaney watched her close the window and angle the slats of the Venetian blind against the still bright rays of the sun.

She hurried out of the private hospital room, leaving Delaney alone with the woman who lay on the bed, tubes coming out of her arms and monitors keeping a constant check on her.

The woman groaned slightly as she opened her eyes and propped herself up on the pillow, focusing on her visitor. She smiled, her voice a soft, croaky whisper.

"Jack."

Delaney stepped forward and put a basket of fruit on her bedside cabinet. "Hello, Wendy."

"You brought flowers last time. You going off me?"

Her voice was undeniably sexy with that husky croak in it, and Delaney laughed. "Never going to happen."

"I don't blame you, you know."

"Maybe you should."

"We're family, Jack. Never forget that."

"I know."

"What's going to happen to the boy?"

Delaney looked at her for a moment. "Nothing good." He looked out of the window and saw Wendy's husband walking across the car park with Siobhan.

"I've got to go, Wendy."

Wendy looked puzzled. "You just got here."

"I know. I've got a funeral to go to."

Delaney walked towards the door.

"Jack."

He turned back as Wendy flashed him a sympathetic smile.

"I'm sorry about what happened. But you can't stop taking care of yourself. Not now."

Jack didn't reply; just nodded and left the room.

Two o'clock in the afternoon, north-west of London. Some trees still had a thick coat of green with flashes of gold here and there, while the top branches of others stretched out like skeletal fingers of coral, scratching the sky, all of it heralding change. That fine line between summer and autumn. A season no longer dictated by the calendar since carbon emissions had made global warming a hard reality. The sky leaked a vivid blue here and there, jagged streaks of pale cobalt showing through an off-white cloth of cloud, and below that were thicker clouds, fat and scudding as the cool winds blew, rattling the dry leaves from the tall trees. Cool enough now so that Delaney pulled his overcoat tighter around himself. A black woollen overcoat to match his black suit and his black tie and his dark eyes as he looked down at the open grave at his feet.

The wind lifted a little, picking up some leaves and making them dance across the grass, and bringing the familiarity of a particular perfume. Delaney looked up to find Kate Walker standing beside him.

"You came, then?"

Delaney shrugged. "Seemed the least I could do. He took a bullet for me."

Kate stooped down to lay a wreath by the grave.

"He said there would be no one here to put flowers on his grave."

Some two months after he had disappeared, the body of Bill Hoskins had been discovered in an abandoned well on a run-down farm near Henley. A young child had gone missing after an argument about being allowed to watch an unsuitable film on television, and every nook and cranny in the area had been searched. The missing child turned up safe and sound, hiding out in a Wendy house in a friend's garden.

Bill Hoskins, however, was found in far worse condition. Two months' exposure in the summer's heat had not been kind to his already undernourished body. The autopsy revealed that he had been shot once, in the heart.

Kate stood up and looked at Delaney. "Why didn't you return any of my calls, Jack?"

"I thought it best."

"Best for you?"

"Best for you, Kate. When I saw you shot . . ."

"I was wearing your Kevlar vest, Jack. You made me put it on. If I hadn't, I'd have been dead."

"I know. And I'm sorry, but it made me realise. I'm bad news, Kate. You don't need me in your life."

"They told me you've handed in your notice. You're going to move, is that right?"

"Yeah."

"Move where?"

Delaney shrugged again, the words bitter in his mouth. "Out of this city."

"And there's nothing I can say?"

"I'm sorry."

Kate looked at him angrily, blinking back tears. She nodded to the open grave. "Why don't you climb in there with him and be done with it?"

She turned on her heel and walked away. She didn't look back.

Delaney watched her go, a painful knot forming in his stomach. He wanted to call out, ask her back, but couldn't bring himself to do it. He'd been a liability to every woman he'd slept with over the past few years. His wife, Jackie Malone, Wendy, now lying in an intensive care hospital bed. He wanted Kate back, but he knew what was causing the knot in his stomach. Fear. And he didn't feel any better about himself for knowing it.

He waited until Kate was gone from sight, then walked thirty yards in the opposite direction and knelt beside another memorial.

He took a single red rose from the inside pocket of his coat and laid it on his wife's grave. "I'm sorry." His voice a pained whisper. Then he stood up quickly and walked towards the gates of the cemetery.

★ ★ ★

Outside, Diane Campbell leaned back against her car, a trademark cigarette hanging from her carmine lips and a lazy blue cloud of smoke floating towards him on the cool breeze. If he was surprised to see her, his face didn't register it. Campbell ground the cigarette under her heel and snapped another out of the packet, flicking it into her mouth and offering the pack towards Delaney. Delaney took one and bent low so Campbell could light it for him before she lit her own.

"I heard you'd be here."

"You come to wish me luck?"

"I've come to ask you to take back your resignation."

"That's not going to happen."

"You're a good detective, Delaney. You know that."

"Yeah, I do."

"We need you on the force. *I* need you on the force."

Delaney shook his head. "Made my mind up."

"I said I was sorry."

"Doesn't change anything. This isn't about that."

"You're absolutely certain?"

"Haven't been more sure of anything in my life."

Campbell took a deep drag on her cigarette, then looked at Delaney sympathetically. "There's something I need to tell you."

Delaney saw the look in her eyes. "What is it, Diane?"

"The forecourt robbery. The guys who shot your wife . . ."

Delaney could feel the wind roaring, the blood pounding in his ears as he gripped her arm, tight enough for her to wince. "Tell me?"

"We've got a lead, Jack."

Unspoken

Sam Hayes

A mother with a secret: Mary Marshall would do anything for her daughter Julia. A devoted grandmother, she's always been the rock her family can rely on. Until now. Mary has a past Julia knows nothing about, and it's come back to haunt her . . .

A husband on his knees: Murray French is walking a tightrope. A solicitor struggling with an alcohol problem, he's about to lose his wife Julia, and his children, to another man. Someone successful, someone they deserve. Someone who's everything he's not. Can he ever get his family back?

A woman in danger: just when Julia Marshall thinks life is starting to turn around, she stumbles upon the brutalised body of a girl she teaches. And as the terrible present starts to shed light on her mother's past, Julia realises her family's nightmare is only just beginning . . .

ISBN 978-0-7531-8242-0 (hb)
ISBN 978-0-7531-8243-7 (pb)

No Kiss for the Devil

Adrian Magson

A young woman's body is found dumped in the Essex countryside. Investigative reporter Riley Gavin recognises her as Helen Bellamy, a former girlfriend of her colleague, PI Frank Palmer. Ex-military policeman Palmer is accustomed to death, but this is different; this is the brutal murder of someone he was once close to. He knows only one way to deal with it: find the killers.

Meanwhile, Riley's next job is a profile of controversial businessman "Kim" Al-Bashir. She soon realises that there are sinister forces working against him, and if she doesn't tread carefully she could end up losing her assignment. And, like Helen, quite probably her life.

ISBN 978-0-7531-8190-4 (hb)
ISBN 978-0-7531-8191-1 (pb)

Shafted

Mandasue Heller

Larry Logan is a small-time TV star with a mile-wide ego. Gutted when his latest show is axed, he's less than impressed when the only work he can get is fronting a fake game show — actually an undercover police sting to entrap criminals.

His reluctance evaporates when the show rockets his career back to prime-time stardom. And when lovely, shy Stephanie enters his life, he thinks he finally has it made.

But then it all begins to go wrong. Larry is arrested, on-screen, for a shocking crime. He's shafted some dangerous men — is this their revenge?

ISBN 978-0-7531-8164-5 (hb)
ISBN 978-0-7531-8165-2 (pb)

Secret Sins

Kate Charles

Life may not be getting any easier for curate Callie Anson, but it is definitely getting more interesting. Her relationship with policeman, Marco Lombardi grows ever warmer, even though he seems to be keeping her away from his close Italian family. Then her beloved brother, Peter, gets a bit too close for comfort when he moves in.

Professionally, Callie becomes involved with the problems of a new parishioner. Morag Hamilton is worried about her granddaughter Alex, a lonely, isolated 12-year-old spending too much time on the internet.

Meanwhile, Detective Inspector Neville Stewart puts his personal problems on hold as he deals with Rachel Norton, a pregnant woman whose husband has gone missing. With the birth of his first baby only days away, why would Trevor Norton go out jogging and not return?

But Trevor's disappearance may not be what it seems, and just when Neville thinks he's solved it, someone else goes missing — young Alex Hamilton.

ISBN 978-0-7531-8092-1 (hb)
ISBN 978-0-7531-8093-8 (pb)

The Fireman

Stephen Leather

Young, talented, in love with life — why should Sally have thrown herself 15 floors to her death? But as suicide is the verdict of the uncompromising Hong Kong authorities, Sally's brother, a London-based crime reporter, begins his own investigations.

As he delves into the details of Sally's unaccountably opulent lifestyle and her mysterious work as a journalist, he is forced to recognise a very different girl from the fun-loving kid sister he remembers. He uncovers a trail that leads him through the decadent haunts of Hong Kong ex-pat society, the ruthless wheeler-dealing of international big-business and the violent Chinese mafia underworld — to an ultimate, shocking act of revenge.

ISBN 978-0-7531-7964-2 (hb)
ISBN 978-0-7531-7965-9 (pb)

ISIS publish a wide range of books in large print, from fiction to biography. Any suggestions for books you would like to see in large print or audio are always welcome. Please send to the Editorial Department at:

ISIS Publishing Limited
7 Centremead
Osney Mead
Oxford OX2 0ES

A full list of titles is available free of charge from:

Ulverscroft Large Print Books Limited

(UK)
The Green
Bradgate Road, Anstey
Leicester LE7 7FU
Tel: (0116) 236 4325

(Australia)
P.O. Box 314
St Leonards
NSW 1590
Tel: (02) 9436 2622

(USA)
P.O. Box 1230
West Seneca
N.Y. 14224-1230
Tel: (716) 674 4270

(Canada)
P.O. Box 80038
Burlington
Ontario L7L 6B1
Tel: (905) 637 8734

(New Zealand)
P.O. Box 456
Feilding
Tel: (06) 323 6828

Details of **ISIS** complete and unabridged audio books are also available from these offices. Alternatively, contact your local library for details of their collection of **ISIS** large print and unabridged audio books.